City of Crime

City of Crime

Edited by David Belbin

Five Leaves Publications

City of Crime

Published in 1997 by Five Leaves Publications,
PO Box 81, Nottingham NG5 4ER

Designed and set by 4 Sheets Design & Print
Printed in Great Britain by Antony Rowe

ISBN 0 907123 12 0

Five Leaves Publications
acknowledge financial assistance from
East Midlands Arts

Cover photograph by John Stuart Clark

This book is fiction. Any resemblance between the
characters and real people is coincidental.

Contents

Introduction
David Belbin

In literature, at least, crime pays. Crime of one kind or another dominates the best seller lists in a way that other genres rarely manage and fiction hardly ever does, unless it won a big prize the week before. Is this because all the best new writers are turning to crime? Or is it because crime fiction is so intrinsically interesting? After all, crime stories promise escapism and entertainment with a degree of realism and social conscience — areas which serious or *literary* fiction increasingly ignores.

Of course "literary" fiction (there ought to be a name for it which doesn't require inverted commas — maybe that's part of the problem) has always dealt with crime. It's one of the big subjects. So why not put together an anthology of new crime stories where half the writers are from the crime world and the other half aren't? Which would come off better? Would readers even be able to tell the difference? That's the idea behind this book.

The authors I approached included best sellers, a Booker prize winner and the creators of successful crime series. Some had never appeared in book form before. Others had published novels or screenplays but never written a short story until now. All of them were enthusiastic about the idea behind this collection. Most (but not all) came up with stories which meet the single criterion set by the Crime Writers' Association for its awards — they include a crime. Beyond that, it's hard to generalise about what you'll find here. The stories feature authentic police work and obsessive relationships, together with terrorism, treachery and more than one murder. Around half of these stories have a kind of 'twist in the tale', but they aren't necessarily the stories by the crime writers.

All of the authors included have a strong connection with the city of Nottingham, which is the *city of crime* referred to in this book's title. Nottingham has produced two of the finest short story writers of this century, DH Lawrence and, more recently, Alan Sillitoe, who contributes a brand new story, *Brothers*.

But what about *city of crime?* I'm not sure why Nottingham seems to have become the country's crime capital. Maybe it's because some spurious statistics designated it the most violent place in Britain. Perhaps it has something to do with the presence of both an annual crime film festival, *Shots in the Dark* and an accompanying crime writers' convention, *Shots on the Page*. But the main reason must be the large number of crime writers setting their books in the city. All of them are featured in this collection.

The short story is a brilliant, but high risk form. The writer has to do so much, in such a small space. In the best short fiction, every word counts, with an intensity more akin to the poem than the novel. The writer's view of the world is starkly exposed, as is his or her ability to entertain. I hope that this volume both entertains you and introduces you to many authors whose work you'll want to investigate further.

Cheryl
John Harvey

Cheryl had a scarlet embroidered leisure suit with padded
shoulders and a matching belt, which she liked to wear
when she delivered meals on wheels to the elderly, the
housebound and the infirm. Cheryl thought it her mission
to bring a little colour into their lives; she thought it
cheered the old farts up. And it was true, although she
hadn't been doing the job long, four months this coming
week, she would have needed more than the fingers of
both hands to count the number of faces that smiled, positively beamed, when they heard the beep-ba-ba-beep of
her horn, the rhythmic jabber of her finger on the bell. Not
that she was letting it go to her head; she wasn't the Angel
of Old Lenton. At least, not yet.

The truth was, though it paid less, she liked it as well,
if not better, than any job she'd ever had. Bar work, wait-
ressing, a discouraging six months serving up double
sausage, double egg, bacon and chips in the police canteen,
five years — Cheryl still couldn't believe it — on the night
shift at Pork Farms. That had been when her Vicki was little and sleeping over at her gran's in the Meadows. Once
Vicki had started at the juniors, Cheryl had gone to work
there, playground attendant first and then dinner lady.
That, she supposed was what had put the idea into her
head, meals on wheels.

When it had been time to go to the comp, Vicki begged
her mum not to follow there, too. Reminders about writing
to her dad and tidying up her room while doling out the
mashed potatoes. So Cheryl, whose first real boy friend, a
pipe fitter from Bulwell, had taught her how to drive, if little else, and who'd had a driving licence since her eigh-
teenth birthday, if rarely a car, took a test to show the
supervisor she could tootle along at thirty without shaking
up several dozen foil-wrapped dinners, filled in a form

3

with the fountain pen she more usually saved for notes about late payment of the rent, and gratefully accepted a uniform overall which she almost never wore.

Drab, too drab: not the way Cheryl saw herself at all.

As she drove, Cheryl played tapes in the van. Not that it was fitted out with a stereo, of course, but there was this natty little cassette player from Dixons she hung from the handbrake: Jackie Wilson. Sugar Pie DeSanto. Aretha belting out and sometimes, when she was feeling soft and hopeful, 'Say a Little Prayer For You'. Once she had clapped her Walkman on old Tommy Vickers' head and boogied him round the room to 'Let's Get It On', Cheryl keeping time to the slivers of treble and bass that slid through the headphones, singing along at the top of her voice, 'don't want to *push*'. Tommy had had to lie down afterwards for quite a long time.

This particular morning it was raining, that fine rain like mist which dulls the sky and seeps, almost unseen, under the skin and Cheryl needed her scarlet suit and her music more than ever. She was playing Dusty, *Dusty in Memphis;* proof, if proof were needed, that white girls can have soul, the voice, yearning and strong. 'Breakfast in Bed.' Cheryl braked sharply so as not to nudge a cyclist turning left off Lenton Boulevard and taking too wide a line. Her Vicki would still jump in with her now and then of a Sunday, those days she forgot she was near thirteen and it was no longer cool, jump right in amongst the pages of the *News of the World* and settle down to tea and toast and if they were feeling specially wicked, the pair of them, bacon cobs slavered all over with brown sauce. The kind of breakfast Dusty was singing about though, the kind you shared with a bloke, well, it wasn't to say she didn't have offers, but with a kid Vicki's age it was difficult, specially since Vicki's gran had passed on. No more easy all night sleepovers. For either of them. More often now it was quick kebab, a glance at the watch and oops, sorry, got to be getting back.

Cheryl's patch spread all around the Radford Flats

where they lived, down past the Raleigh cycle works and through Dunkirk towards the railway. Her first call this morning, though, was Lenton. Sherwin Road. Mary Cole, who'd been living there alone since her husband died not so long back and Mary herself had a stroke. She was over it now, well, she could move at least, with the aid of a stick, five minutes to get from the back room to the door in a sort of grudging shuffle, one side of her still set, paralysed really, Cheryl supposed. Once in a while, Cheryl had seen her blink back a few tears if something was said that reminded her of Ted, but normally she'd find a smile and even a joke sometimes about the cod.

This morning, the trip to the door was slower than usual and at the sight of Cheryl, bright red on her doorstep, Mary broke down into tears, great gulping sobs which shook the half of her body that could still respond.

Cheryl helped her back inside, put on the kettle and sat her down. 'You're not a social worker, Cheryl,' her supervisor would say, 'You're not a home help. There are others paid to do that. Trained. You have meals to deliver. Quick, in and out.' Easy to say, Cheryl thought, when you're in an office most of the day rustling papers; not so easy sitting here watching the tears try to find a way down this poor old dear's twisted mess of a face.

Gradually, over a cup of strong sweet tea, the story emerged. Ted Cole had borrowed money the winter before last, sixty pounds that was all; at least all Ted had wanted was sixty, but the man who'd called round about the loan had talked him into borrowing seventy five, which meant Ted having to repay the neat round sum of a hundred at a fiver a week. Which was fine from his pension and hers and whatever they got from social security. Only then, Mary fancied a few days away at Mablethorpe, just a week by the sea, maybe that caravan site back down the coast, the place they'd stayed before, and Ted hadn't felt he could begrudge her that. Nor a few presents for the nieces and nephews when they made the trip across from Glossop. Before you knew where you were it was winter again.

Ted now owed a total of three hundred and seventeen pounds, which he had been struggling to pay off at seven pounds fifty a week, when he'd gone out in the frost one morning to fetch the *Mirror,* ten Embassy and a pint of milk and keeled over with his heart.

The first Mary had known about the loans, any of it, was when the collector knocked on the door and expressed his condolences. 'He were a lovely chap, Ted. Lovely. Tell you what I'll do, this last two weeks, the repayments, I'll say nothing. Stick it in out me own pocket, sign of respect. So if you'll just get your purse, love, it's seven fifty, and we'll start as we mean to go on. Your Ted, he used to meet me in the pub, like, but easier for you, I dare say, if I come here.'

This man standing there, face like steamed pudding and rings on the hand he stuck out towards her, rings that were heavy and dull.

'You should have told him,' Cheryl said, 'now there was just you on your own, you couldn't easily manage.'

'Well, I did. Because it was difficult. It was hard.'

'And what did he say?'

'Oh, he was nice about it. Understanding, you know. Firm, but fair. I'll say that for him, he was always fair. He offered to make a new arrangement, just for me.'

'Nice of him.'

'He said there was this new scheme for people like me, finding it not so easy, you know. Said how he would wipe out all the old debt, all the money Ted'd owed, and make out this new loan I could pay back little by little, just how-ever much I could afford. He showed me this paper, I remember, well, of course, I never really understood it. But five pounds a week, he said, we'll try that for a start. And well, well... Mary plucking at the table cloth now and not quite able to stop the tears. 'At first it was fine, but then I started to fall behind, and today, today he came right in here, into my home and, I've swept it up now, but he took a china pot from that shelf there, mine and Ted's anniversary ware it was, and dropped it, right there on the

6

floor. Sorry, he says, clumsy. These clumsy old hands of mine. Do more damage sometimes than they've a mind. Next week, Mary, he says, ten pound. You'll not let me down. And then he left.'

Mary heaved a sigh and groped for Cheryl's hand. 'I was frightened.'

'Of course you were,' Cheryl patting her, nodding, all the while thinking, you bastard, you cowardly bastard. Asking her, before she left, 'This paper you say he gave you, you haven't still got it, I suppose? That or something with his address, a card?'

She pulled out the card, cheaply printed, from behind the cups and saucers at the side. 'I'll just borrow this, Mary, for a while, okay?'

Mary looked alarmed. 'Wouldn't want to cause any trouble.'

'Don't you worry,' Cheryl said. 'It'll all be fine.'

The offices of the Sheriff Finance and Loan Company were on the Alfreton Road above a burned-out tandoori takeaway and adjacent to a lock-up shop trading in second hand electrical goods and vinyl albums on which the names Neil Sedaka and Roger Whitaker were writ large. There was neither carpet nor lino on the stairs.

Sonia White was just scrolling another invoice into the Olivetti when Cheryl knocked and barged right in. Sonia was around Cheryl's age, thirty nine, skinny where Cheryl was, well, amply covered, and not only having problems striking the right keys but enjoying a seriously bad hair day into the bargain. The ends of her fingers were blotched white with Tippex.

'Mr Dunn?'

Sonia blinked. 'No.'

'When are you expecting him?'

'Nobody of that name works here.'

Cheryl produced the card she had taken from Mary Coles' kitchen. 'This says he does.'

Sonia eyed Cheryl with suspicion. 'Mr Dunn sometimes

works for us. He never works here.'

Cheryl was getting fed up with this, royally pissed off. 'How does this arrangement work?' she asked. 'Fax and mobile phone, or perhaps you're a dab hand with a weegee board?'

The blinking increased, accompanied now by a pronounced tilt of the head. 'Mr Dunn telephones here and speaks to Mr McStay.' The sign on the door behind her, one of those instant engraving jobs they specialise in at shoe repairers, read Jason McStay, Manager.

'And,' suggested Cheryl, 'Mr McStay tells him to go out and terrify an old woman, half crippled and living on her own, frighten the life out of her for the sake of five fucking pounds.'

Sonia pursed her lips. Cheryl half expected her to say, 'Language!' and tut-tut. She was the sort, Cheryl thought, for whom the expression 'having relations' didn't mean a visit from your gran or a great aunt.

'Is he here?' Cheryl asked, pointing towards the inner office.

'Not presently.'

Jesus, Cheryl thought. 'And when will he be here, or is he busy off somewhere threatening old ladies, too?'

'There is no need to cast aspersions,' Sonia said, getting older by the minute, 'Mr McStay is a perfectly respectable businessman and, besides, you can't see him without an appointment. He never sees anyone without an appointment.'

'Oh,' said Cheryl, 'and how do I get one of those?'

'Write a letter, stating the nature of your business and we will contact you in due course.'

'I'll bet,' Cheryl said. 'I'll bet you will, my arse.'

That evening, Cheryl left Vicki watching *EastEnders* with a friend from school who lived two floors up, and went to Sherwin Road on foot. Mary was bearing up, happy enough to have Cheryl mash tea and butter toast, but worried sick about where she was going to find ten pounds.

'Relax, sweetheart,' Cheryl told her. 'Don't you worry. I'll look after it, I promise.'

And the way Mary had looked at her, squinting up from the one good side of her face, had made Cheryl all the more determined that she would.

There were only two pubs she thought Ted Cole would have walked to for his regular meetings with Reggie Dunn, The Happy Return and the 17th-21st Lancers. Never The Grove, too full of students and student nurses. Cheryl called in both of them and Dunn wasn't in either, but, just as she'd guessed, he was known. 'You tell him I'm looking for him,' Cheryl said. 'Cheryl Wheeler. Just you tell him that.' Staring at the barman hard, daring him to make some crack.

Three days passed and nothing happened, nothing out of the usual. Vicki went to school and came home. Cheryl drove her van round the streets of mostly terraced houses, the rent-controlled flats and the back-to-backs. On the Thursday evening, for a treat, she walked with Vicki to the chippie and carried it back, warm through the wrappings of paper, cod and chips twice, two pickled onions, a can of Vimto and a Pepsi. Somebody's birthday, Cheryl thought, when they found the lift still working. It didn't matter, the whole block had been tarted up something righteous, even moved them out for a spell while the work was done, lifts were lifts all the same which meant, more often than not, not working.

Up on the eighth floor, Vicki jumped past the slow sliding door and out onto the balcony and before Cheryl could follow her an arm slammed across in front of her, one foot braced to keep the lift door open. 'Hear you been looking for me?' Reggie Dunn's flat, round face glaring in.

'Vicki!' Cheryl shouted, but all the girl could do was stare, mouth wide, at her mother trapped on the far side of the man's spread body. Reggie Dunn, tall, fat, strong.

'Vicki!' Cheryl shouted again.

'Never mind her,' Dunn said.

Vicki didn't move; didn't run.

9

'You been mouthing me in my local, running round my boss, making all these lyin' fuckin' allegations. Sticking your tart's nose where nobody asked it to go. In my affairs. And you got to learn that's not on.'

Cheryl ducked her head. 'Vicki, run and...'

His hand caught her round the neck, forcing her back. 'Never mind fuckin' Vicki. Never mind her. What you want to think about is me. Me. Reggie Dunn.' His knuckle was pressing hard against her windpipe, making it difficult for her to breathe. 'If I ever, ever, hear of you interfering with me again, the way I do my job, anything, your life won't be worth livin'. Right?'

And faster than he had any right to be, pushing her roughly back, he pressed the bottom button on the lift and sent her down; Vicki's face, shocked and pale, the last thing Cheryl saw before the door slid closed. Vicki and that bastard alone on the eighth floor balcony.

The lift seemed to take hours to descend and when it had, Cheryl wasn't prepared to risk it again. She raced the stairs, lungs rasping, backs of her legs aching by the time she swung around onto the open walkway and there was Vicki, leaning over the railing, staring down, hands clenched fast, her still child's body racked by sobs and tears. Chips and broken pieces of fish, some stamped in, lay strewn across the floor, paper wrapping itself around the metal rails, the backs of Vicki's legs. Of Dunn there was no sign.

Cheryl caught her daughter fast and cursed and cried and kissed her hair.

Resnick had the CID room to himself. The door to his own office, a partitioned-off section of the long, rectangular room, was open, revealing a desk crowded with papers, Home Office bulletins and memoranda, case files and rosters and scraps of paper on which his sergeant, Graham Millington, had scribbled important messages in a hurried and largely indecipherable hand. Around him, typewriters waited silent, VDU screens tilted blankly save for the rhythmic blip of cursors and in ragged tintinnabulation, telephones rang and continued to ring unanswered. Although the windows facing onto the Derby Road were unhealthily closed, the constant drum of traffic underscored everything, accented every now and again by the clash of gears as an articulated lorry approached the Canning Circus roundabout.

Kevin Naylor and Lynn Kellogg were out on the Broxtowe Estate, investigating an attack on the house of a widower who was suspected of having grassed to the police about one of his neighbours. Broken windows, excrement smeared across the front door and pushed in parcels through the letter box, vilification tagged on his walls in fluorescent colours, four feet high. And all the man had done was wave down the local Panda patrol and complain about his bike having been nicked from his back yard, the second in as many weeks.

Millington himself, new boy Carl Vincent in tow, had hurried off in the direction of Angel Row, where a posse of eight or nine youths, the youngest no more than nine years old, had steamed through one of the major clearing banks, waiting for one of the staff to pass through the security doors and barging past him, while others vaulted onto and over the counters. Several hundred pounds missing, one clerk elbowed in the face, a have-a-go customer knifed in the thigh, and all in around three minutes flat.

It was the third such incident in the city centre in the past month; all the kids wore sweat shirt hoods around their heads, scarves across their faces; limber, lithe and fast; black, white and shades between. Caught on the security cameras, their exploits would have made an excellent commercial for one of the new alcoholic lemonades or Pepé jeans, but when it came to identification they were next to useless.

Turning, Resnick picked up a telephone at random and identified himself. Forty-five minutes later, Cheryl Wheeler was sitting opposite him in his office, Cheryl dressing down according to the seriousness of the situa-

11

tion, wide black trousers, denim shirt, boots with a three inch heel. Outside, Millington and Vincent had returned and were interviewing the parents of one possible suspect, a youth of fourteen who had already been taken into care twice. 'What'd you have me do,' the father was saying, 'tie the little bastard to his bed, burn all his soddin' clothes?' He had tried both and neither had worked.

'I know you, don't I?' Resnick said. 'We've met before but I can't think where.'

Cheryl's mouth widened into a smile. 'It was here in the canteen.'

'Right. Carole? Caroline?'

'Cheryl.'

'Of course.' Resnick's turn to smile. Charlie Parker with Miles Davis and Max Roach. Nineteen forty seven. 'Cheryl.' One of those bouncy little blues themes Bird used to love to play. 'Tell me about it,' he said. 'From the beginning, tell me what happened.' Impressed by Cheryl's fire as he listened, the righteousness of the anger brimming inside her, the love.

'Why didn't you come in last night?' Resnick asked when she had finished. 'Report it then?'

'I was bloody scared, why d'you think? And I wasn't going to leave her, Vicki, I wasn't going to leave her and no way was she moving out of that flat, not if I'd dragged her kicking and screaming.'

'He didn't touch her?' Resnick asked, the second time.

Cheryl shook her head.

'You're sure?'

'She wouldn't lie. Not about a thing like that.'

'And you?'

Unbuttoning the top buttons, Cheryl pulled back her shirt to show him the bruises, colouring well, to her neck. The most prominent, purple, the perfect size and shape of a large thumb.

'I'd like to have some photographs taken. If you've no objection?'

'Suit yourself. Go ahead. Take as many as you like. Just

12

so long as that bastard ends up inside.'

'You would be willing to give evidence? If he were charged.'

Her eyes widened. 'What d'you mean, if?'

'There was no one else saw what happened, no other witnesses?'

'My Vicki, she was there all the time.'

'You might not want her,' Resnick said, 'giving evidence in court, standing up to cross-examination. Always supposing the CPS would want her on the stand.'

Cheryl swept back the chair as she rose to her feet. 'You're going to do soddin' nothing, that's what you're saying, isn't it? You're going to let the bastard go scot-free.'

'No, Cheryl,' Resnick said, 'That's not what I'm saying at all.'

Sonia thought it would be a good idea if she had one of those signs like the one's on her boss's door, the one that said Jason McStay, Manager, right there on her desk. Free-standing. Easy to shift then, when Sonia had a dust and tidy. Not Receptionist, though; Secretary. No tone. Personal Assistant to the Manager. No, that was too long, they'd never fit it all on. But, Sonia White, Managerial Assistant, that would be fine. Real class. She would ask Mr McStay when he came back in. At least then, people wouldn't gawp and talk to her like she was part of the furniture; that woman who'd been in the other day, all scarlet nails and scarlet mouth and that ghastly leisure suit. Sonia shuddered. Women like her gave a new meaning to the word cheap.

Five minutes later when the door opened and McStay came in, a bit of a face on him, Sonia hesitated that fatal second too long.

'Get us a coffee, Sonia. Two sugars. It's a bastard of a day.'

'Yes, Mr McStay.'

What she did was nip across and buy him a cream slice,

refresh her lipstick and bring in his coffee and cake with her best professional smile. 'Mr McStay, I've been meaning to ask...'

He hardly seemed to listen, uncertain whether to utilise the plastic knife in his drawer since his last Kentucky Fried Chicken dinner or bring the whole thing to his mouth and hope for the best.

'So, I mean, Mr McStay, what d'you think?'

'I think anyone with half a brain, walking in and seeing you plonked down behind the typewriter can see you're the sodding secretary, so what's the point?'

She'd scarcely got over that when a big man knocked and entered. Quite a nice suit, Sonia thought, a little old-fashioned but she didn't mind that; shame though about the stains on his tie. She wondered if he were the new collector Mr McStay had set on: a nice look about the eyes that might charm a few of the old dears at least.

When Resnick showed her his warrant card, she knew she'd been barking up the wrong tree. 'Mr McStay doesn't normally see people without a written appointment,' she began, but her heart wasn't in it. 'I'm sorry to trouble you, Mr McStay,' she said into the receiver, 'but there's a policeman here to see you.'

Resnick smiled his thanks and went on through.

In the course of McStay's journey from Belfast to Glasgow via Tyneside and Sheffield and a few minor diversions between, there were times when he'd drifted close to the wind. Since setting up Sheriff Finance and Loan here in the city, he'd had more than a few warnings — employing personnel with a penchant for violent behaviour, exceeding the duly constituted Codes of Practice, failing to pay National Insurance contributions for all of his staff as well as some little negligence over taxes; the arson attack on a persistent defaulter was little more than a rumour and remained unproved, though not for want of trying.

So McStay sent Sonia in search of more coffee, which Resnick tasted but didn't drink, laying out the case against one Reginald Alexander Dunn, currently in

14

McStay's employ.

McStay was shocked, almost apoplectic with apology. He had no idea of the tactics that Dunn had been using and neither did he condone them in any way, shape or form. And to attack a member of the public, threaten her little girl. 'You leave it to me, Inspector. I'll deal with it forthwith. The last thing I want, the name of this firm dragged through the mire. Business like mine, well, you can imagine, trust and confidence of our clients, that's what it depends upon. No, he's in here and I'm telling him straight. He'll not work for me again.'

Resnick nodded. 'Just one other thing.'

McStay's eyebrow twitched.

'Standard loan contracts, the kind your firm uses. You do issue contracts?'

'Yes, yes, of course.'

'All the time?'

'Everything above board.'

'Each and every case?'

'Yes.'

'So the papers concerning Ted Coles' loan, they'll be here on file?'

'Somewhere, yes. Sonia can...'

Resnick leaned forward, just a little. 'Isn't there a clause, in the event of the death of the borrower, the remainder of the debt is set aside?'

McStay could smell something distressingly like his own sweat. 'Usually, yes.'

'And in the Coles' case?'

'I daresay, yes, but, like I say, I can check.'

'So you've been collecting on a contract that was legally null and void, in addition to persuading an elderly stroke victim to take out a second loan to cover that non-existent debt?'

'I think, I mean, I can see there's almost certainly been an administrative oversight and...'

'And you'll make restitution immediately? Full financial restitution?'

15

'Well, naturally, yes.'

'Plus, I daresay, a bonus to compensate for your client's deep discomfort?'

'I think we could see our way...'

'A generous bonus?'

'Yes, yes, you have my word.'

'Resnick rose to his feet. 'I think what I'd be happier with, if it's all the same to you, let's have the figures down on paper. Nice and clear. Signed. You know the kind of thing.'

'Graham,' Resnick said, back at the station. Resnick had nipped into the Gents to relieve himself and found his sergeant doing something decorative to his moustache with a pair of nail scissors. At least it meant he couldn't whistle 'Winchester Cathedral' at the same time.

'Boss?'

'You remember that arson attack, February? Halal butchers on the Ilkeston Road.'

Millington wiggled his upper lip, rabbit like, in front of the mirror. 'Loan shark we liked for it, if it's the one I'm thinking. McFall?'

'McStay.'

'That's him. Sheriff something-or-other. Robin Hood in reverse sort of a thing. Steal from the poor and keep McStay in Alfa Romeos.'

'Right. Well, I think we might be able to squeeze out a little insider information.'

Millington slipped the nail scissors down into their plastic leather-look case and looked interested.

'Reggie Dunn,' Resnick said. 'Late in McStay's employ. I thought perhaps you might find the time to have a word.'

'Over a friendly pint.'

'That sort of thing.'

'Happy Return, then. Not been in for a while. Might give Reg Cossall a call, not so far from his place. He might fancy a chat with Dunn himself. Both Reggies, after all.'

'Thanks, Graham,' Resnick said, rinsing his hands

16

under the tap.

McStay hadn't called round on Mary Coles himself, hadn't had the stomach for it. He sent Sonia instead, even thought it had meant giving in to her about having some poncey sign stuck on her desk.

'Yes, Mrs Coles,' Sonia had said. 'Five hundred pounds, representing a repayment plus a substantial and generous bonus. And your old loan contract cancelled and returned. Now if you'll just sign this form absolving the firm of any further liability, I'll be hurrying along.'

And she smiled her prim little purse-string smile and watched Mary fumble with her pen.

'The thing is, Reggie,' Millington was saying, Cossall close alongside with a large scotch, Millington himself with a pint of mixed, 'it's because we don't want to see you ending up with someone else's shit on your shoes, we're going out of our way to give you a hand.'

'Photographs of that woman you nearly strangled in Radford,' Cossall said. 'Don't look good. And then, of course, there's you up there alone with the little girl.'

'Not so little,' Millington mused.

'Thirteen.'

'Almost.'

'I never laid a finger.'

'Course you didn't,' Cossall said, 'we understand that. But out there in this mistrustful world, who else is going to believe it?'

'Eighteen months inside,' Millington said. 'Assault. In there with the nonces.'

'Look, I fuckin' never...'

'Right, right,' Cossall said. 'We know. Graham and me, we believe you. Right, Graham?'

Millington smiled, a terrifying sight. 'Now, Reggie, before you say any more, how about another drink? Bitter was it, or perhaps you fancy something a little stronger?'

Dunn sank what was left of his pint and then a swift

Bells, followed by another, and told them about keeping watch with McStay in his new sports job while Mickey Threadgill and Pleasant John Taylor, McStay's money in their pockets, swaggered down to the butchers across the street and torched it.

It was Hannah's half term and she was off at an English teachers' conference in Harrogate, which meant that instead of spending the evening round at her house on Devonshire Promenade, something he was increasingly likely to do, Resnick was spending a quiet evening at home with the cats.

Of course, he'd put his Charlie Parker on the stereo, the collection with 'Cheryl' as one of the tracks. Not the greatest, perhaps. But honest, genuine. Miles, only young then, sounding a little uncertain in his articulation, hazy; and Bud Powell's piano solo working too hard against the rhythm. But Parker's chorus was fired by the presence of possibility, brilliance waiting for its spark.

Cheryl told the story to her new feller a few weeks later. They were taking a break from dancing, a leaving do for a friend of a friend upstairs at the Irish and the DJ over the top on seventies disco. 'Le Freak.' 'Young Hearts Run Free.' 'You're the Greatest Dancer.'

New feller. She presumed that's what he was. They'd met at the exhaust centre when she'd taken in her van for some running repairs. Grease on his overalls and a great bum. Twenty seven if he was a day. He confessed to her after, it was the leisure suit he'd noticed. She hadn't told him yet how old she was, though he knew about Vicki so he could likely figure out she wasn't exactly Liv Tyler. Closer, Liz Taylor. Still, pray for a little subdued lighting and hopefully the stretch marks wouldn't show. Vicki was sleeping over with her mate Erica and her two kids, a favour returned.

'And they nicked the lot of them?' Brian asked. A nice name, Brian.

18

'All three. Pictures on the paper. Arson. Intimidation. Fraud. Enough for half a dozen episodes of *The Bill*.'

'Let us know,' Brian said, his hand rather high on her thigh, 'when you're ready to leave.'

It nearly popped out of her mouth. 'Right now, sunshine,' but there was Gloria Gaynor winding up through the speakers. 'I Will Survive.' She couldn't let that go to waste now, could she?

'Come on, love,' she said, dragging Brian back out onto the floor. 'Just one more dance, eh?'

Behind the Wall
Stanley Middleton

Soon after I had started school, and that is now nearly seventy years ago, I acquired the habit, when I had nobody to play with, of running up and down our short back-garden path. This, only a few yards in length, lay between a rectangle of flowers on the one side and a small bank of rhubarb, untidy rockery-stone and lilies of the valley on the other. I'd trot backwards and forwards, my mind as lively as my short legs, making up adventures and excitements, combats with Germans and Romans and Red Indians, talking to myself the while, either in commentary or snatches of dialogue or even in small pieces of third-person narrative similar to that in the books I was beginning to read. To this day I can't recall exactly whether this speech rang only in my head or was spoken aloud, muttered breathlessly, as I ran tirelessly, enjoyably for half-hours on end.

Neither my family nor the neighbours declared my behaviour eccentric. I was doing nobody any harm; my mother knew exactly where I was and could check from time to time that I had not deviated into mischief, while visitors coming to see us or the people next door, for the yard was shared, would greet me politely enough with,

'Just having your run, are you, Sonny?'

What they said in private to their nearest and dearest I shall not conjecture now. Perhaps they envied my parents so docile a child, suspecting that their own offspring would have chosen to play their rowdy games in gangs outside the houses of men on night-shift.

As I trotted I could look over the low, round-topped wall to the gardens, three in number, further down the street. They lay at a much lower level than ours for the houses were built on a slope. The garden next to us was distinguished from any other known to me in that it had a circular bed surrounded by brick-paths and quartered with a brick cross. Moreover, it was separated from the other two plots and from its own yard by a fence of green, pointed palings through which a small gate led into the centre. There seemed to my young eyes something rather aristocratic about this arrangement, something ordered, controlled, planned, as opposed to the other patches of marigolds or rose bushes roughly split by a path, 'pad' we called it, in one case paved and in the other of trampled soil.

At the far side of this third garden I could see, could not miss, a bleak brick wall. It rose as high as any of the two-storeyed houses, but was unmarked by ornamentation, and unpunctured by windows. It rose against the sky, and stayed sombre, dull and unlovely, but solid, a huge dividing feature. Its owner was a Mr Park.

I use the word 'owner' advisedly for Park not only owned this property but perhaps a dozen other houses in the street, something unusual enough to be spoken of in my hearing more than once. Most of the other families, like us, paid rent, some directly to Park himself, and so spoke of him as playing a more elevated rôle. This status as a capitalist was not due to any financial acumen on the part of the man himself, but to his father, 'Old Man' Park, who had up to his death lived in the same premises his son now occupied. He had been a builder and joiner, and the wall made up the back of his workshop, his store rooms and stable. For all I know he had built them himself earlier in his career. That had been long enough ago, and even my brother, ten years older than I, and at work, did not remember the horse, though the dray still stood, strong as ever, if rusty and paintless, at the furthest corner of the yard in all weathers. Park's 'grounds' seemed huge; approached by double-gates they were unpaved except for a long 'patio' (we did not use the word) of paving stones outside the back door of the kitchen and the first entrance to the wash-house.

'Old Man' Park had been prosperous enough, but his

business had died with him. He had quarrelled with his only child who had refused for whatever reason to take up his father's trade, had left home, and had worked, rumour claimed, somewhere in Scotland, and had not returned until after his father's death, about the time of my birth, when the son sold up the goodwill of the business, the stock, the horse but not the dray, and found for himself a suitable job somewhere in Nottingham. The work he did was by no means out of the ordinary; he was shop assistant and head storekeeper to a large ironmongery emporium on the London Road, hardly a wonderful occupation for our only capitalist, but jobs were scarce then and were to remain so until the outbreak of the War. He dressed neatly, polished his only shoes, set out from home at a quarter to eight each morning, and was not back, equally neat, until after six o'clock. He worked, it was observed, most Saturday mornings, and sometimes even in the afternoons. He did not patronise the pubs, the cricket-field, the picture-palaces, the churches or the chapels, the billiard-hall or the swimming-bath, but could be seen on bright Sunday afternoons walking across the common land, now a golf-course, with his beautiful wife.

Mr Park, (I never heard his first name), rarely spoke by way of greeting to anyone in the street, let alone to people casually met. His face, slightly pock-marked, seemed dour, set in concrete. He thinned his mouth to a grim line, half shut his eyes in suspicion, never altering his expression in face of the expected, silent hostility of the world. He would nod to my father, everyone did, but never lift his hand to touch the brim or raise his trilby hat, even if my mother was there. The forehead came down; the chin dropped towards his prominent Adam's apple, and that was all. No sound escaped from those compressed lips.

'I wonder what he's so glum about,' my mother would say.

'I wonder.' My father glanced down at my pricked ears.

'He looks like somebody with something on his conscience,' she'd enunciate.

23

'Haven't we all?'

'You speak for yourself,' she'd answer, laughing.

Mrs Park was quite sparklingly different. In the long hours her husband spent at work, she'd cheerfully sweep her pavement or scrub her doorstep, often displaying bright bloomers as she leaned energetically forward. She could be heard singing in a resonant contralto as she hung washing on the line. We all knew her first name, (it was Mary), and she'd speak to small boys, to me even, if nobody better presented himself. She seemed shapely and her limbs shone rounded and strong. She offered a stark contrast to the thin, grim, slightly hunched frame of her husband as they walked side by side, but on those occasions she matched her expression to his, as stoically battle-scarred as he from the vicissitudes of the world. It even appeared to my mother that Mary wore less colourful clothes on these occasions, even though the outings must have been entirely devoted to pleasure. Of the nature of these excursions I have no idea, perhaps merely to breathe the fresh air, the cheapest diversion away from home. She was not, we agreed, local, but betrayed no signs of a Scottish accent, so that we had no idea either of her origin, or where she had met her husband.

The Parks had no children, but the wife, at least, did not show any antipathy towards those who played in the street. Mr Park we all feared not because he had taken action against us but because he ignored us. 'The Skull,' we called him. If we asked him for a cigarette card or the right time he walked past us as if we had not spoken, or he was stone-deaf. Even at the age of seven I wondered how this old man got on with his sprightly wife. Did she laugh or sing when he was at home, and did he respond in any way? I had heard my parents more than once touch on this subject.

'He might be very good about the house,' my father said. 'Useful. A real handyman.' My father had a good word for everybody. 'Thoughtful.'

'But his face. It's like a thundercloud. I feel sorry for

that poor woman.'

'She doesn't seem sorry for herself. She always speaks. Always pleasant.'

'That's what I mean. They're poles apart. What could she see in a monster like that?'

This led my father to compare and contrast, not without touches of malice, the married lives of one or two other notables in the street, to such effect that my mother felt called upon, by means of face-pulling, frowns and despairing gestures, to warn him that small ears were cocked and taking it all in. My father laughed, a deep almost solemn sound this time, as he answered,

'He'll learn. Soon enough. For himself.'

One day in early winter Mrs Park at her front door stopped and enquired why I wasn't at school. On the lookout for conversation she was dressed in her finery, mobcap and apron put away.

'I've been badly,' I said.

'What's been wrong?'

'Ear-ache. We went to the doctor's. He put oil in my ears.'

'Are they better now?'

I answered that I had almost recovered, but pointed, not without pride, to the cotton-wool in the afflicted organs. As I was about to move off she asked,

'Would you like a biscuit?'

'Yes, please.'

'Come on in, then.'

The question did not altogether surprise me in those innocent days. We were not warned to keep away from strangers, only to be polite if they spoke to us. God knows we were suspicious enough of oddities, the mentally deranged, the physically deformed, 'chockers', that is old men of about my present age. The girls skipped to rhymes such as: *My mother said/I never should/Play with gypsies/In the wood,* but we did not apply these rhymes to ordinary life. They were as far from our sort of reality as the ideas I read about a few years later at the grammar

25

school, notions which the grey-eyed goddess Athene put deep into the heart of the daughter of Icarius, the prudent Penelope. Perverts there may have been, paedophiles, and we had heard of them, but they were on a par for us with ghosts or dragons. Dogs or enraged citizens guarding their territorial rights were much more likely to do us harm. These were the times, you may recall, when a woman could walk down the main street to do an hour's shopping and leave her back door unlocked with no dire consequences.

Moreover, it was considered right that children should be given small treats if they had injured themselves. Fall and cut your knee, endure your dabs of stinging tincture of iodine like a man, and before long someone would be stuffing your mouth with some tooth-rotting confection. Mrs Park's offer, therefore, of a biscuit had seemed perfectly proper to me: a reward for putting up with the pain of my recent illness.

Going inside the house was a slightly different matter. The usual pattern was to be left standing out on the pavement where the presentation would be made. One was not often invited into other people's homes; the soles of the unrighteous could trample in mud or blood or worse. Nevertheless, being curious I followed Mrs Park's shapely back and legs into the front room, past settee, marbled mantle-piece, superior leather chairs, through the small corridor and into the living room, where she opened the wall-cupboard, and produced a biscuit barrel. She removed the lid and allowed me to choose. This was luxury, indeed; at home we had biscuits, but they were kept in a plain tin, and were all of one dull kind, arrowroot. I looked, but knew better than to poke about with my fingers. In the end I picked a chocolate delicacy of the sort we had only in our Christmas selection. I thanked Mrs Park who returned the barrel to its cupboard but said no word to me about dropping crumbs as my mother would. I took my first bite with my left hand cupped inelegantly below my mouth. Having established my credentials as a polite, well-brought-up child I was preparing to leave when she said, suddenly,

'You're the little runner, aren't you? That's what Mrs Smith calls you.' Our next-door neighbour. 'And I've seen you sometimes from the window of our attic bedroom.' This was news to me. I continued to munch my biscuit. I had not noticed her attic. 'I used to like running when I was a girl.'

'Yes,' I said.

'I won several races when I was at school. I couldn't do it now. I haven't the puff.' I smiled at her. 'I won the silver cup at the orphanage where I was.' This I recognised as a nugget of information I could pass on with advantage to my mother. 'You don't know what an orphanage is, do you?'

'Yes,' I said. 'A place where they send children who haven't got fathers and mothers.'

'Um.' She looked for the moment as grim as her husband. 'A hell-hole.'

She immediately cheered up, as if her confession had lightened the burden of her memory.

'Do you know what a stable is?'

'Yes. A place where they keep horses.'

'Have you ever seen one?'

'No.'

She narrowed her eyes.

'We have a stable,' she said. I knew this, but did not say so, spoiling her pleasure. 'Would you like to see it?'

'Yes, please.' Absence from school had not proved unalloyed delight. Boredom had soon prevailed.

She beckoned me through the scullery where she unfastened the back door, held in security by a large lock, a small Yale, and two huge metal bolts.

'You'd think it was The Tower of London, wouldn't you?'

We emerged on to the patio. She did not lead me immediately to our destination, but towards the double-gate out into the street. There she pointed out three even larger bolts, and a rock-heavy steel padlock.

'It was Mr Park's Dad put them on,' she said. 'He didn't want burglars filching his money. He was a miser. Do you know what that is?'

'Yes.'

'And his son's damn' near as bad.'

The word 'damn' was absolutely forbidden in our house, and though many in the street and schoolyard starred their remarks with swear words, 'damn' appeared but infrequently. (A few years later, when I was a teenager, I remember the ancient wicket-keeper of the opposing team taking the ball which had whipped past my bat, looking heavenward and sighing, 'By God, youth, that was bleddy close.' 'Was it?' I said, with such nonchalance as I could muster. 'As near your off-stump as "damn" is to swearing.')

Mrs Park showed no signs of having spoken out of turn, but rattled the bolts irritably and flicked the padlock upwards. She nodded to me, a fellow-spirit who understood her frustration and marched me smartly towards the stable door. She tried to pull this open without success.

'It's double,' she said, 'so you could open the top without the horse getting out.'

I could see that.

'But it's all locked, barred and bolted. It was an obsession with him. He couldn't bear any one near his property. And he brought up his son to be as bad. Every penny had to be accounted for. When he was no older than you, he lost three-ha'pence from the change from a pound note. He stopped his penny spending-money for three weeks to teach him to be more careful.'

She had by this time unfastened the end door, and we stood inside. The only light spread from that opening, but we could see quite well because the walls and the ceiling were whitewashed, emphasising the blackness of the one cross-beam. I could see furniture stored: a sofa, two arm chairs, a kitchen table and benches, two marble-topped washing tables with basins and ewers. These items all seemed in better order than those one would find in daily use in the neighbours' houses. They were all spotlessly clean, washed and dusted within the last day or two.

'That's some stuff my husband, Mr Park, had left to him in an aunt's will. We had no room for it inside, so it has to stand out here. "It's too good to sell," he says. 'We'd get nothing for it these days.' So I have to come out here and clean and polish it.'

We moved into the next space past a low partition. On the walls here hung two sets of harness, reins and brushes.

'He calls that the tack-room,' she said and moved me beyond the last division. 'This is where they kept the pony. Look, you can see the double-doors. The floor would be covered with straw then. Not now, I have to keep it all swept out and washed down.' I could smell the disinfectant.

'It's very smart,' I said. I felt proud of that word which my mother sometimes used.

'You could say so,' she answered, laughing gently at me. 'Well, that's the end of the tour. Now I have to make certain that I lock everything up. Mr Park'll check it when he comes home. Every night without fail.'

We emerged into the daylight, and walked together to the kitchen.

'He'd have kittens,' she said, 'if he knew I'd been out to the stable, and left the back-door wide open. Still, he'll not find out.'

'No,' I said. 'Never.'

She ruffled my hair and bending pressed my head warmly against her breasts, an unknown embrace to me. When she released me, we were both smiling.

'Still, I'll say one thing for him; he's as honest as the day's long. Mean as muck, but straight with it.'

Mrs Park guided me through the house and out into the street. I thanked her as I had been taught and she said, 'I wish all the boys in the street were as polite as you. You're a credit to your mother.'

Just before I set off at a run to cover the few yards up

29

the street, she said significantly,

'Honesty is always the best policy.'

In my later years as teacher of English, Latin and Divinity in the lower forms of a grammar school I often, at the end of a lesson just before I dismissed my pupils, offered them some such apophthegm and made them repeat it in the hope that they would retain it. 'Blessed are the meek for they shall inherit the earth' or even 'I before E except after C' or 'And Masculine is found to be/Hadria, the Adriatic Sea.' How successful this device was I have no means of discovering, but I have wondered many times if this 'wrinkle', we used such a term, wasn't implanted in my head that winter afternoon outside Mrs Park's front door.

At the beginning of December street gossip erupted. Mrs Park, it appeared, had been attacked on a piece of waste ground, and a largish sum of money had been stolen from her. She had been to her bank to collect the takings of the Christmas Club she organised. People paid small sums each week throughout a good part of the year; she recorded these transactions on their cards and in a book of her own. The clients had already consulted a catalogue and had decided what sum they would reach and had made their choice: a large tin of fancy biscuits, a box of choco-lates, a flowered caddy of special tea tied with ribbon, a jar of boiled sweets or a china spaniel, half-full of wrapped caramels, which once emptied would stand for the rest of the year, and longer, on the sideboard or front-window ledge as a symbol of affluence. The decisions had been made; Mrs Park had consulted her agent from the whole-sale grocer in town; he would deliver and be paid in cash on Friday evening. Thereafter each mother would hurry home, her treasure hidden under apron or brown paper, to keep it from prying eyes and fingers for the next three weeks. And now, the prudent had been robbed. Indigna-tion ran high, since there were many who claimed that Park could easily have put his hand in his pocket and paid out the thirty-odd pounds lost. He showed no signs of so doing. My mother recalled what I had reported when I had given them an account, listened to with no inconsiderable interest, of my visit to the Parks' house and stable. 'Mean as muck, but straight with it,' she quoted. That at the time had been considered vulgar and condemned as unfit for small ears to hear or small lips to repeat. Now it was blatantly produced as a word to the wise. *Verbum sapienti.* My father shook a lugubrious head.

Imagine, then, a week later when the news broke that Mrs Park had not been attacked at all. The investigating police, sympathetic at first, had become suspicious. A call to the manager elicited that she had been nowhere near the bank that afternoon and had, in fact, kept no account there. She was responsible for the torn coat, the dirt on face and hands; the blow on the head had been self-inflicted. She had been spending the money as it came in on clothes, on finery. Or so the wiseacres claimed. Mr Park grew and remained, it was said, livid with anger. Certainly as he stumped off to work in the morning he spoke to no-one, stared straight ahead, grimmer than before. We saw nothing of Mrs Park; she made no appearances in the street and must have done her shopping after dark. She kept the blinds drawn as if she had a corpse laid out in the parlour. Some reported furious exchanges from within the house, loud enough to be overheard by neighbours. One woman, given to exaggeration, described Mrs Park's screaming as her husband unmercifully beat her. 'You could hear his fists thumping into her chest,' she said.

In January, my father, going up the path to the shed as I was engaged on my 'run', stopped to exchange a word with me. He sometimes did this. We loved each other, but had little idea how to talk to each other. This afternoon, with frost already on the ivy leaves, he seemed grave, disconcerted as he pointed at the high ugly wall that formed the back of Mr Park's stable. He said nothing for a while; we stared together. His forefinger traced the outline in the icy air.

'We don't know one half of what goes on behind other

31

people's walls,' he said. 'Not one half.' We stood there, side by side, (I can imagine it now), lost and disturbed by our ignorance, but not altogether displeased by our complicity. 'Not a quarter.' Again we shared silence. When he spoke finally he was himself, an adult to a child, a father. 'Don't get cold,' he ordered. 'Get running. You'll catch your death standing about.'

That weekend we began to learn what had happened behind those blind walls. One Saturday afternoon Mr Park was chopping logs and kindling at the far end of his yard when the telephone rang. His was the only telephone in the street and dated from his father's days in business. I was surprised that he had kept it. His number was given by people with relatives admitted to hospital. If the patient was thought by the authorities to be within hours of death the nurses would ring and Mrs Park, never her husband, would carry the desperate news round. Word of my own father's imminent death ten years later came through that same number, though not through the Parks. It was a quicker means of communication than that other harbinger of catastrophe, the telegram.

On this Saturday afternoon the phone rang and Mrs Park came out and reported that he was wanted. She seemed, he said afterwards, to be perfectly normal. Muttering complaints he hurried indoors, leaving his wife by the chopping-block. When he returned less than five minutes later she had disappeared. This slightly surprised him, he said, because she had not to the best of his knowledge come back into the house, and there was only the one door. Not very concerned, he continued with his wood-cutting. Half an hour later he had stacked the logs neatly on the stable floor. Before he locked up he walked round to the other doors to make sure they were securely bolted. In the last room, the furniture-store, he found his wife hanging by the neck from the black cross-beam.

She had used a ladder, still in place, to attach the rope to the beam and had then climbed on to a small table which she had dragged a few feet forward. With the rope

32

round her white throat she had kicked the table away and thus had hanged herself. Her final, deliberate movement, the kicking over of the table, must have taken place after he had resumed his work. He informed the coroner that he had heard no sound. She was still alive, he thought, when he cut her down, but he was not sure. By the time she had reached the hospital she was dead. The local newspaper offered a watered-down account of her last hours. She had left no note. Mr Park was reported by his cleaning-woman not to be able to get over the casual way she had told him he was wanted on the telephone.

Mr Park stayed for perhaps another six months before he sold up to a man with a small haulier's business. He was sighted now and then in the town. Not long afterwards I gave up my running along the path. When I went back there a few months ago, both our house and his had been pulled down. Nobody in the street recognised me, but I didn't expect it. I questioned one woman standing at her front door right opposite the place where Park's gates had stood. She had never heard the name. I mentioned my own, but she had not heard of that, either.

Paying For It
David Belbin

Until his wife became pregnant, Andrew had never gone with a prostitute. But the libido made its own demands. Paying for sex was preferable to seducing his wife's friends, or sleeping with his students. Gradually, the idea took a hold on him. The seediness of the act attracted Andrew: sex separated from love or friendship, becoming as impersonal as money. He would not regard it as betraying his wife.

Andrew hadn't always believed in fidelity. When he was a student, in the seventies, monogamy seemed to be a trap, an institution which needed overthrowing. Love, he argued to the women he wanted to sleep with, was a bourgeouis construct, designed to keep the workers in line. Look at the ruling classes, he'd say. They had it away with each other whenever they liked. Why settle for less?

In the late seventies, Andrew often had two, or even three women on the go. A few of them shared his libertine philosophy, conducting their love lives in a similar fashion. Most merely put up with the situation. As the eighties began, Andrew's enthusiasm for open affairs waned. Fewer women were prepared to accept his terms and he got into more and more complicated relationships with those who would. Then, suddenly, everyone was scared of herpes, which was quickly followed by HIV. In 1985, Andrew got his first lectureship, and surprised himself by falling for a bossy, beautiful student eight years his junior.

Fiona was shocked by Andrew's previous promiscuity, but found an explanation for it which satisfied her. Andrew was an only child, whose parents died within months of each other during his first year at University. Indiscriminate sex, Fiona thought, was his way of denying death. But the time for denial was over. She insisted on monogamy.

Sex with students was frowned on less in the mid eighties than today. Nevertheless, when Fiona moved in with

35

Andrew, his head of department suggested that it might be prudent for them to marry. Andrew, having discovered that he had been wrong about the value of romantic love, found that he had nothing against marriage, either (though he made it clear that he was far too selfish to father children).

After graduating, Fiona became a secondary school teacher, and the couple were both successful at work. They moved to Nottingham in 1990. Andrew, by 1995, was a senior lecturer, well-liked by students and staff, with the prospect of a professorship. Fiona was a Head of Year. The couple lived in a Georgian town house near the city centre. '95 was also the year when Fiona hit thirty and became broody. She wanted to move from the inner city to a smart suburb, raise a family.

At first, Andrew resisted. Families frightened him. Bringing up children looked too much like hard work. Fiona respected his fears. Having children had never been part of their deal. But people changed, she said. Andrew didn't know whether he believed this or not.

Then things fell into place. Andrew was offered a post at the city's old redbrick university, which had hitherto regarded his discipline, Media Studies, as a jumped-up subject, beneath contempt. Now they saw how popular it had become and sought to buy an instant reputation. Andrew was being given the opportunity to create a whole new department. He took it. At the same time, there was a scare about the contraceptive pill Fiona was using. So she stopped taking it. By June 1996, Fiona was five months pregnant. That was when she went off sex. It was also when Andrew noticed the girl for the first time.

She stood at the bottom of his street, the run-down end, where working girls were often to be found, opposite the cemetery. But she didn't look like the other girls. She seemed less cheap, somehow, in her white blouse and tight black skirt. She was striking, but not conventionally beautiful, like Fiona. Her shoulders were too wide, her arms too thin, and her hair unfashionably long. She was, Andrew guessed, older than the children who sold themselves for crack money, but younger than the hardened whores who did it to support their kids. Her face was a little too big, he decided, but it stuck in his memory. He wanted her.

For weeks, Andrew resisted. He had never needed to use prostitutes before and, now that he was tempted, it seemed reckless to pick one so close to his own doorstep. He and Fiona had known, when they bought this house, that they would be near a red light zone, but its location, opposite the Arboretum, a short walk from the city centre and the University, was so convenient, the house so fine, that they succumbed. Where else in England could you get a Georgian town house for £80,000? It was worth the occasional hassle that Andrew's wife got from kerb-crawlers. Fiona was blasé about this, saying she felt sorry for the working girls. Theirs was an honest profession, Fiona proclaimed, which would always be around. Better that men use prostitutes than become rapists.

They didn't want their child to grow up around them, however, and put the house on the market. Selling wouldn't be easy. The place was big but had no garden and the area had declined further in the last six years. Their home was worth less now than they'd paid for it.

As Fiona finished the summer term and began her maternity leave, she started going to bed at nine, leaving Andrew at a loose end. The idea of screwing the girl took hold of him. Where was the harm in it? Andrew read somewhere that one in three men regularly used prostitutes. Women expected it. How would Fiona be hurt by this small deceit?

Still, he didn't approach her. Fidelity had become a habit. Andrew couldn't work out whether having the girl was a fantasy, or a plan. It didn't matter. In July, as suddenly as she'd appeared, the girl disappeared.

Sometimes, in those summer months, Andrew cruised the city streets, looking for her. Twice, he thought he'd found the girl. The first time, it was a woman a little older, not bad looking. He'd have slept with her in the seventies. She approached the car, but Andrew found he wasn't tempted. The second time was in late August, on Mapperley Road. He'd slowed down after seeing a woman who looked like the girl. He passed her, wound down his window and waited for her to offer him business.

'What can I do for you, duck?'

Andrew took in the woman's face. It wasn't the girl. This woman was Fiona's age. Her make-up was crudely done, but there was intelligence in her eyes and she was attractive enough to tempt him. Too attractive, Andrew realised. This woman was not for sale.

'I'm sorry,' he mumbled, catching on. 'I confused you with someone else.'

A man in a black leather jacket rapped on his passenger seat window, holding open a police warrant card. The woman stepped back.

'Would you mind explaining what you were doing, Sir?'

Andrew thought quickly.

'I'm sorry officer, I'm tired and I made a mistake. I was driving home from work and thought that this woman was my wife. Naturally, I stopped to give her a lift. But when I saw her from the front...'

'Your wife dresses like that, does she, Sir?'

Andrew glanced at the woman's tight mini-skirt, her cheap, thin blouse.

'Sometimes, yes. It's summer, for Christ's sake!'

'I'd have thought she'd get some bother, if she walks home this way. Can you show me something to confirm where you live?'

Andrew gave the plain clothes man his driving licence, thinking up a lie in case the officer asked him where he worked. This road wasn't on his way home from either University. But he was all right. The man made some kind of check over his radio, then handed Andrew's licence back.

'Better let you get home to your wife, Sir. Sorry to have detained you.'

Andrew could tell that he was unconvinced, but they were letting him go. This was compensation, he decided, for the many times that Fiona had been hassled by kerb crawlers.

Andrew was about to say that he was grateful. But then he saw the cynicism in the eyes of the male officer, the contempt on the face of the woman. He drove home.

After such a close call, Andrew stopped cruising the streets. He settled for masturbation, fantasising frequently about the girl. By September, he was having trouble summoning up her image for such reveries. Fiona was due in a few weeks. The new semester was about to begin. Andrew decided he was over what had been ailing him. No need to feel bad about it. Nothing had happened, except in his mind.

Fiona went to stay with her mother for a few days, giving Andrew time to prepare for his new job. He worked sixteen hour days. There were few distractions. Most of his University circle were still on holiday, while the couple's teacher friends were busy with their new term, which had already begun. He found that he missed Fiona badly.

He didn't notice when the girl first returned. One day, she was just there, in the same place. Only her red lips, and the way she stood, legs apart, made it clear what she was. Andrew wanted her more than before.

Even so, the first time he noticed her, he resisted. But she was there the next day too, a Friday afternoon. Andrew went to use the phone box opposite the end of his street, where he made an imaginary call. He watched as she went off with a bespectacled man who he recognised: a city solicitor. After fifteen minutes, the same man dropped her off.

Andrew wanted to go over then and there, proposition her. But it was madness. What if someone spotted them? Andrew wasn't friendly with any of the neighbours, but Fiona had acquaintances. If one of them were to see him with the girl, tell his wife... He decided to walk past her, get a good look. Later, maybe, when it was dark, he would come by in the car, and... a blue BMW stopped. With a smile, the girl got in. She seemed to attract a better class of customer, Andrew realised, professional men wanting to unwind at the end of the working day. He waited in the phone box for a long half hour, but she did not return.

Nor did she appear on Saturday or Sunday. Andrew cursed himself for not having her while he had the chance. He had been faithful by default.

Fiona was due back from her mother's on Monday evening. Andrew was to pick her up at the station just after eight. He drove home from the University at four. Looking forward to his wife's return, he picked up a bottle of Pouilly Fume, her favourite wine. Fiona would have one glass with her supper and he would finish the bottle after she'd gone to bed.

The girl was standing on the corner as Andrew turned onto the street. She was bending down, doing something with her shoe, and didn't look in his direction. Andrew's mind was on Fiona. Had he expected the girl to be there and thought it over, he might not have stopped. But he didn't think. The girl, hearing the squeak of his brakes, looked up, and approached the car. Close up, there was something vulnerable about her face, something sweet but damaged. Andrew leant back and opened the door.

'Get in, please, then get down. I'm taking you to my house.'

She hesitated for a moment.

'Please,' he said. 'I live round here.'

'I know,' she said, shutting the door and ducking down. 'I've seen you.' Her voice was almost accentless, not local. Andrew did a detour, turning onto a sidestreet and approaching his house from the far end of the road, so that he passed the narrow alley which was used only by the bin men and burglars. He stopped the car.

'It's the house at the end of the alley,' he told the girl. 'Wait for me in the back yard, while I go round the front and let you in.'

'All right', she said, as though this was familiar behaviour.

I'm mad, Andrew told himself, as he found a parking space. The high, hollow hum of the burglar alarm welcomed him to his home. There was a double flash on the answering machine, but Andrew ignored it.

40

'How long do you want?' the girl asked, as soon as she was inside.

'An hour,' Andrew demanded, greedily.

'Fifty.'

He didn't haggle and paid in advance.

'Where do you want me?'

Andrew was so attracted to her that he became nervous, his hands clammy. He held out a hand. She looked surprised, but took it, then followed, like a child being guided by an adult.

'Nice place,' she said, looking at the landing walls, with their framed photos of forties' film stars and jazz musicians.

'Where would you have taken me?' he asked, 'if I hadn't brought you here.'

'Apart from the car? There's a flat I borrow. You'd have had to pay an extra ten.'

The spare room was made up. The bed was new, three quarter size. He and Fiona had slept in it once, to test that there was enough room for guests, but they had never made love on it. Now the girl sat on the edge and undressed. Andrew asked her her name.

'Does it matter?' She replied.

'I want to call you something.'

'Sharon.'

She didn't look like a Sharon, more like a nude painted by Degas. Her breasts were heavy, a stark contrast to her slender arms. Her nipples were a bright, pinky red. Andrew found himself shocked by this sudden intimacy, reminding him of his shallow seductions in the seventies. But she was revealing everything too quickly.

'I'm Andrew.' He wasn't sure why he told her his real name. 'Leave your knickers on for now, Sharon.'

'You're the boss.'

He meant to hold her, work up to the event, but she was undoing his flies.

'Do you want me to..?' He nodded. For a moment, he had confused a transaction with a seduction. While she worked, he noticed a small, brown mole on her neck and felt a strong urge to kiss it. But he didn't.

'Are you ready?' Her tone was tender but polite, like a nurse about to give an injection.

'No. Not yet. A little more.'

Andrew wanted to stretch time, to make the hour last forever.

'Talk to me for a little while,' he said. 'Tell me about yourself.'

She frowned and he knew that anything she told him would be lies.

'Where are you from?' He asked.

'Reading.'

'How long have you been working the beat?' He'd read somewhere that this was what the girls, and the police, called it.

'I don't, except when things are quiet. I've got a mobile number. You call me up. I only answer if I'm free. Then I get a taxi to wherever you want me to be. Do you want it?'

'Yes, please.'

She produced a scrap of paper from a tiny pocket in her skirt, removing a condom at the same time.

'You don't have a pimp? Most of the girls round here seem to.'

"Sharon" shrugged. 'A couple of thugs have tried it on. One of them showed me a gun, tried to get me to come with him. But they've got no hold over me. I don't do drugs and they don't know where I live.'

'Sensible.'

'Do you want me to suck you again?' She kept her eyes on him while she spoke. He liked that.

'No. Let me hold you.'

Their embrace was gentle and so absorbing that Andrew didn't notice her remove her panties or slip on the condom. She straddled him and the sex began. It was more exciting and more satisfying than he had expected, or hoped. He felt passion. He felt dirty. He felt like singing.

After they'd been fucking for a while, the girl began to grind her thighs together, trying to make him come quickly,

42

but Andrew asked her to stop. When they were finished, and he'd paid her, they had used practically the whole hour.

'I'll call you,' he said, as he let her out the back.

To his surprise, she smiled girlishly and blew him a kiss.

'I'll bet you will.'

He was closing the back door when he heard the front one open.

'Andrew, are you there?' It was Fiona. 'Didn't you get my message on the machine?'

'I only just got in myself,' he shouted, hurriedly rearranging his clothes.

'I got an earlier train. I had to take a taxi.'

'Never mind. You're home now.' He called, blessing his luck, then hurrying into the hall and taking his wife into his arms.

'You're all sweaty,' she said. 'Has it been hot here?'

'Yes,' he told her, adding the promise, 'I'll take a shower.'

Andrew saw the girl several times over the next two weeks, though never again in his home. He would phone her mobile from a call box and arrange to pick her up. They would go to a desolate room in a drab house off the Woodborough Road. If the room wasn't available, they made do in his car. Twice, they used a phone box, which was exciting, but risky. The second time, as Andrew finished, they were interrupted by drunken, mocking yobs and had a humiliating run back to the car.

The girl seemed to enjoy chatting with Andrew, and treated him with tenderness. She never told him her real name, though, and deftly deflected questions about her past and private life. She was, by contrast, happy to talk about her other punters.

'Sad, most of them. Their wives don't do it any more, or won't give them head. They're always justifying why they're with me, as though I care. Some of them want to treat me like a daughter, which is just freaky. They want to pretend I like them, that I'm not just doing it for the money. It's only sex, but they want to make it more.'

She sounded young, naive, when she opened up like that.

She was, Andrew guessed, nineteen or twenty, and assumed that all men used prostitutes. Andrew wondered about her parents, whether they had an inkling of what she doing, how they would feel if they did.

'Open your legs,' he asked one time, when they were in the rented room. When she obeyed, he began to eat her, his tongue caressing her clitoris with loving precision.

'Stop! Stop!' She ordered.

When he looked up, she was crying. He held her, and they did not fuck that day.

'Don't do that again,' she told him, when he dropped her off in the usual place, a short walk from the Victoria Centre bus station.

Afterwards, he didn't call her for days. Fiona might go into labour at any time, and there were many meetings with his new colleagues, preparing courses. Andrew's department, it was suddenly decided, had to offer an option to second year Humanities undergraduates. Andrew had the lightest timetable and ought to do it himself. But what on? Years ago, Andrew had published a slim book on punk, the music of his University years. He dug out and dusted his notes, then raided the attic for seven inch singles. He played them after Fiona had gone to sleep, reliving his youth. Not much of the music had aged well. Andrew was surprised to find how little nostalgia he felt for those days.

The semester started on a Tuesday. Andrew resented the hours he spent out of the house, worried that Fiona would go into labour without him. But he missed the girl, too. When Fiona's mother came to Nottingham to help out, Andrew at last had a chance to call her. He drove to a phone box, and dialled her mobile number. What he wanted was a final, thrilling fuck before he began his new job, entered fatherhood.

'The number you called has been disconnected. BT has not charged you for this call.'

At home that night, after his wife and mother-in-law had gone to bed, Andrew was almost glad that it was over. He'd been with the girl eleven times — twelve, if you counted the

44

last occasion, when they didn't screw. Now that she was gone, he could admit it to himself: he'd been obsessed with her. Even now, he only had to think of the girl to become hard.

Those three weeks — his prostitute days — had been a time of madness, Andrew decided, a kind of limbo, where his libido had ruled his life. But now they were were over.

A week later, the baby had still not arrived. Fiona was constantly grouchy and Andrew was glad to go to work, begin lecturing again. His *Punk Rock* course was the most oversubscribed option in Second Year Humanities. When Andrew arrived at the lecture hall there was no need to pass round the usual attendance sheet. It was clear that all of the signed-up students were there, together with curious undergraduates, several post-graduates, and a few staff.

'I'm going to talk about a movement which was effectively over before most of you were born,' Andrew announced, buoyed up by the big audience. 'We're going to start by listening to its death throes.'

The song began, ugly, out of tune, the singer attacking the garbled lyric with a disgust which taunted the listener to react with the same feeling. Andrew scanned the audience, enjoying their expressions. Some looked bewildered, others had an embarrassed smile. Several grinned, as if to show that they got the joke. Many listened in calm concentration. One or two took notes. None of them seemed to be enjoying the music.

Andrew glanced at his notes. He would start by saying that the track was *We Are All Prostitutes* by The Pop Group. Then he would talk about punk rock and the ideas it came from. In those dog days of the last Labour government, the punks had foretold the collapse of socialism. Punk saw romance as a myth, invented by retailers to sell their products. Everything was for sale. In a society where money was the only way of denoting value, we were all prostitutes.

In a dissonant din of screeching violins, the track faded. Andrew opened his mouth to begin.

Then he saw her. She was towards the back of the hall

45

and had had her hair cut. But it was definitely the girl. Andrew's mouth opened and closed. She was a student. She might even be one of his students. And she knew exactly who he was. Andrew consulted his notes.

'I thought I noticed a little stage fright,' his head of school commented afterwards. 'But interesting. I expect there's a book in it.'

The book had already been written, by Andrew, but he said nothing, too busy scanning the backs of the heads of departing students, wishing now that he'd taken an attendance list.

'I passed this round for you,' the Professor added, handing him two lined, A4 sheets full of names and departments. 'Petty, I know, but it can be useful to keep a record.'

Over lunch, Andrew went through the list twice. There was, of course, no "Sharon".

Andrew arrived early for the next week's lecture, hoping to spot the girl. It was twenty minutes before he noticed her. She'd slipped in late and was sitting at the back, where she could escape easily. Andrew gazed at her as he spoke. In the student uniform of jeans and sweatshirt, she looked younger than on the street, more beautiful.

As he'd expected, the girl left immediately the lecture ended. Andrew pushed his way through the students who were waiting with questions. Two had books for him to sign. 'Next week, next week', he repeated, adding, disgracefully, 'my wife is having a baby'. The ruse worked, and soon he was running across the grass at the back of the Portland building, through a sea of similar looking students, trying to identify a body which he knew better naked.

Then he was beside her. She didn't seem surprised to see him.

'We have to talk,' he said.

'I knew I shouldn't have come,' she answered, looking at the grass.

'Can we walk? By the lake, maybe?'

'No. Someone might see. How long have you got?'

46

'A meeting at four. Nothing until then.'

'Drive to the Victoria Centre.'

In the car, she told him her real name: Emma.

'You live here alone?' He asked, when they were inside her Victoria Centre flat, high above the city. Emma nodded. She brought a bottle of Becks from a well-stocked fridge.

'When you live alone, there's no-one to ask where the money comes from.'

'How long have you been...?'

'I started this June, at the end of my first year. I was skint, in debt. There were no jobs going. My Mum's on benefit. She couldn't help.'

'That's awful,' Andrew commented, lamely.

'Not really. It's like you said in your lecture last week. "We're all prostitutes." Most people hate their jobs. So most jobs are a form of prostitution.'

'But sex shouldn't be a job. It should be...' He stopped when he saw the disdainful look on her face.

'Women always find a way of making men pay,' she told him.

'I don't believe that,' Andrew said, not sure what he believed.

'I do. Only fools give it away. All the time I was growing up, I saw the way men fucked my mother about, swore I'd never let them treat me that way. There's nothing wrong with what I do.'

'I didn't say there was,' Andrew told her, 'but it can be dangerous.'

'Not so very dangerous. I only get into a car when I feel safe. If a punter's all right, I give him my card. I soon work up enough business to keep me off the streets.'

'You don't work in term time?'

'I take the work seriously,' Emma said. 'And, in term time, I'm more likely to be spotted by someone I know. Anyway, I paid off my overdraft in a week. I figure if I work three months a year I'll have enough to see me through my degree and study abroad.'

47

'Why do my course? Did you know I was one of your.. clients?'

Emma laughed. 'As if. I figured you worked for Central TV. You've got that flash git look about you. I came to your course because of my Mum. She's always going on about the punk days. She bought into all that 'fuck love' theory you were on about. Also, there's a bit of a buzz about you at Uni. Some of the other girls fancy you.'

'Do you?' Andrew asked.

Emma smiled enigmatically. 'You want someone my age,' she told him, 'you don't have to pay for it.'

'I know,' Andrew said. 'But I want you.'

Emma looked uncomfortable. 'That time when you tried to... you know. It freaked me out.' She went silent. He looked around the flat. It was nearly stylish, with a framed Picasso print on one wall, fresh flowers perched on a new-looking coffee table. But he couldn't help thinking about where the money for the rent came from.

'I don't go with prostitutes,' he said, eventually. 'But I had to have you.'

Emma didn't seem flattered.

'Why me? I'm not beautiful. I've got spots, in case you hadn't noticed. My body's out of proportion. I'm nothing.'

'You're not. You're gorgeous. If you knew how much I wanted you now...'

She put a finger to his lips and pulled him towards her.

'Are you safe?' she asked, when she'd undressed him.

'I've not had a vasectomy.'

'I don't mean that. I'm on the pill.'

'I'm safe,' he promised her.

'Can I see you again?' he asked afterwards. 'I mean, like this?'

'I don't take clients during term time,' Emma said, coldly.

'I don't mean as a client,' he told her. 'I have feelings for you.'

'Feelings?' Emma leant forward. The way her breasts

48

dangled tantalised him. 'Romantic love is a lie,' she told him, using his own words, or a parody of them. 'A way of getting women into bed. I really fancy you, Andrew. I enjoy your company. I could fall for you big time. But I'd only get hurt, wouldn't I?'

'I...' He could not deny it. He loved his wife, and would never choose to leave her, especially not for a student whom university regulations prohibited him from screwing.

'Go,' she told him.

'I wish...'

He looked down at her phone, meaning to memorize the number, but it wasn't written on the hand-set.

'Andrew?' For a moment, he thought that she was going to ask him to pay. But she was holding out a slim volume. It was his book on Punk. 'Would you sign this? Put "To Veronica." That's my Mum.'

He got to his meeting five minutes late.

'What the hell are you doing here, man?' the head of school asked.

'I'm sorry. I..'

'Have you come from the hospital?'

'Hospital?'

'They've been trying to get you for hours. Your wife's gone into labour.'

The Queen's Medical Centre was opposite the university campus. It was quicker to run there than take the car and search for a parking place. Andrew, breathless and sweat-drenched, reached the maternity ward ten minutes after hearing the news. The delivery, they told him, had been quick but painful. His wife and daughter were fine. A sister put the baby in his arms.

'Where were you?' Fiona asked. 'I called in plenty of time.'

Andrew had been working out the lie during every moment of his run to the hospital.

'I drove home to see you for lunch and the car broke down,' he said. 'By the time the AA had turned up and sorted it out, I had to get back for my meeting. That's where

I heard.'

'I wanted you there with me.'

Lucy was an ideal baby, crying only when she was hungry, waking just once a night. Andrew's heart filled with love for her and Fiona. He resolved never, ever to sleep with Emma again.

The University allowed Andrew a week's paternity leave, so he missed the next of his "Punk" lectures. When it resumed, Emma did not come. Nor did she come to any more of the series. Andrew was relieved. He didn't want his resolution put to the test.

In December, Andrew and Fiona agreed a house sale and had their offer accepted on a place in Beeston. In January, just before the semester restarted, the couple began to make love again.

A CID sergeant was waiting outside Andrew's office when he arrived at work on the first day back.

'You know a student called Emma Hardy?' he asked, once inside.

'Name doesn't ring a bell,' Andrew replied, calmly. He didn't know Emma's surname and, if it was her, they hadn't done anything illegal.

'How about this?'

The photograph was of Emma, looking about fifteen. Andrew bluffed it out.

'Yes, I think.. a girl like this was at one or two of my lectures.'

'I see.' The officer made a note. 'There's someone I'd like you to meet. Can you be at the station for two this afternoon?'

Andrew checked his diary.

'I've a...'

'It's important.'

'I'll cancel it then. Can you tell me...?'

'Two.' The officer told him, brusquely, and left.

All morning, Andrew tried to work out what was going on. Before going to the police station, he decided to visit

Emma. First, he had to broach the Victoria Centre's security system.

'There's no-one here of that name,' a disembodied voice told him.

Confused, Andrew killed time by walking around the city, trying to work out what the police wanted from him. Had Emma freaked out and made some kind of allegation against him? Rape, perhaps?

In the police station, Detective Inspector Greasby was civil.

'There's someone who wants to see you,' Greasby said.

Andrew was taken into the CID room, where a woman of about his own age, who he assumed was a police officer, stared at him intently.

'Yes,' she told the Inspector. 'That's him.'

Andrew stared back at her. There was something familiar about the woman — the knowing eyes, the slight wobble in the lips. He guessed, correctly, that she was Emma's mother.

In an interview room, the Inspector asked questions about Emma.

'Look, what's going on?' Andrew wanted to know. 'I mean, if there's been some kind of crime, I want a solicitor.'

'We're trying to establish whether there's been a crime or not. When did you last see Emma Hardy?'

Andrew calculated. People were bound to have seen him talking to Emma outside the Portland Building in October. He gave the date.

'I can be precise because my daughter was born that afternoon.'

'Then you're the last person to have seen Miss Hardy alive, Sir.'

'Emma's dead?'

The Inspector stared at him, taking in Andrew's manner, his behaviour.

'That's what we'd like you to tell us.'

Andrew asked for a solicitor.

The solicitor who came was an old friend, Max Carter.

Andrew admitted to Max that he had slept with Emma, explaining the situation, making it clear that he had not known Emma to be a student when it happened. He did not tell him about their last encounter. The solicitor told Andrew not to give a statement until he'd got more from the police.

'If you've been straight with me, I can't see that you'll be in any trouble. Thing is, the police and the girl's mother want to know what's happened to her. Once we tell them that she's a prostitute, the picture becomes clearer. Girls like that go off all the time.'

'Emma's not a common prostitute. She took her degree seriously.'

'What I don't understand,' Max said, ignoring Andrew's comment, 'is why they brought in the mother.'

That night, released without charge, Andrew was tempted to tell Fiona what had happened. But it was easier not to, and, finally, he didn't.

Next morning the police came while he was still in bed.

'It's a mistake', Andrew promised his wife.

The police had an order forcing him to give intimate body samples. When Max visited Andrew in the cells, he was less sympathetic than the day before.

'Why didn't you tell me the girl was your daughter?' He asked.

'When did you find out?' Detective Inspector Greasby wanted to know.

'I had no idea.'

'Maybe you fucked her because she reminded you of her mother?'

'I didn't recognise the mother when I saw her yesterday.'

'But you don't deny that you had a sexual relationship with Veronica Hardy in 1976?'

'We had a brief thing,' Andrew admitted, against Max's advice.

'You knew that she'd dropped out of University?'

'Yes, but I didn't know she was pregnant. I certainly

never made the connection with Emma.'

'When did Emma tell you who she was?'

'She never told me. I still don't know if I believe...'

Traces of Andrew's semen was found on Emma's sheets, showing that he had had sex with Emma after finding out that she was a student. He had lied, to his solicitor and to the police. It was bound to come out. Whatever else happened, he would lose his job.

Emma, or her body, was not found. She had vanished from Nottingham, taking little from her flat. Her bank account had been cleared out on the afternoon Andrew saw her last. He could have done that, the police argued, to make it look like she had run away, or been robbed by her pimp. They seemed convinced that she must have had a pimp.

'How did they know about me?' Andrew asked Max.

'There was one of your books on the coffee table in the flat, signed, dated and dedicated to the girl's mother. '

Emma's disappearance was reported when she didn't go home for Christmas, Max said. It took until January for her flat to be searched. The solicitor assured Andrew that he had a good defence.

'The only evidence against you is circumstantial. The jury will be prejudiced against you for sleeping with your daughter, but the defence will give many examples of a syndrome which might have affected you. Surveys show that, with a brother and sister who've been separated for a long time — even with a parent and child, where there's been an adoption — often the first thing they feel when they meet is an overwhelming sexual attraction. We'll argue that something of the sort happened between you and Emma.'

After two and a half days, Andrew was released by the police, who did not have enough evidence to charge him. But the damage had been done. The story was all over the papers. Fiona, who had been cheated on, lied to, and publicly humiliated, wouldn't let Andrew visit their new house, or see his daughter. The university suspended him.

Andrew booked into a hotel and took to drinking. A

month on, Emma was still missing and his wife still refused to talk with him. Fiona had now discovered, perhaps through Max, that Andrew had been stopped for kerb crawling, and that he had slept with Emma in their house. She began divorce proceedings.

In March, Andrew moved to London, where he found an affordable bedsit and some temporary lecturing work. He had no criminal record, but was too notorious to get a university job. He might change his name and build a small career, but he would never regain his reputation. He would never see his wife and child again. No court would give a man access to his baby daughter after he admitted having carnal knowledge of her older sister.

Only the idea that Emma may still be alive, and might somehow need him, kept Andrew from killing himself. If Emma were alive, she was most likely to be in London, where it was easiest to be invisible. He collected call girl cards from phone boxes then rang, disguising his voice. On rare occasions when the woman answering sounded like Emma, he would go to see her.

She would have changed, he knew, but not how. He kept seeing traces of her in women on the street — her hair, the way her shoulders moved, something about the walk, perhaps, or the way she stood. He kept remembering nuances he hadn't been aware of noticing at the time.

Once, near King's Cross, he saw, from behind, a woman in a cheap winter coat. Her hair was like Emma's, only more grey. The walk was right. He'd decided that she was too small when a crowd of people pushed past her and she ducked her head in that distinctive way Emma had, a kind of flinch. He ran to her. She looked around, with fear at first, but then with recognition.

It was Emma's mother, Veronica. Andrew had slept with this woman, fathered a child with her. Yet he remembered little about her. She was one of many. He'd fucked her, not because he had to, but because he could. Now she looked pale, finished, like the ghost of her own daughter. He persuaded her to go for a drink at the station bar.

'Have you heard anything of her?' he pleaded when they were sitting.

'Would I be here if I had?'

He stared at her, trying to formulate the question. 'Why didn't you..?'

'Tell you? I didn't know it was you. There was another guy I saw more of, a lecturer. I moved in with him after I got pregnant. Later, he tired of me and had the tests done. Emma wasn't his. We split up.'

'So I'm definitely Emma's father?'

Veronica didn't acknowlege the desperation in Andrew's voice. 'Maybe,' she mumbled. 'It was a long time ago. There were always other guys. Sometimes I was too stoned to remember.. I got my timing screwed up.'

She sounded like a teenager, Andrew thought. 'But you told the police...'

Veronica's voice became more formal. 'I told the police that you were probably her father, but without you both doing the tests, there's no way of knowing.'

'When did Emma find out about me?' Andrew asked, choked voice muffling his confusion, his anger.

'She had no idea, until that last day you saw her. She rang when you'd gone, told me about some book you'd written. Then she said she'd met you...' Veronica stopped, staring at a woman running for a train. It was not Emma. 'It sounded as though she liked you, so I warned her. I said, "I used to know that man. Don't get involved with him".'

'And what did she say?' Andrew whispered.

'"Is he...?" I'd always told her that I wasn't sure who her father was. But she never believed me. When I was silent, she said, "it's him", and I said "maybe". Then she hung up.'

Andrew stared ahead, saying nothing. Veronica asked a question.

'Why do you think she became a prostitute?'.

'I don't know,' he lied. 'She said there was nothing wrong with it.'

'And you think that's what she's doing now?'

Andrew didn't answer. It hadn't occurred to him that Emma had any choice but to sell herself. He doubted it would have occurred to her.

'I'm Emma's mother,' Veronica said, her hollow eyes staring down the platform at a departing train. 'I blame myself.'

"Where are you staying?' Andrew asked, finally.

'I'm still in Reading. I come here on a day return, whenever I can afford it. I daren't move, in case Emma decides to come home.'

Andrew reached into his pocket for something to scrawl his address on.

'If she does get in touch, will you contact me? I'm...'

'Why would she want to see you again?' Veronica snapped, getting up to go, her drink untouched. 'Haven't you done enough already?'

Andrew waited until she was out of sight before leaving the station. He walked without direction. Shortly, he found a phone box cluttered with cards. When it became free, he went inside, took some coins from his pocket and cradled the receiver. He took a few deep breaths, then began to dial, endlessly searching for the one woman who would not sleep with him.

The Ticket
Raymond Flynn

Afterwards, nobody was quite sure how, or when it started. Looking back, none of the CID were able to pinpoint any single moment, any particular incident leading up to the time when it became common knowledge throughout the station: Brian French was working his ticket.

At one moment he was out there beavering away with the rest, having a moan once in a while, a passed-over, vaguely boozy detective constable with twenty-five years service, openly looking forward to his thirty, and two fingers to the lousy job. The next, he was a liability: idle, swinging the lead, just looking for the nearest exit, mate.

Not that anyone really blamed him, on a personal level that is. In his day he'd been efficient, reasonably popular in the department, slightly standoffish perhaps, a bit moody at times; but a pretty good bloke on the whole. A Queen's Commendation for bravery, somewhere in his distant past. He was, however, well hated by somebody, somewhere upstairs.

The details were unclear, half lost in the myths and legends of the bad old days, but Harry Goddard, one of his former detective sergeants, was now an assistant chief constable, and rumour had it that they hated each other's guts.

Occasionally, it was said, a long, vindictive arm reached down from on high to rub Brian's face in the manure. Certainly, he'd suffered more pointless transfers than most; rule by furniture van. His triumphs were seldom, if ever, rewarded with praise, and brick-bats, threats to return him to uniform duties, winged their way towards him with monotonous regularity. According to canteen gossip, the only reason Brian French had never been sent to draw his big hat was that Harry Goddard would be deprived of all his fun once the threat had been carried out.

'He'll never get promotion,' said the detective inspector, with that mixture of sympathy and relish he reserved for other people's misfortunes, 'not as long as he's got a hole in his arse.'

Not that Brian was in the running; he'd stopped attending promotion boards, even as a day out, years before.

Working his ticket. Not exactly an unknown phenomenon: well, talking about it anyway. Twenty-two years have come and gone; the disgruntled plod attends the cheese-and-wine at Headquarters, and somebody dishes out the cupro-nickel impression of HM's head attached to the blue and white ribbon. Well done thou good and faithful servant. Eight years to go; then sod off, draw the pension, and go and join the security industry at three and a half quid an hour.

And that's when it starts; the huddled, half joking conspiracies in the canteen: stress, ancient injuries inscribed on records of service, bad backs. Like the Fraud Squad fraud, the impossible convoluted crime of the decade whereby the commercial branch makes millions prior to resigning *en-mass,* leaving nobody sufficiently competent to investigate the scam, the road to the lucrative early bath is usually trod only in dreams.

Brian, however, was making his bid, or so they said. Nothing spectacular at first. In the twenty-fifth year of his service he spent ten weeks off sick. Anybody can run out of luck, of course; get two bad doses of influenza in a season, spend a couple of weeks at home to recover from a smack across the head with a base-ball bat, but Brian French, six foot one, ruddy faced, and built like a brick outhouse, began to droop and whine. A day here, five days there; his absences were noticed, and he was becoming about as much use as a chocolate fireguard whenever he condescended to appear.

'When are you going to see Roddy Crossley about those burglaries?' Detective Sergeant Rawlings would ask. Or,

'Have you got that file ready for Crown Court?'

And the reply was always the same, 'Haven't got around to it yet, Sarge; I'm snowed under. First thing tomorrow, without fail.'

And somehow, tomorrow seldom came.

A bit moody from time to time, standoffish, yes; but the man became downright unsociable within a matter of months.

'Going for a pint, Brian?'

'Er — no; no thanks. Rawlings is after me. Got all this paperwork to finish.'

Sometimes they'd find him an hour or two later, alone, half a dozen empty jars before him, in the back room of a pub, unfrequented by police.

He'd developed this odd habit: feeling his wrist. Every now and again, throughout the day, he'd draw back his chair a trifle, and under cover of his desk he'd take his left wrist in his right hand and check his pulse against his watch.

'You all right, Brian?' asked a young DC on one occasion; he was worried.

'Yeah.'

'Course he's alright.' George Cork, a hearty, cross-grained detective con. who'd known Brian for years snorted crudely, banged himself noisily on the chest, and muttered, 'Keep ticking, you bastard; rock on!'

Everybody, including Brian, laughed, but they still caught him doing it day after day.

The youngest DC went sick. Mumps. Everybody made the usual jokes, predictable as well as callous, cops. The morning he came back Brian met him near the sergeant's office.

'Feeling better, now?'

'Yes, thanks.'

'Is it right what I hear: you've had the mumps?'

Warily, expecting the joke, 'Yeah.'

'What's the symptoms?'

'Feels hard under your ears; sort of wooden. Stiff neck,

swelling on one or both sides of your jaws.'

'Sounds painful.'

'Very. I had to take a lot of aspirin.'

Within twenty minutes Brian was across at the health centre opposite the station. His symptoms were just like mumps, he said. He didn't get a sick note; he didn't keep his mouth shut. Once again, everybody laughed.

Then there was the punch up; not quite so funny. Saturday night and the *Green Man* exploded. Drug dealers, rather than thieves falling out. Iron bars, knives, the lot. The uniforms howled for the cavalry, assistance from other Divisions even, to bail them out. Nothing loath, the CID office scrabbled through drawers, collected handcuffs and staffs, and exited smartly to join in the fray. Not so, Brian.

Holding out a great, meaty paw he turned to his colleagues and said, 'Sorry I can't help out, but I've been getting pins and needles lately; my left arm's gone numb.'

'Think of a word,' said George Cork as he climbed into the sub-divisional van, 'containing the letters c — t — n and u; and I don't mean coconuts!' And most of the other passengers felt the same.

It's a rare outfit that doesn't carry one or two spare parts; the guys (and gals) who are going to perform miracles — tomorrow. From the Paper Tigers, whose wonderful files somehow never contain *quite* enough evidence to get their prisoners before the courts, and their authors into the nasty witness box for cross-examination, to the super-jacks with the super informants who promise miracles in the form of detected crime once their snouts can be persuaded to come across (about once every third leap year) the police force knows and cherishes them all.

The bosses occasionally try to root out the dead wood; but pips and crowns are no guarantee of life and growth either. In any case the workers will sometimes go to extraordinary lengths to protect the rest.

'Something', said a philosophical George Cork afterwards, 'to do with this job fucking up the the best of us in the end. There but for the grace of God, my old sons.' But most of his hearers were just as smashed as he was at the time.

Saturday afternoon; the two–ten shift, and a skeleton staff in reserve. Everybody else is busy making arrests down at the match. Even the shoplifters have joined the red-and-white-scarved people's militia, so they can fall out with the Leeds United fans.

'What you got there, Brian?' George, bored; drawing a moustache on the detective sergeant's girlie calendar. Any mischief will do.

'Nothin' much!' Hurriedly, Brian French stuffs a photocopied sheet of A4 into his desk, and screws another scrap of paper into a tiny ball, aiming accurately for the waste-paper bin. 'Fancy a cuppa?'

'Yeah; why not.' He adds a pair of glasses and a pipe to the nude, and as soon as Brian wanders out of the room, kettle in hand, he pounces on the waste basket, extracts the paper ball, and stares uncomprehendingly at a mass of scribbled calculations.

Shameless, he raids his colleague's desk, and all is revealed. A photocopy of the Police Federation chart; pension rates; commutation tables; three and a half years enhancement for retiring sick. Evidence: rock solid at last. George, a founder member of The Serious Rumour Squad, soon spreads the news.

The following week, Brian arrested the Linnaker twins for burglary; a pair of twenty-year-old toe-rags who deserve everything they get, but nobody could describe it as an orthodox interview.

The custody sergeant, who heard it at the other end of a long corridor and through a couple of brick walls, went white. He could visualise the headlines in the tabloid press; he sent for the DI to calm Brian down. Nobody was pleased with him, but this time he was pegged: a man determinedly working his ticket on grounds of psychological stress.

The force welfare officer came out to have a chat. They

61

were together for ages, and, to be fair, the WO stuck up for him with the divisional commander, refusing to discuss Brian's personal business. Discipline, he said, was undoubtedly up to the management, but welfare did not involve trotting off and telling tales to the boss. And the word came down from on high. Direct from Harry Goddard; 'Keep an eye on French; if he so much as twitches in an aggressive manner, he's out!'

It was the Rosemary Carter murder enquiry that did for Brian French. Her husband reported her missing from home on the Sunday night. By Monday morning the Major Incident team was out, and they were taking a very hard look at her loving spouse. The neighbours had reported hearing a double explosion early on the Saturday afternoon, and husband Robert, together with his shotgun, disappeared shortly after he made the report.

The whole station was humming by the time Brian got to work. The parade room had been cleared out, lockers had been stashed in the corridors, civvies had been rooted out of their offices, and an Incident Room had been set up with the area detective superintendent in charge of the enquiry. The sub-divisional CID, the divisional CID, and anybody else's CID he could beg, borrow, steal or kidnap had been summoned for a briefing, and the parade room was solid with listening detectives when Brian French made his grand entrance.

He was carrying a child's skipping rope at the time; the evidence from a juvenile shop-theft at Woolworths. He flung back the parade room door, beamed at the assembled company, and skipped the length of it singing,

'Gunpowder, strawberry jam and kippers,
Here comes Sally without her knickers,'

in a cracked tenor voice. A stunned civilian scenes of crime officer opened the door for him at the far end, and his voice and the slap, slap, slap of the rope gradually faded away along the corridor outside.

The detective superintendent paused in his briefing, waited politely for Brian to depart, and murmured, 'All part, no doubt, of life's rich pattern.' Then he carried on.

It was the police surgeon for Brian after that, and an early retirement date.

'This is the happiest day of my life,' he said, when the news came through.

The CID saw him off in style, just as they always do. A buffet at the local pub, a cut glass decanter and half a dozen tumblers; a massive bunch of flowers for his wife. Why not? It takes guts to pull a stunt like that!

The area detective superintendent, fresh from his successful murder hunt, Gawd bless 'im, made the speech and handed over the presents.

Brain replied. He'd had a few by this time, but nobody took exception to what he said. He'd enjoyed his service, and he'd met more good guys than double-dyed bastards on the job. So far as the latter was concerned, he was sure everybody would know who he meant. They knew all right; they cheered, and even the detective superintendent was heard to mutter, 'I'll drink to that!'

He was sorry, said Brian, very sorry for any bother he'd caused.

Then he sneaked off early, let himself into the CID property store, took Robert Carter's shotgun, placed a plastic bag over his head so he wouldn't make too much of a mess for somebody else to clear up, and he blew out his brains.

Grace
Robert McMinn

A few years ago, there was a reunion at Bletchley Park of those who worked there on cracking codes during the war. These people had the necessity for secrecy inculcated into them so thoroughly that they had never spoken of their war work to anybody. One husband and wife, married forty years, discovered that they had been wartime colleagues only when the reunion invitations arrived in the post. There are two things I can't imagine about that. One is the idea that you could keep a secret for so long. The other is the idea of being with someone forty years.

Love is like judo, it's a passive art. This summer has been a bit traumatic and fraught, and the upshot of it all is that Linda threw me over and moved out a couple of weeks ago. It is supposed to be a trial separation, but we both know she's not coming back, so I'm thinking of putting the house on the market and moving back to Nottingham. Actually, my neighbour Joe, who knows Sam, who works with Linda's sister Terri, tells me that Linda has moved in with a guy she works with. I don't know if they're doing it, but I wouldn't be surprised. During these months when I've been caught up in my own affairs, she has been acting oddly and going out a lot. I haven't been inclined to read anything into her behaviour, but draw your own conclusions. So, whatever. Things are pretty much over between us, and I'm here on my own now, which is different, and a bit scary. It just occurs to me that Terri is a pretty stupid name for her sister to have. I'm not even sure what it's supposed to be short for. Terylene?

I've been spending my evenings daydreaming, playing my guitar in the back bedroom and breaking off occasionally to blow smoke out into the garden. It's so quiet that I can hear the motorway five miles away, and every train that goes past across the industrial park holds out the promise of escape. Three nights ago, I heard noises in the back garden: burglars attracted by the open back windows; but when I turned the light on they leapt over the fence like gazelles and jumped into a car waiting down on the main road. I phoned the police but they were too busy playing dominoes or something to bother with it. I don't like it here anymore. It's not as if she left anything worth stealing. I wanted to call after them: come back, look around, the place is empty.

When it all started, I was still working in the Derby office. At one point, after being caught playing table tennis when I was supposed to be working, I was transferred up to help with the post room and the maintenance work. There was a lot of scandal about my 'disgrace' and the move was supposed to be a real punishment, a career *cul-de-sac,* but I enjoyed working up there, and the best thing about it was being able to wander around fixing things, and meeting lots of people when they came to the office to do work. There was even more opportunity to goof off, and I could have started a table tennis tournament for all anybody paid attention to what I was doing. Shortly after I got up there, management decided to rationalise the switchboards and struck an agreement with the people in the office on the second floor that they would send someone up to assist for two or three hours every morning, depending how busy the post room was. It was summer, then, too, and the person who got sent up was a summer casual, a recent graduate who was just doing the job until something better came along. She was about five-eight, with shoulder-length curly brown hair. She was regular-sized, but she had large breasts which made her look bigger than she actually was. I think she'd been there about four days and had been quite enjoying herself, but was a bit pissed off when they sent her up to us on the Friday. What was weird about it: that was the same Friday me and Linda were picking up the keys to our house. Odd that I should meet the reason for our breakup on the day we were moving in together.

As one who had recently been sent up there for 'punishment', I sympathised with her on that first day, but I didn't say much to her. Rowena, the main post room person, was having one of her Bad Days, so it wasn't a very friendly welcome. The only social conversation was some talk about me and Linda moving down to Milton Keynes; people were confused as to why I had only taken a half day off, but I explained that we couldn't pick up the key till 5 anyway. So she knew from the beginning about Linda.

We moved all our stuff over the weekend, and my life was totally changed by Monday when I came back into work. Linda had managed a transfer from work with no trouble, and so it was the first day for about two years that I wasn't meeting her for lunch. There was loads of post on that Monday morning, as usual, so I went round to help sort it, as usual, and the only difference was that Grace, the girl from downstairs, was sitting at the switchboard, trying to remember how to use it. In fact, the first time we really spoke was when she got into a pickle with a call, and I showed her how to put someone on hold. She thanked me *grace*fully, and I remember noticing how *rich* she sounded.

I don't want to sound too much like a pretend working class hero, but I know I always sounded more High Peak than High Tea, and Grace sounded to me like Jolly Hockeysticks and Pimms No. 1 in the hospitality tent. Sorry: *marquee*. I was a bit put off, chip on my shoulder intact from my recent 'punishment', but she seemed to take a liking to me because I had been so helpful. I think then she started looking forward to coming upstairs, because, when Rowena was in a good mood, we had some good times up there. It always amazes me when people take to me, but after all, they see what they want to see.

It was only about two days later that Rowena had another Bad Day, and decided about half an hour after coming in to go home and sleep it off. That left Grace and me on our own, and I sat next to her to open all the envelopes while she coped admirably with the switchboard. I knew she was smart because you never had to

67

show her how to do something twice. I sat next to her that morning and she started talking to me. In her head, I guess we were having some kind of conversation, but I swear to god I understood only about one word in ten. She spoke so fast, and there was so much background noise that I kept having to ask her to repeat things.

But you can get used to anything, and with Rowena off for a couple of days, I was soon tuned into Radio Grace, and learning a lot about her. It turned out she came from Little Eaton, about ten minutes from where I grew up, and though we had gone to separate schools, it felt like we had much in common. She was a bit younger than me (named after Grace Slick while I was named after John Kennedy), but seemed to be more worldly. She spoke English, French, Spanish and Italian. I'm not sure if her accent was as hard to understand in all the countries of Europe, but she knew a lot about *Romance*.

At the end of her second week, I was so antsy about having lunch on my own that I blurted out, 'I feel like going for a drink.' Grace stood up from the switchboard and looked over the desk at me and simply said, *'Yeah!'* with more enthusiasm than any woman had previously shown at the prospect of a drink with me. Rowena discretely had other plans, convinced by then that Grace and I had something going.

Meanwhile, back at the ranch-style Wimpy home, Linda and I were in the thick of decorating. I said nothing to her about Grace, and how much fun she was to work with, even at the very beginning. It was like I knew that there was something there. Moving from Grace in the office to Linda at home was such a huge contrast; it was like moving from Kim Delaney in *NYPD Blue* to Elizabeth Montgomery in *Bewitched*. But it was a move I convinced myself I could cope with. In conversations at home, Grace was just referred to as *someone from downstairs*. I suppose I was no different from any other married man having a fling with someone at work, but you like to feel you're cleverer than that.

It was funny when we started to meet for lunch every day, because that was how things had started with Linda. As a summer casual, Grace had no flexibility about the time she went to lunch, and was only supposed to take an hour. But, Machiavellian in her cunning, she was able to manipulate her boss into being very lenient with her. He was the guy who sat in the corner office downstairs, the one with the prosthetic arm and the glass eye. Grace said she tried hard when she was talking to him not to stare at the plastic arm, but it was a losing battle, because when you looked up to his face you found yourself staring at his glass eye. In any case, the guy fancied her as his bit on the side, and was always suggesting things the two of them could do together. I think Grace had actually been for a lunchtime drink with him once, which was possibly why she was so enthusiastic about having me as an excuse. She said,

'I couldn't get out of my head the idea of what might *fall off* or *drop out* of his body if I had sex with him.'

And she said,

'Then I started wondering if he took the arm off *before* he had sex, or afterwards. You know: sex, cigarette, remove arm, then sleep. Or: remove arm, have sex, put arm back on again, smoke cigarette, remove arm, sleep. Or what? What do you think?'

We started to go out every day, and never just for the hour that Grace was allowed. From the very first time, we went to a pub around the corner and down the road rather than the one everyone from the office went to. I was aware that people would talk, knowing that I had just moved in with Linda. Grace just seemed happy to avoid anywhere that might feature a man with a plastic arm.

I always felt I was above that kind of thing, but I have to admit to being very attracted to Grace's breasts. She wore baggy trousers and a baggy top all the time at work, but she couldn't fool me. I used to sit and watch her over at the bar when it was her round, and liked to imagine her naked. I also liked to imagine what might fall off or drop

69

out of *my* body if we did it. Trying not to stare at her tits while she was talking was pretty easy, though. Looking into her eyes, you weren't distracted by the glassy vacancy of an artificial eye, but by an intense colour blue. I always liked the combination of dark hair and blue eyes. I don't think she dyed them, or whatever it is people do.

Towards the end of her summer there, the prosthetic arm guy had started to get slightly bitter about her long lunches, but Grace had another job lined up by then and was just serving her time. His threats meant nothing to her.

I had given up smoking when I started seeing Linda. One of my things is that I get very self destructive when I'm single (he said, making himself sound like Errol Flynn), and a girlfriend with all my bad habits is always going to be bad news. Grace smoked Marlboro and drank Guiness. On my lunches with her I made free with her cigarettes and drank Irish whiskey straight. It was an Irish pub we'd chosen for our liaison, and we wanted to fit in *(as if)*. Sometimes I'm sure I drove home to Milton Keynes over the limit, but who gets breathalised at four o'clock in the afternoon? I used to have a great time driving home that summer. On a good day, I could do it in an hour and a quarter, flashing under those surveillance cameras without a care at 80 or 90 mph, but there were roadworks on the motorway during those months, and I sat in the heat in the queue listening to tapes in the car and mulling over the things Grace and I had talked about that day. A record I was really into at that time was that odd album CBS released when Dylan left the label briefly in the early 70s. *Dylan* featured odd cover versions like 'Big Yellow Taxi' and 'Mr Bojangles', and I loved it because of the husky way his voice sounded. Having just taken up smoking again, and being impressed with Grace's linguistic powers, my favourite activity was to croon 'Spanish is the Loving Tongue' to the traffic cones as I drove slowly by.

How can I explain to you how it felt to live that summer? I had applied for a transfer to the Milton Keynes

70

branch, but my 'disgrace' meant that it took 18 of your English months to come through. And that summer, I swear, I just didn't care. It was the perfect affair for me. No sex was involved, so it wasn't as if I was arriving home with the scent of a woman all over me. True, my hands were dry from endless washings with the nasty piss-coloured liquid soap in the office toilets to rid myself of the smell of fags, and I was forever cleaning my teeth, sucking mints and gargling mouthwash, but I was having the best time of my life: cigarettes and whiskey and *smart* conversations.

But it was — I can't think of the words — not about to last that way forever. The salad was wilting in the bowl, the milk souring in the fridge. Even after Grace's contract ended, and she had two weeks to wait till her new job in London started, she would come into town and meet me for lunch. On the last Friday before she was due to start, I came out at noon wearing a Panama hat and met her in the doorway to Marks and Spencer. Linda had given me the hat as a present, to keep the sun off my head when my hair was short. *We* thought I looked pretty good in it. Grace said,

'I'm not going anywhere with you if you're wearing that stupid hat.'

She was right. I looked ridiculous. I carried the hat and threw it in a bin as we walked down Sadler Gate. We went to the pub as usual. The conversation went something like: I can't do this if it's going to be an affair; I can't be someone's *mistress*. And then: I can't do this to Linda; she's meant too much to me, given me stability and saved me from myself; I love her, I can't leave her.

It was a conversation on the edge of tears that lasted two hours and several whiskeys. It might have been better if we had held hands or something, but we just stared across the table into each other's eyes. We walked slowly back to the office, emotionally drained and feeling bad. And yet: exhilarated too. The emotions I was feeling were so extreme, like nothing I had ever felt for Linda, and I

71

knew it was good, all of it, even the bad stuff. It was almost an out-of-body experience: I was hovering above myself approving of the emotional wreckage below. I was proud of myself for being able to feel such intense sadness. I asked Grace to wait outside the news kiosk while I got some mints to mask the whiskey on my breath, and when I got outside she was nervously hopping about, wanting to be gone from the scene. She tried her best to make it pleasant and I ruined it. She said,

'Well, you'll have to come to see me when I settle in. I'll show you the sights.' I said,

'Shall I bring Linda?'

And she turned and left. It was a deliberately inappropriate remark for me to make. I flattered myself that Grace was having trouble accepting the situation. I thought I could see tears of denial in her lovely eyes. Actually, she just had a lot more class than me, and knew not to make a bad situation even worse.

I went back to work, extremely late but not caring. I left at the earliest opportunity and embarked on one of my drunken drives home, feeling *excellently* sad. *Adios mi Corazone.*

For the rest of the time Linda and I had together, I thought more about Grace than I did anything else. I was *gone*, and I might as well have left Linda back then, when I had the chance. It was I who was having trouble accepting the situation.

I was finally transferred, and my promotion came just about six months later. I was in a new environment without my poor reputation, and the 'punishment' was over. But Linda and I were already leading pretty much separate lives, and one Sunday, a week or so before my first trip to the North London training centre, she took the car to her dad's and left me on my own to get up to no good. So I bounced off the walls for a little while, then phoned Grace.

Actually, I looked up her mum in the phonebook and phoned her. Actually, I went to the kitchen cupboard first, and got the bottle of brandy we keep for cooking and had a few slugs of that, then phoned Grace's mum. I was holding the bottle in my hand when she answered. I said, 'My name's John and I used to work with Grace. I'm trying to contact her and wondered if you could help.'

Grace's mum (suburban wit): 'Hold on John. I'll see if I can contact her. She's sitting in the kitchen.'

She was visiting for Sunday lunch. It was so exciting to hear her voice. I still cannot believe that I had the guts to call, as spineless as I have been in other areas of my life. I told her about my coming to London, and we arranged to meet. It was very precise: 6 pm at the top of the steps to the Green Park tube station, next to the Ritz Hotel.

I didn't count on several things, country hick that I am. The most important were the London Transport strikes, which were on that summer as they apparently are every summer, as reliably as Spanish air traffic controllers. It was always on the national news, but who outside London pays any attention or cares one iota? The strikes had all been on Wednesdays, but foolishly we arranged to meet on that day. I arrived in Stanmore on the Monday, prepared to go to my digs that evening and settle in. What happened was that the strike that week was changed from Wednesday to *Tuesday*, and we were all sent home that night, and told not to return till Wednesday. So I got on the train and went home, calling a surprised Linda from the station at 8pm. She was an absolute age in coming to pick me up, and talked nervously all the way home. Draw your own conclusions.

On the Wednesday I was due to meet Grace, then, I had not yet settled into my digs, so I was unable to leave the training centre at four and hop directly on the tube to Green Park. Instead I had to walk, on an extremely hot day, carrying all my stuff, the two miles to the digs where I was forced through an inherited predisposition to politeness to make conversation, accept a cup of tea and a *cheese and beetroot* sandwich, and generally waste time that I should have spent travelling.

73

After a quick rinse at the bathroom sink and a change of shirt, I had to walk another mile to the tube station, arriving just ten minutes before six o'clock. You might ask yourself, why on earth didn't I take taxis that day, to speed my transfer at least between training centre and digs, between digs and tube station? The truth is, I had just £10 to spend. It was towards the end of the month, I had already exceeded my overdraft limit, and my expenses for the training course wouldn't come through for another month. This was one of the more pathetic things I hadn't thought about when planning to meet up with Grace. The final thing was that, even if I'd had more than £10 in my wallet, and even with the trains working that day, it took over 40 minutes to reach Green Park. Then, already more hot and bothered than I had ever been, I was forced to mount all the staircases and escalators at breakneck speed in my attempts to get to Grace. Of course, there was nobody there when I got to the top, though I am sure that I saw her getting onto a bus across the street as I hit daylight. I was too breathless to call out.

Nevertheless, I stood there for another forty minutes, even asking the ice-cream vendor who was there if she had seen anyone resembling Grace. I was like anyone who suffers denial over being stood up: no pride or circumspection. Instead you become convinced that something terrible has happened to your loved one to prevent her arrival. Actually, something terrible *had* happened: I was forty minutes late and it was Grace, not me, who had stood for that time feeling the eyes of passers-by upon her as she concluded that I had choked.

I walked slowly up to Piccadilly Circus, but daren't go any further in case I got lost. I drank some coffee and walked back, then made my slow way back to the landlady at the digs. I stopped on the way to call Linda, wanting to tell her all about my day and perhaps for the first time realising the gulf between us, how little of our lives we were actually sharing. We both had our secret work to do. I wrote to Grace (again, *c/o* her mum's house) and explained what had happened, begging for another chance a few weeks later.

The simplest thing to do was to take a day off, pretend to go to work and get on the train to make a day of it, but instead we arranged the exact same thing, this time allowing an extra half hour for the vagaries of transportation and idiots. As it was, I arrived a good two hours early, sporting a brand new watch and a small bottle of paracetamol. Grace arrived ten minutes early looking every bit of two years older, the strain of city life showing in the dryness of her hair and the pallid colour of her skin. Still, she was beautiful, and her eyes were the same colour blue.

She was carrying a briefcase and a carrier bag, wearing something with shoulder pads, looking tired. Her hair was straight and slightly longer than I remembered: like Kim Delaney in the movie *Body Parts* rather than *NYPD Blue*. We walked down Piccadilly towards the Circus. She was talking and I understood maybe one tenth of it. After two years, to finally be with her was almost too much joy to bear.

At a pub in Soho, we drank a couple of beers and then walked round the corner to queue at a cheap and popular Italian restaurant she knew. In the line, I began to calm down. Waiting there in the queue she stopped babbling at last and looked at me. 'You are...' She hesitated.

I can remember only the warm evening and the crowds, the smell from the restaurant kitchen, the laughter of couples.

'...exactly the same,' and then she smiled, letting me know that she meant it as a compliment.

Everyone sat shoulder to shoulder, it was a good way to be, thigh to thigh on long benches in the warm downstairs. It felt great to be with someone who felt so at home there and I didn't feel like such a bumpkin this time. Grace, living in Dulwich and fluent in all languages known to humankind, made the order and asked for a carafe of house red. She poured the wine into glasses when it came and I remember that as she held her glass she slid a napkin from beneath the cutlery and screwed it up nervously in her other hand. We drank steadily and started to reach out cautiously, to touch across the table. There hadn't been any physical contact before. Already things were different, better. At the very moment we finally held hands, the man sitting next to me fell asleep, face down in the middle of his meal, leaving his companion bewildered and lost, looking apologetically at Grace and me. We just smiled, like any tolerant couple who haven't a care in the world. Again, it was an experience, one I was watching like a third party from above with my inner eye. I was in London for only the fourth time in my life, I was with another woman, I was eating in a restaurant, I was holding hands with Grace and contemplating the rest of my days.

Later, we kissed, she buried her face in my chest and talked to me about her situation, about her boyfriend Max and his level of commitment. It felt good to hear her ripping him apart, airing her grievances, comparing him unfavourably to me. I stepped over winos and vomit — drunks and chunks — and garbage, watched as a street woman pulled down her pants and pissed in the doorway of a shop, dodged as a purse snatcher careened past pursued by an agitated law enforcement officer, and felt that everything was right with the world. I remember looking at the Homeless with something like pity for the amount of *stuff* they carried everywhere with them, those carrier bags full of who-knows-what. Here was I, I thought, prepared to give up *everything* for Grace, wanting to travel light, to dump all my baggage and fly.

There was a full moon in the sky, which pleased me no end because my new watch was one of those with the phases of the moon. I kept showing it to Grace and she smiled indulgently. We kissed and touched a lot, and managed everything without breaking contact: crossing the road, manœuvring round obstacles, even the ritual exchange of phone numbers. She walked me to the station for the last train north and we kissed goodbye. In my pocket: both her home and office phone numbers, so keen

76

was she for me to stay in touch. It was like things were about to happen for us, atoms in motion, energised by the summer heat.

A week later, Linda left. Which is about where we came in. What set it off, the day after I got back from London, still full of *Grace*, I forgot it was Linda's birthday. Which upset her more than you might think. It was like she was waiting for me to forget it. Even though for a large part of our lives we had been doing the usual things, somehow it was obvious that there was no longer a reason we were doing them together. We went shopping together as usual, even had two weeks in Scotland, but for the whole summer we lay next to each other in bed without touching and never spoke about this big thing between us that was creating long silences and tense conversations: our secret work. I have rolls of film from the holiday somewhere which I cannot bear to have developed, and the house is half empty from all the things Linda took away: one lamp where there were once two, half the number of records, only one change of linen for the bed. She left me a chair to sit on and the TV, but apart from that we never really had much furniture. If I talk to myself, the house echoes.

I walk around not knowing what to do with myself, bursting into tears at odd moments. It's the most ludicrous things that bring it on: adverts, signature tunes, tricks of the light. Most of the time I feel fine, but then something sets me off and I realise I've been on the edge of hysteria for days. I go for walks but there's nothing to see round here; I write letters which are like the announcement of a death in the family; but, actually, this was what I wanted, wasn't it?

It was a week ago that I phoned Grace at work to tell her that Linda had left, and I wish I'd handled it differently. I forgot that love is a passive art, and I just threw her with the news. I could tell from her panicked reaction that it was the last thing she was expecting to hear. I should have kept it to myself for a few months at least, waited until Grace asked, 'How's Linda these days?' Then

I could have casually mentioned that she left some time ago, by which time Grace might have been used to me again. It was as if, two years on, she was now prepared to have an affair, to be a mistress, given that we would be equals in our cheating ways. But confronted with the news that there was nothing stopping us from my end, she realised how much Max meant to her.

So this is what is happening with me. I was sorting through some crap today, because I had the theory that throwing things out would mean they weren't around to make me feel bad, and I was just in awe at the amount of stuff Linda and I collected and kept from our courting days. She left behind a load of the handbags she had bought over the years in charity shops, bags which matched whichever *retro* look she was into at the time, and inside several of them I found ticket stubs, corks from bottles of wine, scrunched up notes and other items of memorabilia. I felt like a medium touching them all, putting myself in contact with the spirits of the dead. Why do we hoard things so? I even found an old diary Linda was keeping when she first met me, filled I'm sure with all the teenage turmoil and excitement of sneaking out of the house to meet me when her dad disapproved. And you know what? I threw it in that black binbag like it was on fire, I didn't want to see any of it. I felt as if to read a single word would start my whole universe unravelling.

Yesterday, I got an apologetic letter from Grace. It started, 'Dear John,' and went downhill from there. She hadn't known I was really so close to splitting up with Linda. She had taken my talk of the dying relationship in the same spirit as she had meant her dissatisfaction over her own. To be sure, there were things about Max that left her feeling lonely and untouched, but she was never going to give up the life they had built for themselves in favour of the dream of a man who found it so easy, apparently, to step from one relationship to another. *In daylight, what seems possible under the moon seems uncertain and even a little mad.* That's a direct quote. She typed her letter, so

78

there was nothing to read into the handwriting. She spent three pages imparting the simple news that she will not see me again. And she did an odd thing. Or at least, it seemed odd until I was chucking the stuff out of the house this morning.

In the envelope was a paper napkin from the Italian restaurant, the one she screwed up in her hand when she was drinking from her glass. At first I thought it was some kind of hidden message, that for some reason she couldn't say in her letter what she really wanted to say, that I was supposed to meet her at this restaurant at some appointed time. It's a long while since I received a letter from someone in these circumstances and every word seemed like overdetermined code. I looked at the initial letters of sentences and paragraphs, trying to see what she really meant: Bletchley Park would have been proud of me. But then I realised: the napkin was just something she kept in the same way that Linda and I kept the cork from our first bottle of wine, the cinema tickets of every film we saw together, and the silly love notes we sent when we were hot for each other and not doing it yet. Grace kept the napkin, but sent it to let me know there was no point. That was the code she wanted me to crack.

The Good Neighbour

Catharine Arnold

She was there from the beginning and now it is hard to imagine the neighbourhood without her. Now, whenever a net curtain twitches or I sense eyes watching me from behind a Venetian blind, I think of Elma. As the spirea trembles against the garden fence, as though brushed in passing by some invisible entity, I almost expect to see her greying chignon and ascetic features emerge from the other side of the bushes, and anticipate that characteristic greeting: 'Ah, Rebecca', as the silver hoop earrings refract rays of light and the crystal round her neck responds with its unearthly gleam.

Now Elma has gone — but on long summer evenings, when the twilight stretches the shadows of old fruit trees across the lawn, and the neighbourhood fox steals up close to our french windows under cover of the overgrown grass, then I feel she is still with us, watching over us, and I find it impossible to believe that she has really gone away.

When we moved up from London we discovered that the leafy Victorian suburb on the outskirts of Nottingham did not possess an official Neighbourhood Watch. The reason for this soon became apparent. Elma Chandler *was* the Neighbourhood Watch. Inevitably she attracted other less affectionate epithets than this, including busybody, nosy parker, witch (courtesy of the local children) and interfering old bag. This latter designation was commonplace among the dozens of individuals unfortunate enough to be confronted by her on a variety of imagined misdemeanours. These included the smoke emissions from their bonfires and barbecues, the noise levels of their stereos and their effrontery in parking outside her house — although she seldom used her own car, an old black Rover, which sat on the drive for weeks on end. On a daily basis Elma succeeded in antagonising pubescent skateboarders,

81

delivery men, labourers digging ditches for television cables and employees of the local gas, electricity and water companies. Within weeks of moving to Sherwood I had only to hear a commotion in the ostensibly quiet residential street to know that Elma, with her thin, androgynous body, birdlike features and distinctive earrings would be haranguing some unfortunate man — for it was usually a man — who was attempting, desperately, to complete his task.

'Missed her vocation in life, that one', my husband would say, with the complacent wit of a man watching the sport from his armchair after a good meal. 'Should of been a traffic warden. Where's that bottle of wine?'

It had been Charlie's idea to move back to Nottingham, where he had been born and bred before taking off for London. There was always plenty of work in the building trade, he maintained. As a qualified solicitor I could get a job anywhere, and he didn't want our two small daughters growing up in what he called The Smoke, an archaic description becoming ever more appropriate given the increasing pollution levels down there.

Stressed and exhausted from trying to juggle motherhood and the law, I was ready for a break. Several years with the Crown Prosecution Service had left me cynical and jaded and I was even contemplating giving up the profession altogether. For the time being I was happy to sink back into domesticity and a large house in Nottingham was far more appropriate for raising a family than our cramped two-bedroom flat in Fulham.

None of our friends were surprised when we left London. Our marriage was already regarded as so unconventional that they had given up being shocked by anything we did. We were the first to admit that we were an odd couple — I am a diminutive Jewish lawyer from an academic family, and Charlie is a builder with impeccable working-class credentials, built along the lines of the proverbial brick outhouse and possessed of more humour, wit and creativity than all the men I dated at Cambridge

82

put together. If I had had any worries that leaving London would put a strain on our relationship, I was soon too pre-occupied with the mechanics of moving house and the activities of Elma to give them much thought.

We picked the worst day to move. Although it was the height of a legendary dry, hot, summer, rain sluiced down from the moment the van arrived, ensuring that we left Fulham in a stressed and irritable state which only wors-ened as our journey up the M1 progressed. We got stuck in a tailback and lost the removal van. Sophie, our three year old, started crying and demanded to be taken home. Char-lie became frustrated at the delay and his size eleven feet thumped the pedals ominously. His balding head shone in the way it always did when he was angry and I broke all my rules and lit a cigarette in the car, with the children there, which made me feel guilty for the rest of the jour-ney.

But something strange had happened when we eventu-ally got to Sherwood and turned the corner into Webb Street. The removal van was parked outside the large Edwardian semi which was to be our new house, and our furniture and boxes were already being carried in. Two men were bearing our wardrobe up the front steps whilst a stick-thin woman with a grey bun and glinting eyes was directing traffic and issuing orders like a real pro. I emerged from our car, astonished.

'You must be Mrs Ashfield!' The grey-haired woman's voice rang out, cultivated, clear and distinctly Establish-ment. 'Welcome!'

'Who are you?' I demanded, testily. 'And what's our front door doing open?' I was tinged with London-induced paranoia, and convinced that some almighty mistake had occurred which would result in our having to spend the night in a hotel.

The woman smiled reassuringly, as if I was the same age as Sophie. 'My dear, you mustn't worry. I have a spare set of keys. I directed the men myself. It was imperative that the van unload as soon as possible.'

'Well, that's all very well, but —'

She smiled graciously as the rest of my family emerged from our car, crushed and mutinous, viewing her with disfavour. She extended a hand to Charlie. 'Mr Ashfield! Welcome! And these must be Sophie and Isobel. I'll just go and put the kettle on.' She went into the house — our house — as if she owned the place. Charlie and I exchanged glances.

Once we had squeezed in past the furniture and packing cases — which I had to admit were being arranged with admirable professionalism — we found her in the kitchen, where she had poured out mugs of tea and opened a box containing a large chocolate cake. The cake improved Charlie's opinion of her no end. When she proceeded to bring out a bottle of claret, he was even more impressed.

'It's traditional,' she said, with the same slightly deranged smile. 'When someone new moves in, we always bring cake and wine. It's a custom.'

That's when I noticed the large bouquet of flowers on the window ledge.

'Those too,' she said, smiling eerily. 'Welcome to Webb Street.'

'Tradition?' said Kate, outside the school gates the following week. 'Tradition? First I've heard of it.'

Kate, a freelance journalist with two young daughters and an air of humorous frustration, had introduced herself on the first day of term. She lived five doors down and we had become instant friends in the manner of stressed-out professional women still adjusting to the ravages of life with small children. 'Elma's weird,' said Kate, as we made our way back through the playground after depositing our youngest offspring at the nursery. 'She means well but she just can't stop interfering. It's because she's home all day.'

'Doesn't she work?'

'She used to have a job at that New Age bookshop in town, but she gave it up after her father died, so she could look after her mother. Then her mother died.'

'How awful. So how does she manage?'

'Her parents left her quite a bit. Her father was a doctor. And she used to have some job or other in the Civil Service, down in London, so I suppose she's got a bit put by. It's a pity she gave up the bookshop, though. Now she's on her own and she's got nothing to do all day except meddle with people's lives.'

'That's rather sad.'

'She's a sad person. Sometimes she stays indoors for weeks. We hardly ever see her. She calls these times her "hibernations". I get the impression that she just sits in her chair all day, watching everybody through the windows.'

'Creepy.'

'Isn't it?' Kate stuck her thumbs in the tops of her jeans' pockets and flicked back her long red hair, looking rangy and tough, as if she should have been setting off to cover Bosnia or the Gulf, instead of submitting a DIY column to the local newspaper. 'God, I'm bored.'

'Why don't you go back to work?'

'I'm trying, but it'll mean leaving Nottingham, and I like it here. Even if my neighbours are weird. Come on, let's go to Birds and pig out on cake.'

I was going to say that Elma soon became a regular visitor to our house, but it would be more accurate to describe her as a permanent fixture. During the first few weeks I was glad of her presence. She was genuinely fond of the children, reading to them in her distinctive, high-pitched voice from old-fashioned books that I suspect were hers as a girl, beautifully illustrated but slightly foxed editions of Beatrix Potter and A A Milne, and a disturbing book of moral tales entitled *Struwwelpeter*. She let them run riot in her large, overgrown garden with its drooping rose trellises and heavy-headed sunflowers, and encouraged them to fuss over her six cats. Sophie and Isobel, who were still over-excited and disturbed by the move, and missed their London friends, appreciated her company, while I spent all day unpacking interminable crates of books and wrestling furniture upstairs.

Charlie was busy elsewhere during the day, helping one of his old pals restore a huge, creepy, rambling house a few streets away which had remained untouched since the 1930s. The reclusive octogenarian owner had finally died — the body had been discovered, rather grimly, some weeks after the event — and now the house was giving up its secrets. Charlie came home every night smeared with cobwebs and full of tales of rooms stuffed with newspapers, cupboards full of Dresden china and mice in the sideboard. He hadn't even started on our place. So I was grateful to Elma for all her help. If her comments sometimes irritated me, I tried not to show it.

'Dear, dear, what *are* we going to do with you?' she would ask, as I realised at 5pm that there was nothing in the house but stale bread and ancient bacon and we were out of lightbulbs and I needed to make a hasty foray to the supermarket, which would be better accomplished as a solo mission than a family outing.

'Let me look after the children for you while you go shopping,' she would offer, managing to make it sound as if I was swanning off to the Paris collections instead of driving to Sainsburys.

'Children need routine, you know,' she observed on another occasion, turning up at seven at night to find us all tucking in to a Chinese takeaway as *Top of the Pops* roared away in the background and Sophie strutted around in my old high heels intoning the dubious lyrics of a gangsta rap act. 'They need routine and a balanced, nutritious diet. Oh, and you shouldn't be eating this Cantonese rubbish. Try the Vietnamese place at the other end of the High Street. Very authentic. They're Boat People. I know about these things.'

There wasn't much Elma didn't know about. Whatever the topic, she seemed to be impressively — and irritatingly — well informed. Particularly about the neighbourhood. As well as unsolicited advice on housework and childcare, Elma also took it upon herself to warn us about our neighbours, gravely informing Charlie that marauding gangs of teenage boys were often to be found in the area, apparently looting houses and stealing cars. She herself had a highly sophisticated burglar alarm which was forever going off without reason, and, according to Charlie, who had put in some new window locks for her, enough security equipment to start a small shop. She was also, as I soon realised, completely without fear. On one occasion I looked out of the window to see what all the noise was about and watched her approach and break up a posse of lads who were whooping and posturing as they kicked a ball down our street. They did not represent a real threat but, as strapping fifteen year olds brimming with testosterone, they would have intimidated me. Another time I saw her tackle a drunk who appeared to be threatening to beat up his girlfriend. United by Elma's abuse, they shrugged and walked off.

But she was still scared of somebody — or something — breaking into her house.

'Well, she's got her art, hasn't she?' said Charlie, as we soaped one another in the big old-fashioned clawfoot bath that was one of the reasons I had wanted this house. 'Some nice pieces. She's got to be worried about being burgled.'

'What sort of stuff is it?' I was yet to be invited into Elma's house, and was intrigued. The children, too, were denied access, but given their energy and vigour and Elma's legendary art collection, this was hardly surprising.

'Oriental, most of it. One or two old English pieces, some antique silver, the genuine article not EPNS, a very attractive mahogany drop-leaf table — and then all these silk paintings and prints. And she's into all this Peace movement stuff. You know — CND stickers on the windows, you've seen them, stained glass things with doves on, and rainbows — a bit naff, really. Said she used to be big into Greenham Common and that.'

'Greenham Common? I thought she used to be a Civil

Servant.'

'She did.' He began to lather two days' growth of beard and reached for the razor. 'She cracked on she was a secretary or clerk or summat at the Ministry of Defence — MI5 and that.'

'Oh, come on. She must be joking.'

'Well, somebody's gotta do it.'

'So she was like Miss Moneypenny?'

'Yeah — but Miss Moneypenny gone radical. She got disillusioned around the time Greenham came along, and left her job, and went down the airbase to support the peace protesters. Spent quite a bit of time down there. Women tell me everything, you know that. Us builders, we're like doctors and hairdressers. She was dead forthcoming when I told her how I used to hang around with them Travellers and how I'd been at the Battle of the Beanfield. Said my heart was in the right place, even if I had sold out. Some of the stuff she comes out with is a bit wild, though.'

'What sort of stuff?'

'Says she knows things about the Government, and she wants to leak it to the papers. Or write a book. She says the reports she's read about weapons testing would make your hair curl.'

'It sounds incredible,' I replied tartly. 'If it's true. She wouldn't be the first person who decided to invent an exciting past for herself.'

He was hauling himself out of the bath now, water sheeting down from his hirsute body, magnificently animal. I never had to explain to my girlfriends why I married him. And I could see that even Elma might be impressed enough to want to make her past sound more glamorous for him.

'Elma reckons there's been some right goings on here,' he continued, draping himself in a towel.

'What, in this house you mean?'

'Yeah. When the Naylors had it. Said there was a lot of screaming in the night.'

'It was probably just the Naylors having sex.'

'And she said they left in a hurry.'

'Well of course they did. We wanted to move in. We'd sold the place in Fulham.'

'She made it sound more sinister than that.'

'I think Elma's already proved she's got a vivid imagination.' My forensic training, coupled with my innate scepticism, was catching up with me. 'She's got nothing to do all day except watch people —'

'And make up stories about them?'

'When she's not making up stories about herself.'

I was intrigued about our predecessors despite myself, and made a point of asking about them next day, when Elma popped round with one of her characteristic offerings — home-made apple jelly, golden as preserved sunlight, presented in a little glass jar with a gingham top.

'What were the Naylors like?' I asked, filling the kettle. At the mention of their name Elma made a fluttering gesture and touched the crystal at her throat. 'Oh, my,' she replied. 'The Naylors.'

'Well?'

She glanced around, as if afraid that the children might be listening, but they were engrossed with playing mud pies on the terrace.

'I was very glad when they left,' replied Elma. 'In fact, I tried to get them to leave.'

'What did they do? Loud music? Wild parties? Lots of rowing?'

'I don't think they were very nice people, dear. They seemed to have some very unattractive habits. Odd people coming to the house.'

'I suppose it's possible they were drug dealers,' I suggested, drawing on my criminal experience. 'Unlikely, but —'

'Not drugs,' said Elma with authority. 'I know about drugs.'

I looked at her sceptically. What on earth would anyone like Elma know about drug dealers?

'I lived in London for years,' she replied, as if reading my mind. 'It wasn't any of that sort of thing. No grass or smack or speed. I would have known about that.'

It was disconcerting to hear her talk like this, but I was prepared to believe she knew what she was talking about.

'I was worried about their children,' she continued. 'I think there was a lot of cruelty. In fact, I urged them to leave.'

'How?'

Elma sighed, glanced down at her sandal-shod feet, folded her arms defensively.

'I said that if they didn't stop beating their children, I would report them to the authorities. I also offered them money to go.'

'You offered them money!' Now she really was crazy. 'How much?'

'Nothing much, but enough to get them into temporary accommodation for a few months until they sold the house.'

'Elma, I'm sorry, but that's the most stupid thing I ever heard. Why do that? If you were so worried about the kids, you should have gone straight to social services.'

'I didn't like to think I would split the family up. I just wanted the husband out of the way. I tried to buy him off. He was the one who caused all the trouble. He was a monster, Rebecca. An utter brute.'

'So what happened in the end?'

'Well, clearly, they sold the house — you're here, now. And I later heard Mr Naylor had left Mrs Naylor.'

'What happened to them?'

'Who?' This from Sophie, emerging from the garden, crusted with dried mud. 'Who are you talking about? Who's been screaming? And your burglar alarm's gone off again, Auntie Elma.'

'That keeps on happening! I'll see you later, Rebecca.'

It was the following night when Charlie started the rewiring. We had been in for a month by this time, but his reputation had preceded him and he was getting work all over Sherwood, which was full of dilapidated Edwardian houses bought in a spirit of enthusiasm by young couples who subsequently found themselves desperately in need of a good builder.

Why he had to start taking up the floorboards at nine o'clock on a Saturday night is beyond me, but that's Charlie. Unpredictable. I think there was some vague idea about investigating the state of the wiring prior to a trip to the merchant's on Monday morning — but as it was, I was glad the children were in bed when he started work. I was lying on our bed watching a rerun of *NYPD Blue* while Charlie prised up a floorboard and found a little recess underneath.

'Aye-aye, what we got here! This where they kept their stash? Oo-er, *missus.*'

'What have you found?'

'Dirty pictures.'

'Oh, it's probably some saddo's soft porn collection.'

'Nothing soft about this,' observed Charlie. 'This is serious stuff.'

The woman was dressed in the regalia of S&M — corset, suspenders, stockings, dogcollar, high-heeled boots, all of which looked slightly incongruous with her bony, intelligent face. And she wasn't just standing, or sitting. She was wearing a harness and suspended, rather painfully, by the look of it, from the bracket in the bathroom.

'So that's what it's for. I was going to get a pot-holder for that.'

'Looks if they were into more than foliage plants,' replied Charlie.

'It's horrible. It looks so painful.'

'It's meant to be painful, Becky. That's why they do it.'

'Who was she? Do you suppose she lived here?'

'Maybe she was Mrs Naylor.' By this time Charlie had got out his torch, and was poking around under the floorboards. 'I got some more!'

He plunged his hand in without flinching and brought

out a handful of grimy prints. They featured the same woman in various poses and an angry expression, which was entirely understandable. In one picture, she was bound and gagged, but her pants were missing so that her genitals were clearly displayed. She looked vulnerable and cross.

'That's what they call a Continental shot,' said Charlie.

'I'm sure they do. Where would you get stuff like this developed?'

'There's a whole scene. Contact mags, sex clubs — you'd be surprised.'

I had encountered references to pornography in my criminal work, but I wasn't ashamed to admit that it had disturbed and frightened me. I was even alarmed by Charlie's apparently extensive knowledge of the subject, but he had seen a lot more of life than I had. 'Do you think those scars on her back are real?' I asked. Despite myself, I was fascinated. 'That would explain the screaming.'

Charlie looked at me.

'Don't you remember what Elma said? She said sometimes she could hear screaming. At night. It must have been — when they were doing this.'

'In the bathroom. With the planthook.'

I shivered. Charlie put his huge, comforting arm round me and patted my shoulder. 'I'll nip out to the pick-up and get the tow-rope, then, shall I?'

'Charlie.'
'Yeah?'
'You awake?'
'No.'
'Only I was just thinking. You know what Elma said. About the Naylors leaving in a hurry.'

'What about it?'

'Do you think they did leave?'

Charlie turned over in bed, draping a heavy arm around my body. 'Go to sleep.'

'What if they didn't leave?'

'Beck —'

'What if there's more than just photographs under the floorboards?'

We ended up going down to the cellar at three o'clock in the morning, Charlie moaning and fastening his towelling bathrobe as I carried the torch.

'There's nothing down here, Becky,' he repeated, as I made my way down the rickety wooden steps. 'If there had been, I'd know about it. And it would have come up in the surveyor's report.'

'I just have to know.'

'Look, I'd know if there were dead bodies.' Charlie was cheerfully robust about such matters, rather like some of the pathologists I'd worked with. 'Dead bodies create all sorts of problems — smells, mainly. And gases. It's much harder to conceal stiffs than people think. If you're selling your house, that is.'

'Even so —'

Charlie put on the overhead lights — a couple of naked lightbulbs that threw grim stark radiance on the bare brick walls. In addition he ran the flashlight into the recesses of the cellar, which was gloomy and cobweb-ridden and stretched the length and breadth of the house. We were going to turn it into a utility area and playroom, eventually. 'Look at that. No rising damp. No disturbed areas in the concrete floor. No new plastering for — oh — at least ten years. Anyroad, do you think I would have bought this place if I thought it had bodies in the cellar?'

'Well, no —'

'Not unless it would of got me a few grand off the price, like.'

I gave up.

'And Elma's got an overactive imagination,' remarked Charlie, as we went back to bed.

'I can't help wondering what happened to them,' I replied, settling down against his reassuring bulk.

'You and your imagination,' said Charlie said, shaking his head. Next day he found another packet of photographs in the plasterboarding behind the sink.

I spent the following days in turmoil, desperate to know what Charlie would find next. My most obvious course of action was to ask Elma — but Elma was nowhere to be seen.

'She's hibernating,' said Kate, when I confided my anxieties at the school gates. We both paused, visualising Elma curled up in a nest of straw and shredded newspapers, like Isobel's hamster. 'Now and then she likes to withdraw for a bit. I think she gets depressed.'

'But do you think she's all right in there?'

'She does this now and again — never comes out. It's always around the time her parents died.'

'I really do have to know what happened to the Naylors.'

'Why don't you write to them? Your solicitor should have a forwarding address.'

'That's a good idea, but it'll take too long.'

'There's been nothing in the papers about them. If something happened to Mrs Naylor, then nobody knows about it —'

'Yet.'

'Becky, has anyone ever told you you're paranoid?'

'All the time.'

As soon as I had dropped Sophie at nursery I went round to Elma's and banged on the door. I could hear the sounds sink down into the silence, like ripples widening in a dark pool, as I hammered away with the brass dolphin doorknocker. I knew she was in there. I suspected she was watching me. As I walked away, irritated, I sensed the flicker of a Nottingham lace curtain and span round. But the windows were lifeless and untouched behind the dense green foliage. Cursing, I headed back to our house.

There was no sign of life for three days. I kept expecting her to pop her head out of the window when I started my car — but the outside of the house remained as enigmatic as ever.

'But why can't we play in Aunt Elma's garden?'

'She's not feeling very well.'

'But if she saw us she would feel better!'

'Not necessarily.'

'If she's really ill, she won't notice,' observed Isobel, with the mixture of self-interest and shrewdness that already boded well for a career in the legal profession. 'She'll have to go to the hospital, then she won't know.'

The possibility that Elma was indeed so sick she needed help began to bother me. What if she had fallen, like the poor man in the house round the corner who had started rotting away before the police broke in? Perhaps she was in a coma, or had succumbed to a heart attack?

I decided to think it over while we went shopping. The mechanics of taking both daughters, a small bike, a doll's buggy containing an anthropomorphic rabbit in a dress and a carrier bag full of library books was sufficient to distract me from my anxieties about Elma for the time being. Just getting round the Co-op unscathed drove all other preoccupations from my head. Then, as we were walking down the High Street towards the branch library, with the girls calling out salutations to their schoolfriends left and right, I saw her.

She was wearing an impeccably well-cut navy suit and carrying a briefcase, but she had those tell-tale signs of primary maternal preoccupation that I recognised so well. In this case they took the form of a double pack of disposable nappies in the other hand and what looked like a bottle of spirits shrouded in cerise tissue paper wedged under her arm. But it was definitely her. It was the woman from the photograph.

At first I was overwhelmed with relief. She was alive, then. He hadn't killed her. She wasn't under the lawn, or in the cellar, or beneath the paving stones of the terrace (all of which, Charlie had maintained, were totally undisturbed).

But then I started to worry about her children. As she retreated down Mansfield Road, I called out to her.

'Mrs Naylor! Mrs Naylor!'

She hadn't heard me, kept on walking. I was powerless to give pursuit, weighed down by bags and toys and two small children. *'Mrs Naylor!'*

She stopped then, turned round, looked me up and down as if wanting to know who on earth I was and what on earth I was doing haranguing her in the middle of the local high street at four o'clock in the afternoon.

'It's me,' I said, idiotically. 'Becky Ashfield. We bought your house. Remember?'

She walked towards me, securing the bottle of spirits, still looking doubtful.

'Why, what about it? Is there something wrong with the house?'

I realised how I must look — tattered, paint-spattered jeans, trainers, Star Trek T-shirt, baseball cap. I hardly looked like a mature, professional woman capable of inspiring confidence.

'I just wanted to see if you were all right,' I found myself saying. 'Moved into your new house okay, and everything.'

She looked defensive, adjusted the bottle again. I could see she was desperate for a drink, and after what she'd been though I didn't blame her. 'How is Mr Naylor?' I asked, going for it

Her defence collapsed. From looking rigid and antagonistic, she suddenly seemed to slump, shaking her head with a wry look of recognition.

'Bloody Elma!' she said, drawing closer, and putting down the nappies while she fished in her bag for a cigarette. She held the packet out to me, and I accepted — only in the interests of getting her confidence, you understand.

'Well, you may as well know,' she said, lighting our Silk Cuts for us. 'I left him, the bastard. He was giving me such a hard time.'

I nodded sympathetically. I had done more than my share of matrimonial.

'That's why you weren't in a chain. We said we were

going into rented accommodation, but actually we split up as soon as we'd sold the house.'

'Was it — erm —, cruelty?' I asked. 'Unreasonable behaviour?'

'I'll say he was unreasonable. What we do in our own home is our business. It was when he started selling my pictures that I got angry.'

'What?'

'I like — erm —,' glancing down at my children and rummaging for a euphemism. 'I'm assuming you found some of the pictures. What I didn't like was the betrayal of confidence. Sending pictures of me to a dirty magazine. And getting them printed. What sort of a husband is that?'

Charlie nearly choked on his bitter when I told him.

'What did I tell you!' he spluttered, wiping foam off his chin with his dust-ridden T-shirt. 'There's you imagining this is the most sinister address since 10 Rillington Place and all it was was her feelings got hurt. Women!'

'Well, I'm just glad she's all right, anyhow. Apparently, they're living up in Mapperley Park now, with her mother. The children are much happier and she's dating a dentist.'

Charlie wasn't surprised that I had gleaned so much information from a brief encounter in the High Street. Like him, I have the gift of inviting confidences. It is obviously useful in my line of work but sometimes I end up knowing more about my friends and acquaintances than their own families.

'Well, now you know what we can do if money gets short,' said Charlie, opening another can of beer — the contents of the previous one now liberally adorned his work clothes. 'Remind me to get some film for the camera.'

Elma appeared the following day, leaning on a walking stick. She was thinner than ever, and there were dark circles under her eyes. She looked like someone who had emerged from some grim ordeal, three months in a foreign prison, perhaps, or radical surgery. I put my hand on her arm to steady her as she came into the garden, and was horrified by the thinness of her forearm.

'Are you all right, Elma?'

'I will be, my dear. I will be. Where are those marvellous children?'

'At school, Elma, same as they always are at this time of day.' I wiped the paint off my hands with a rag, hoping that none of the terracotta emulsion had transferred itself to Elma's sleeve. 'You haven't been well.'

'I've been... there are times when I need to withdraw from the world. My little retreats, I call them.'

'Hibernation.'

'I see you've been talking to Kate. She's a good woman, but somewhat over-imaginative. She does tend to sensationalise things, but I suppose that's because she's a newspaper-woman. I've met quite a few of them.'

'Really?' I clambered back onto the stepladder and continued with my painting.

'They used to come and hang around the Common, during the protest. Sometimes they'd send women reporters disguised as peace protesters, to infiltrate us. You could spot them a mile away, of course. They didn't care about the cause. All they wanted was a good story.'

'So what exactly were you doing in those days?' I asked.

'I was a secretary in the intelligence service,' she said simply. 'My family have military connections, and I was transferred after an initial spell in the Home Office.'

'You must have seen a thing or two,' I responded, humouring her. Now I knew she was all right I was more interested in getting the ceiling finished before it was time to go and collect the girls. I didn't really believe her reminiscences of life in the secret corridors of power.

'I did,' said Elma. 'Up there — by the ceiling rose — you've missed a bit. And really, you should have put newspapers down before you started.'

'We're sanding the floorboards.'

'Would it not have been better to sand the floorboards first, before you did your decorating?'

I felt irritated beyond measure. Elma was clearly better.

98

'I'd best be off now,' she said, as if, for the first time, she sensed my vexation. 'I'm writing my memoirs, you know.'

'Is there much call for that sort of thing?' I was standing on the marble-topped mantelshelf by this time, stretching precariously into a corner with the roller, so not paying full attention to what she said.

'Oh, I think they will attract a great deal of interest, Rebecca.' She always used my full name. 'I've had a bit of a set-back because of a fault in my computer — I've no idea what caused it, though I do have my suspicions. Anyway, I have already had a chat with a literary agent, in London. She thinks she can get me a good deal, but the material is so sensational it might not be possible to publish in Britain. We may have to get in published in Australia — like they did with *Spycatcher*. I'd better get back to it.'

'Your book is like *Spycatcher?*'

'It could cause even more of a stir.'

'Can you do that? Didn't they make you sign the Official Secrets Act?'

'I'm past caring about formalities like that, my dear. I have nothing to lose. It's time people knew the truth. Mind you don't fall, now.'

The next day I had a phone call from my sister, saying that our grandmother was dead and I was needed in London. To be honest, Granny Berlinner and I had never been that close — a similarity of character and resulting conflict of personalities ensuring that we could always get enough of each other's company. Half an hour, once or twice a year, was more than sufficient. But the rest of my family were shocked and upset by her sudden death, and I felt obliged to go and comfort them. I said I would drive down the following day and Isobel and Sophie, who regarded any trip back to London as a bonus, were to come with me.

It was unfortunate that as a result of recent events I had neglected to put my car through its much needed

99

MoT, or thought to give it a trial run before setting off to London. As it was, we put in bags and cases, I strapped up the children — and the damn thing wouldn't start. A visit from the AA man confirmed that my car was in no condition for a trip to London, and I couldn't face dragging the girls down on the train. Getting the bags and children out again, I went and knocked on Elma's door.

'Of course you may borrow my car,' she said, reassuringly, squinting above her half-moon glasses at the sorry wreck of my D-registered Escort. 'But you really should trade that vehicle in soon, Rebecca. What would happen if you had a real emergency? Be prepared, that's my motto. Here are the keys.'

'Er — when was the last time you took it out, Elma?'

'Last Tuesday, to Tesco. You shouldn't have any difficulty. Now, I must get back to work. Have a safe journey.'

Elma's twelve-year-old black Rover was in surprisingly good condition, considering how little she used it. But it was obviously a bad day for me and automobiles. As we drove down the M1 in the pouring rain, Sophie grizzling in the back seat, I was disturbed to see dense black smoke emerging from under the bonnet.

'The car's on fire!' remarked Isobel, straining in her car seat to look at what was going on. 'How can it smoke if it's *raining?*'

'I don't know,' I said, swerving onto the hard shoulder and dragging the children out. A horrible and I hoped unfounded suspicion was forming in my mind. Rain lashed down as I helped the girls scramble up the embankment away from the traffic, Sophie sobbing with confusion and fear. I was just reaching for my mobile when the car exploded.

It was several hours later, cold, wet and tearful, when we got back to Sherwood in the AA van.

'What's going on?' demanded Isobel, eager for more drama. 'Look, an ambulance! And police cars!'

I saw the strips of police tape and groaned. Just what

100

we needed after all this. A crime scene on our doorstep. The ambulance was leaving, but the siren was switched off, which was a bad sign. I woke up Sophie, who burst into tears, and we made our way to our own front door. Charlie was waiting for me. He embraced me silently, with uncharacteristic emotion, and I had never seen him so scared, or so relieved, to hold us in his arms.

'What's happened?' I said, completely forgetting about our own drama. 'What's going on?'

'It's Elma. She's dead.'

'Did she collapse?'

'The police are here.'

'The police always come for a sudden death. It's routine.'

'It wasn't like you think,' replied Charlie. 'Not natural causes. She was found bludgeoned. Someone beat her to death. They reckon it was a burglary gone wrong.'

I looked up at the black windows of Elma's house, with their tracery of Nottingham Lace curtains. For a second, I thought I saw a pale face gaze out, then realised I must have been mistaken. A trick of the light.

'The burglar alarm went off,' said Charlie. 'You know how she's been having trouble with it recently. It was still going on when I came home. I went round in the end, couldn't stand it. I found her. The neighbours said the burglar alarm had been going off all day. But nobody bothered. Because it was only Elma.'

The next day an unmarked removal van parked in our street, and a taciturn group of men in brown overalls emptied Elma's house. The police scene-of-crime tape was rolled up and one by one the items of furniture were brought out like items at a sale. Rolled carpets followed, *jardinières,* pictures in frames. Even the Nottingham Lace curtains were taken down so that the windows stared like blank eyes, empty and lifeless. I saw all this from behind my own lace curtains, recent events making me cautious. Within half an hour of the removal van leaving, another, smaller, van arrived and an estate agent's board was ham-

101

mered into the flowerbed in the front garden.

'How can they do that?' Kate demanded later, at the school gates. 'It was a crime scene! They can't put it straight on the market!'

'They can do anything they want,' I said, sadly, having spent the previous, sleepless, night, putting two and two together, remembering the Hilda Murrell case, and producing some very disturbing arithmetic. 'They murdered Elma. They tried to kill me. And my children.'

'Now you sound crazy!'

'Think about it. These people's methods are not subtle. They primed Elma's car to explode the next time she used it. Except I came along instead. And when that didn't work, they battered her to death and made it look like a robbery.'

'But why?' Kate's professional interest was taking over.

'Because, to use a cliché, she knew too much. I thought all her stories about working for British Intelligence were just hysterical attention seeking, but someone else — lots of people — seem to have been prepared to believe her. I don't know what she saw or did, but she was threatening to publish her memoirs and someone took her very seriously indeed. I just wish I had.'

'Where do you think her memoirs are now?'

'I don't think they'll ever be found. If she even got around to starting them. I just wish I'd believed her. If I had, maybe all this could have been prevented.'

'Perhaps,' replied Kate, sceptically. 'Perhaps her memoirs cost Elma her life. But they nearly cost you your life, don't forget. And your children.'

It took a while for the house to sell. The property market had hit an all-time low, and nobody local fancied moving in to a place where the owner had been beaten to death, however unpopular she may have been. The police inquiry was inconclusive, and nobody was ever charged. Explanations as to the cause of Elma's car's sudden conflagration were also unsatisfactory, with the police even-

102

tually attributing the damage to an electrical fault. It was some weeks before I felt like driving again, and now I always look underneath the car before getting in.

Charlie considered buying Elma's house and converting it into flats, but I felt uncomfortable about using her old home this way. So the wild garden became even more overgrown, and the CND stickers began to peel off the windows, but at least I was able to do something for her six cats. Unscathed by the sinister group who had stripped the house and removed all traces of Elma's presence, the animals immediately moved in with us next door.

Elma's house stayed empty through Christmas and New Year, looking ever bleaker. Then, one day in March, the SOLD sign went up, and a team of decorators arrived to erect scaffolding and paint the outside. The following Saturday, another van arrived, bearing a Scottish address, and a large family arrived with it, at least four children crammed into the back of a Montego estate with a barking, feathery-coated Irish setter.

I gave it an hour, then I went round and knocked on the door.

The mother, who was about the same age as me, and tight around the eyes with stress and exhaustion, regarded me suspiciously.

'I've bought you a pot of tea and a cake round,' I said, hoping I did not look too eccentric. 'It's kind of a custom round here. Oh, yes, and I know this sounds daft, but I'm supposed to give you this, too.' I handed her a bottle of wine.

She took one look at me and I wondered if she was going to slam the door in my face, or call the police, or both. Then she turned over her shoulder and shouted: 'Hamish! Come here!' Then she smiled.

'And we'd heard folk down here were unfriendly! Come away in.'

Three children were running up and down the echoing floorboards, while a determined toddler was scaling the stairs. Sports commentary blared out of a transistor radio,

103

and the dog was barking and capering around in circles, its tail representing a threat to any delicate items of china. I thought of Elma — and I resolved to say nothing of the events that had taken place here before. I hoped Elma didn't mind. I like to think she was watching.

A Cold Coming
H.R.F. Keating

'It is someone urgent-urgent wanting you. Some angrezi it is sounding like.'

Inspector Ghote was not sorry his wife calling out had cut short his morning shower. In December in Bombay the water has a distinct chill to it. He wrapped a towel round his middle and hurried to the telephone, feeling the cool stone of the floor on his bare feet.

An Englishman wanting him? But who?

And urgently...?

'Ghote speaking.'

'Ah. Ah, thank God, it's you. Henry Reymond here.'

Mr Henry Reymond? The name was somehow half-familiar. Who the devil...?

'Inspector? Inspector? Are you there? Can you hear me?'

'Yes, yes. I am hearing. Why not?'

'Well... Indian telephones.'

'Our system is one hundred percent first-class.'

Ghote had let himself voice some resentment. Who was this Westerner to decide that if something was Indian it must be inefficient, however much Bombay phones had once been a nightmare of crossed lines and sudden cut-offs?

And then some recollection of that half-concealed frigid disapproval told him who this Reymond Henry, Henry Reymond, was.

Yes. Years ago he had met the man. A noted British author, or so the papers had called him. From somewhere in U.K. called Nottinghill or Nottingham, something like that. In Bombay on some sort of exchange visit with an Indian author. And... and there had been a murder next-door to the flat the fellow had been lent. The Shivaji Park case. And all those years ago he himself had been landed

105

with no more than the task of keeping this Henry Reymond, who wrote, yes, crime stories, out of the way. The fellow had been being one damn nuisance. And had gone on plaguing him himself with his high-and-mighty questions-this and questions-that about every awkward aspect of Bombay life.

'Mr Reymond,' he brought himself to say — Indian hospitality must never be less than wholehearted — 'you are altogether welcome. You are in Bombay itself, yes?'

'No, no. I'm in Delhi. Er — New Delhi. I'm here on a tour for the British Council. Three of us poets.'

'Poets? Were you saying you are poet? But I am thinking it is crime books you are writing. Some hero who is collecting something. Yes, shells. You are writing books wherein this shellswallah is all the time solving very-very fantastic mysteries.'

'Mr Peduncle. My detective.'

Now it was the Englishman's turn to sound offended.

'Yes, yes. I was once going through one of those books. *Mr Peduncle Caught in the Meshes.* Very good.'

'Ah, yes. Well, thank you.' The noted author seemed less hurt. 'Well, you see, it's like this. A couple of years ago, finding the Peduncle books were bringing me in a rather decent income, I decided to try a bit of an experiment. I wrote a crime novel in verse. A long poem really. Set in India, actually. In the days of the Raj. And, well, because of it the British Council asked me to come on this tour.'

'And you would be visiting Bombay also, yes?'

'Well, yes. Yes, eventually. Only... Well, this is what I'm ringing about actually. You see, I've been arrested.'

'Arrested? But what for are they arresting?'

'It's — It's — Well, the thing is they think I've committed a murder.'

'But why are they thinking such? And what for are you telling me this per telephone?'

'That's it. That's it exactly. You see, no one here would listen to me. Or to the chaps from the High Commission either. And then I remembered you. You're the only Indian police officer who's ever paid any real attention to anything I said.'

Ghote remembered in his turn. How — warm Indian hospitality being day by day more and more worn away — he had battled and battled to find answers to those on-and-on damned questions.

'So that's why,' the now familiar British voice went on, 'I'd like you to get on to the Head of Crime Branch here and tell him that he's being utterly ridiculous.'

The words, in that bang-bang voice, had entered Ghote's ear. But it took several seconds, it seemed, before such an outrageous request entered his mind.

For him, for a simple inspector from Bombay, to telephone the Head of Crime Branch at the Centre and to tell him — To tell him what he was doing was utterly ridiculous. It — It — It would be like telling Bombay's Number One film star he was incapable of acting, or, worse, of dancing.

'But, Mr Reymond — But, sir... Sir, what you are asking is a marathon impossible thing. Cent per cent.'

There was a long silence at the other end of the line.

And then the voice that came trickling into his ear was very different from the one he had heard up to then.

'Inspector... Inspector, please. Please, I didn't do it. Inspector, you know me. We knew each other well back then in Bombay. We were friends, weren't we? You know I'm not someone who could ever kill anybody.'

Ghote thought.

What his bugbear of long ago had said was certainly true. In so far as he could ever state that any human being was incapable of murder, he would have said it about the big, flabby, cucumber-cool, unexcitable Englishman he was recollecting more and more clearly with every passing minute.

So — the thoughts went click-clicking through his mind — if Mr Henry Reymond, who was now it seemed a distinguished poet, had been arrested on suspicion of com-

107

mitting a murder which it was almost impossibly unlikely he had committed, then whoever was responsible in far away Delhi was on the point of causing an international incident. The British newspapers would kick up one worldwide tamasha.

So... So, if there was anything he himself could do to get the business quietly forgotten, then it was up to him to do it. No one else in the whole of India probably knew more about Mr Henry Reymond than he did.

And he thought, just perhaps, there was something he could do. If he went to his own boss, Assistant Commissioner Pradhan, and explained to him what the situation was, then just possibly Mr Pradhan might phone his opposite number at the Centre and convince him he ought to go much, much, much more carefully.

'Mr Reymond,' he said, 'I will to my level best do what I can. Kindly await development.'

So it was that, scarcely more than three hours later, Inspector Ghote found himself aboard an Indian Airlines plane bound for Delhi. He felt not a little confused. Never for a moment had he thought that trying to circumvent an international incident would mean he would be dispatched himself without a moment to draw breath to the distant capital. And to do what? To somehow make sure, a task agreed to by the Head of Delhi Crime Branch, that a noted British author had beyond doubt not murdered one Professor V.V. Goswami. To disprove in fact the belief, held it seemed by the whole of the Delhi police, that Henry Reymond had committed murder in order to obtain possession of a certain valuable document — if only just one poem, hitherto unknown, handwritten by some deceased foreigner by the name of Eliot, Eliot with some initials in front, could possibly be so maha-valuable.

But when the plane swooped down to the airport and he stepped out on to the tarmac a yet greater surprise awaited him. It was cold. Sharply and bitterly and horribly cold.

108

In an instant, shivering like the leaves of a pipal tree in his simple shirt and pants, he realised that, of course, he had read in the newspaper — Was it only yesterday: It somehow seemed already weeks away — that Delhi was in the grip of a colder than usual December. Bitingly chill air from the Himalayas mingling with the ever-increasing fumes of the capital's jockeying and jolting traffic had covered the city in freezing immovable smog. Roofless beggars were dying from exposure by the dozen. Everyday life had come to almost as much of a standstill as it customarily did in the intensest heat of summer.

However, he had his duty. He marched off, flapping his arms round himself in a vain attempt to instill some interior warmth, and found an intrepid-looking Sikh taxiwallah.

'Police Headquarters,' he barked out between chattering teeth.

'A cold coming we had of it, just the worst time of the year for a journey and such a long journey... And the camels, dah-di-dah refractory.'

What on earth was this Mr Brian Quayne saying? Perhaps it had not been such a good idea to hear what the two other poets had to tell rather than talk first to his friend, Mr Henry Reymond, if friend he was.

'Please, I am not at all understanding. What it is, please, about camels that are — What was it you were stating? Refractory?'

'Well, Inspector,' the paper-thin, chalk-faced, big-beaked poet said, blinking at him through a pair of round spectacles, 'when we first arrived in Delhi we saw camels here and there. Can't say I was really expecting to somehow. And if the wretched beasts weren't refractory in this awful cold, then I don't know why not. Even if old Tom Eliot was thinking of a slightly less freezing journey than ours. Sharp, that's what he says in the poem, after all. *The ways deep and the weather sharp*. Okay, I suppose, for stuff from the pre-electronic age.'

Ghote felt he was beginning to glimpse a meaning in what the fellow was saying. But this poem he was quoting, was it the one Henry Reymond was suspected of murdering to get hold of, or not? This Tom Eliot, was he, or was he not, the world-famous Eliot? The one with the initials. T something. T.F. Yes, T.F. Eliot.

But never mind all that.

'Yes, yes,' he said, rapping it out impatiently, 'such is all very well. But what I am asking, Mr Quayne, is are you believing your fellow poet, Mr Henry Reymond, was killing one Professor V.V. Goswami.'

'Damn it all, Inspector, it's totally obvious a fat idiot like Reymond would never have the guts to murder anyone. Unless it was one of the paper tigers he stuffed into that rhyming travesty he's so absurdly proud about.'

'So what it is you are saying was happening?'

'The whole business is totally absurd. How I got caught up in it I'll never know. The foremost poet, though I say it, of the Electronic Age. Beating my brains out to produce work with all the implacable logic of the computer, and I find myself involved in a ludicrous business about us all having to hide our copies of some ridiculous book and then having them all found and brought back to us, as if we were in some demented French farce.'

'Mr Quayne, kindly be telling me, if you are able, exactly what was occurring? Facts only.'

Across the poet's chalky face there came for an instant a flush of pinkness, whether of shame or anger it was impossible to tell.

'Very well,' he said in a rather more businesslike manner. 'It was like this. After we Three Wise Men from the West had given our reading at the British Council there was a reception for us at Professor Goswami's house. Little spicy bits brought round by a creepy-looking servant and nothing at all to drink. If you don't count orange juice.'

Ghote once more felt an urge to defend Indian hospitality, even offered by a creepy servant, if creepy the man

110

really was. But, before he could find the right words, with a shudder of distaste the British poet went back to his account.

'And then each one of us was given, or we had thrust into our hands more like, by someone called Mrs Namita Rai a copy of her poetical works, entitled — would you believe — *In the Footsteps of Mr Percy Bysshe Shelley.* Well, naturally, none of us wanted to lug something like that all round the rest of India. So, as it turned out, we each of us contrived discreetly to leave our copies in various parts of the hotel we had been put up at, the Imperial. I hid mine in an inconspicuous corner of what they call the Business Centre, where I was sending off some faxes. Arnold Brudge stuffed his down the side of one of those big sofas in the foyer and that idiot Reymond left his in the tiny hotel bookshop. In imitation he said, kept on saying, of that Edgar Allan Poe story *The Purloined Letter.*'

'I am well-knowing that tale,' Ghote put in, keeping his literary end up.

'Well, everybody knows it. But the thing was — and this is just about as stupid as you can get — the bloody books had been dedicated to each of us by name. So in less than an hour they were all three brought back to our rooms by a bowing and scraping, tip-seeking hotel servant.'

Ghote saw the joke. And kept a straight face.

'But why are you telling all this?' he asked. 'Kindly stick one hundred percent to point in hand.'

The foremost poet of the Electronic Age drew in a sharp sigh.

'This is the point,' he snapped. 'The bloody ridiculous point of it all. You see, we were invited to Professor Goswami's again next day. Plunging out into the bloody cold smog just to drink a cup of milky damn tea and look at this Eliot poem that had somehow found its way to India and been totally forgotten ever since.'

'That is Mr T.F. Eliot, expired?'

'Expired?' The poet gave a cold giggle. 'Yes, I suppose

you could say that. Now we've entered the Electronic Age, Eliot and all his stuff has pretty well expired.'

'So what was happening, please, at this second visit to late Professor Goswami?'

But it was from Arnold Brudge and not Electronic Age Brian Quayne that Ghote eventually heard his most coherent account of how a copy of Mrs Namita Rai's poetical works had led to the arrest on suspicion of murder of his erstwhile friend Henry Reymond.

'Henry Reymond,' said the massive man opposite, wide chest stretching a rough wool, high-collared, tree-brown pullover to bursting point, two slabs of raw red hands flat on the table in front of him, 'that fat slob, he'd faint dead away if he so much as saw a hawk swoop to its kill. He'd piss himself if he heard a dog-fox scream in lust. He'd puke at the smell of a decent bit of blood.'

'Yes, yes,' Ghote had answered sharply, feeling he ought at least to defend a little his friend of long ago. 'But, please, I was asking what was happening when you, all three, were going to Professor Goswami's to examine this poem they are saying is so valuable.'

'Oh, that. Well, you see according to bloody Henry Reymond he had taken with him his copy of *In the Footsteps of Mr Percy Bysshe Shelley*. He says he wanted to hide it in the room where that wretched woman made him accept it. But, because apparently I'd told him to for God's sake shut up about his stupid Edgar Allan Poe, he never said a word to either of us about his sneaky little plan. Then, after Goswami was murdered that night — probably some intruder, I don't know — the police found the bloody book in the room. It was conspicuous enough for God's sake, hand-bound in fancy red silk. But now Goswami's servant swears it wasn't there before the murder. Dare say the fellow could be right, the way he was going about all the time with a cloth over his shoulder looking for something to dust.'

The mountainous poet gave a snort of contempt. Ghote

felt puzzled.

'But you, Mr Brudge,' he asked, 'were you seeing Mr Reymond leave that book there? Can you provide confirmation itself?'

His question was answered with a single long, muffled roar. Only on the end of it were words.

'. . . bother with anything bar Nature. Not what a great slob like Reymond might be doing.'

Ghote's hopes sank away. The poet of the Electronic Age had been just as unhelpful over this point. And it was a vital one. If no one who knew Mr Henry Reymond had seen him hide that silk-bound volume among Professor Goswami's crammed bookshelves, then the chances of persuading the Delhi police that his old acquaintance was not a murderer were slim almost to vanishing point.

'So,' he asked desperately, 'you cannot be stating definitely whether or not this book by Mrs Rai was in Professor Goswami's room prior to the event of murder?'

'Said I can't, didn't I?'

It felt like being crushed by a wall of ice.

'Thank you, Mr Brudge.' He roused himself. 'And may I say I am hoping one day I would read some of your very-very nice poetry.'

'Not *nice*. Christ's sake.'

Ghote retreated.

Perhaps Mr Henry Reymond himself would, asked the right questions in the right way, be able to produce some proof he had not returned to Professor Goswami's in the dead of night in order to steal this new-found valuable poem. Then it would be clear he had not been disturbed by the professor, had not let fall the works of Mrs Rai and had not then, as the Delhiwallahs believed, struck the professor down.

But now all the poet of the once-upon-a-time Raj could do, ask him what he would, was to bleat out that he had never left his hotel room that night, and that he had, he had, he had put Mrs Rai's book on to a shelf in Professor Goswami's room during his afternoon visit.

113

'Inspector, I know I did. I know it.'

'But, please, was anyone seeing?'

For one moment the crime writer-poet sat and thought. But it was for one moment only. Then panic and hysteria set in again.

'No one saw me. No one. Oh God, I wish they had. Then I'd be believed. But — But, you see, that servant seemed to be everywhere I was when I was about to get rid of that awful book. So in the end I just turned my back and stuffed it into the first place I saw.'

'But where was that itself?'

'Oh, I don't know. I don't know. Somewhere. Anywhere. All I know is Professor Goswami was alive and well when I left. I told him how deeply I admired the Eliot manuscript, and then I made that farewell gesture of putting your hands together — one has to make an effort to show you don't feel superior — and we all three got a taxi back to the hotel.'

'That was the newly-found poem of late Mr T.F. Eliot?' Ghote asked, hoping for some last tiny corroborative detail.

Henry Reymond gave him a chill look.

'T.S., Inspector,' he said. 'Tom Eliot's initials were T.S.'

The icy hiss with which that final letter was pronounced finished it for Ghote. He found he was almost hoping Henry Reymond, despite the assurances of his two fellow poets, had been capable of murder and had attacked Professor Goswami. But he could not quite believe it.

So he went, not without internal trembling that owed nothing to the freezing smog, to see Delhi's Head of Crime Branch, a yet more formidable figure than his own Assistant Commissioner Pradhan.

But, before he had so much as uttered a single word of his report he saw, prominently lying on the huge desk in front of him, what could be nothing else than the fatal copy of *In the Footsteps of Mr Percy Bysshe Shelley*, beautifully bound in glowing red silk. He felt it was an omen.

114

Of ill-success.

The first words he heard confirmed all his worst fears.

'Well, Inspector? My detectives have got it all wrong, is it? A Bombaywallah is going to put us right?'

'No, sir. That is — Sir, please to believe this. The two poets accompanying Mr Henry Reymond, who are knowing him well, sir, both are one hundred percent certain he is a man not able to commit any murder.'

'And you, Inspector, are you going to tell me there is one single human being in this world incapable, given the right circumstances, of committing an offence under Section 302, Indian Penal Code?'

'No, sir, no. I am not saying such. I would never say no one is not at worst capable of murder. But, sir, all the same I also am believing Mr Henry Reymond would commit such only under tip-top provocation.'

'And you think the prospect of getting his dirty thieving hands on this priceless poetical manuscript, now missing, is not provocation enough? Poets are always poor, Inspector. Always needing money for wine, women, song. Even you must be knowing that.'

'Sir, yes, that I am understanding. But, sir, kindly consider this. Mr Henry Reymond is not just only a poet. He is crime writer-cum-poet, sir. He is one very-very famous writer of detective stories. Mr Peduncle series, sir. And, sir, he was telling me. From those books he was making so much money that, sir, he was able to take leave from that work and write one poem in verse, murder story in times of Raj only. So, sir, he is having no need whatsoever of stealing any manuscript.'

'No, Inspector. No, Damn it, there is evidence. This book. Found at the murder scene itself. First-class evidence.'

A ferocious hand slapped down on the red silk.

Ghote, as soon as the hand was lifted, ventured to pick the book up. Perhaps Mr Henry Reymond's name was not actually in it? Perhaps one of the other poets' was?

But, no. There on the title page was the inscription *To*

my fellow poet Mr Henry Reymond. In admiration. Namita Rai. Why had the fellow not paid attention to the book being returned to him at the Imperial Hotel just only because of that inscription? Why had he not had the simple sense to tear out that page? Probably because he had believed in his coldly high-and-mighty way that no-one would ever find the book among all the others in Professor Goswami's room. But he had failed to reckon with the efficiency of the police searchers. Even the Delhi searchers.

He flipped over the page and read the titles of the first few poems.

Ode to the East Wind

To A Seven-sisters Bird

Triumph of Death (Cancelled Opening)

'Leave that alone, Inspector.'

Ghote hastily replaced the red-silk volume.

'And, listen to me. Unless you have something better to tell me than all that nonsense about poets not needing money and this friend of yours not being capable of murder I am going to charge-sheet him. Now.'

'Sir, no. Sir, kindly give me some more time. I will talk to him again. Find if he has some alibi.'

'Alibi? Oh, yes, and what alibi did he produce for us? Asleep in his room at the Imperial Hotel. And not even a woman beside him What sort of a poet is that?'

'Sir, one altogether timid.'

'Eh? Timid? Timid, did you say? Well, I suppose you've got a point there, Inspector. Point of sorts. All right, I tell you what. I'll give you till 10 p.m. tonight. Come back to me then with some sort of decent evidence and I'll give the matter more consideration. All right?'

'Yes, sir. Yes.'

Ghote left. Hurriedly.

But go over and over the circumstances with Henry Reymond though he might, he could not extract from the crime writer-cum-poet one single fact that might prove he had not sneaked out of the Imperial Hotel, gone slipping through the chill blanketing smog of Delhi's night-time streets to Professor Goswami's and, while seizing this poem by Mr T.F. — no, T.S. — Eliot, been disturbed by the professor and in a struggle had killed him.

So it was well before his deadline hour that, sadly, he left the prisoner to his fate.

He wandered out into the bone-chilling night, still convinced nevertheless that Henry Reymond had never murdered Professor Goswami. That red silk-covered book *In the Footsteps of Mr Percy Bysshe Shelley* — what trouble it had caused. All because, in the warmth of fellow feeling for those British poets, Namita Rai had made them the gift of those copies.

And how sad it was that the three of them, with cold-hearted Britishness, had tried to get rid of the books. Poor Mrs Rai. If she ever got to know. And — then the thought struck him — she would get to know. When the papers described every detail of the trial for murder of a famous U.K. poet it would come out that he, and his fellow poets, had all tried to dispose of Mrs Namita Rai's works.

No, he must tell her about it himself. He must tell her now. Break it to her gently. So that she would have not too much of suffering.

He hurried over to Police Headquarters, consulted a telephone directory, found that Mrs Rai's residence was not far away.

A quarter of an hour later he was closeted with the writer of *Ode to the East Wind* and *Triumph of Death (Cancelled Opening)*.

And five minutes after that he was sitting in a glow of delight. He had obtained perfect proof that Mr Henry Reymond had left his copy of Mrs Rai's book at Professor Goswami's while that learned gentleman was still hale and hearty. Proof Mr Henry Reymond had never taken that handwritten poem of Mr T.S. — Yes, T.S. — Eliot so as to sell it for the huge sum it would fetch. No doubt, the professor's servant — Mr Brian Quayne right after all, the fellow must be 'creepy' — had led some dacoit friends to this much vaunted valuable object and so brought about the professor's death.

'But, Inspector,' Mrs Rai had said. 'I am well knowing what those disgraceful Englishmen were doing. Goswami Sahib himself was finding Mr Reymond's copy of my book pushed in among his shelves, and he was being so kind as to tell me what had happened in case I should hear of it from some less well-wishing friend.'

Why I Did It

Peter Mortimer

I can explain why I murdered my wife. It's not the kind of thing I'd do normally. I'm not violent. I don't get into fights. Nor has my life been very dramatic. I'm average. And I'm not offering excuses. It is simply what happened.

When I met Cecilia it was actually the second dramatic event in three months. First off I won the National Lottery. Not the great biggy, and I'm not sure I want to go into specific detail on the amount. Let's just say it was enough to see me alright. Luckily I'd asked for No Publicity, so there was no chance of a queue at my door. When I watched the numbers come up, and realised I'd won, I went into the kitchen, made a cup of tea and a Ryvita spread and thought calmly.

I decided to put the money into a safe interest account, not say a word to anybody and for the meantime get on with my life as normal, or as normal as can be with – well, with a sizeable sum sitting pretty.

I allowed myself little secret smiles each morning as I rode the bus into Nottingham City Centre. I lived in Carrington, in the north of the city, a small flat, and I worked in the offices of a double-glazing firm. It was run by two local blokes who wore sharp gear, gelled their hair, smelt of Brut and would rev their big cars when they parked outside.

They took adverts in the *Evening Post* and signed up a Radio Trent celebrity to say how good their work was. For some reason people fell for it, and business was booming. The work was guaranteed for two years, and I had a suspicion it fell to bits a few weeks after that. But that wasn't my business.

They also had some salesmen who'd boast once they got through a front door, they never emerged without an order. Most people who worked there thought the bosses were a couple of tossers, but of course we didn't say so.

One of the girls in the office was Julia who painted her nails blue and once showed me the flower tattooed at the top of her thigh. When she moved into a new flat with her boyfriend in Bulwell, they threw a party, and invited me. It's a bit of a hike from Carrington to Bulwell on public transport, but I went. I suppose I could have got a taxi, but I didn't want to start getting flashy with my lottery winnings.

It was like most parties. Within half an hour I was stood propped up against the kitchen sink wondering why I'd bothered. The French rolls were soggy with spilt beer, and half the people were out of it on drugs.

Then Cecilia was standing in front of me.

'Come and dance,' she said.

She grabbed my hand and led me into the living room. People were thrashing about to some house band. It made me feel old, and if it hadn't been for Cecilia, I'd have been self-conscious as normal, especially as I danced like a sack of potatoes. But she put her hands on my waist, and made my body sway with the music, just like her body was swaying in its little black dress. She had a red silk scarf tied round her neck.

Everything she said made me laugh, and the things I said seemed to make her laugh. I wasn't used to that. We danced for a couple of tracks, then she leant forward and kissed me on the lips. You know when people say it seemed like electricity passed through them? I'd have said that was crap. But it happened.

'Let's get a taxi,' she said soon enough. And we did. We sat in the back and I felt the warmth and closeness of her body next to mine.

'Where do you live?' she asked, I said 'Carrington', and she leant forward to the driver and said, 'Carrington, please'. We were no sooner back at my flat than this fantastic-looking female was naked writhing with me on the floor and we were making passionate love. Jeez.

I'd say she was more experienced than me, but that

wouldn't be saying much. Everyone else in their late twenties had had ten times more sex than me. In fact I hadn't really done it at all. I'd fumbled around, I'd even slept in the same bed as a girl, but that's what it had been. Sleeping. Sometimes I got panicky, thinking how much everyone else was getting.

Now here was Cecilia. And her love cries were ringing around my flat.

'Do you always have this effect on women?' she asked later as we lay on my single bed. I couldn't reply. She ran her hand down the fine hairs on my belly.

'Know what I think?' she asked, and I shook my head. 'That for every one person, there is this ideal other person. Trouble is, most of the time, they never get to meet. What are you doing Wednesday?'

Two weeks later I asked Cecilia to marry me. She had totally knocked me out. I could think of nothing, or nobody else. The smell of that dark hair, the feel of it brushing against my skin, her mouth opening into that wide smile, those deep dark eyes, pale skin. Even the sound of her shoes clip-clopping down the street. I was in love. Being apart from her seemed absurd, obscene, a waste of time.

She said yes. We had a quick register office wedding, and for the time being moved into my flat though I knew it wasn't satisfactory. It was only then that I told Cecilia about my lottery winnings.

She shrugged her shoulders.

'It's only money,' she said. 'Let's go for a pizza.'

Cecilia's possessions were few. Some clothes, a couple of paintings, a small wardrobe. She worked as a counter assistant in the Victoria Centre Boots, and lived alone in a small bedsit in one of those large converted houses in Mapperley Park. Or at least she did.

I bought a house, brand new, mock-Georgian, on a luxury estate in West Bridgford. As Cecilia reminded me, living south of the river was much more desirable. One night as I sat down working out mortgage rates, repayments etc. Cecilia said, 'Why not just buy it?'

'Buy it? You mean all at once?'

'Why not? Mortgages are designed to suit building societies, not people. You can afford it.' She leant over and kissed me. 'You've got to learn to treat money with disrespect, Lee, otherwise it ruins your life.'

This was only one of the extraordinary things Cecilia said. How had I managed to live my life before her? As if it had all been waiting. A preparation. I bought the house outright. I felt – exhilarated afterwards.

I knew now why people wrote love songs, poetry. They were trying to explain it. Except you couldn't. You could only experience it. And no-one had ever experienced it like I was doing. I wanted to touch her all the time, be with her all the time. The dull ache in my chest meant only one thing. Cecilia was not there.

Two months after our wedding – two months which contained more real life than the other twenty-seven years put together – I said to Cecilia:

'What do you think about children?'

'Children?'

'Yes. For us. How many should we have?'

She tossed her head back and laughed.

'None.'

'None?'

'There are enough children in the world, Lee, without us adding to them. Come here,' and she pulled me down, began unbuttoning my shirt.

'But Cecilia, I thought –'

By this time she was running her hands up and down my bare chest.

'And there's too much thinking in the world, as well. Not enough doing.'

So we did some doing. I pushed the thought of children away for the moment. There was plenty of time and I didn't want to put too much pressure on Cecilia too soon. I could see how a young woman wanted to wait before she began the job of bringing up kids. Things would develop.

Naturally.

It was soon after this I asked her, 'Why do you need to work behind that Boots counter?'

'No real reason,' she said.

'It makes no sense,' I said. 'And you don't need to work there now. In fact, I don't want you to work there any more.'

'Don't you?'

'I'd like you to be here, making our home just right for us. I'd like to be at work, and think of you, being back here.'

'You're such an old-fashioned thing, Lee,' she said. 'It's a good job I rescued you,' and she ran her fingers through my hair (which, I had to confess, was thinning slightly).

Only a short time before I'd come home every night to a cold empty flat. Now I could get used to coming home to Cecilia. I would kiss her goodbye on the doormat each morning, travel in across Trent Bridge to work, and marvel that one man could inherit such good fortune. In the evenings I would return home and find myself increasing my step as I neared the house. Sometimes by the time I was at the front door I was jogging.

I bought a car for Cecilia to use during the day, and the both of us at week-ends. And one week-end, as we were taking a drive out through what remained of Sherwood Forest, she said, 'Lee, we should travel.'

'That's what we are doing,' I said.

'No, the big world out there. What do we know of it, here, in our tiny little corner?'

I hadn't given it much thought. The TV news, documentaries, a small glimpse of those other worlds. But somehow not quite real, not quite lived in the way your own life was lived.

'Africa, America, India.' She counted them off on her fingers. 'Well?'

As regards travel, these were places I'd almost considered on another planet.

'But Cecilia –' I said.

'There's always a 'but' if you want one, Lee,' she answered. We were near Ollerton.

Two weeks later we were in Kenya. When I returned, Julia at work said, 'You're branching out a bit, aren't you? What's happened to old stick-in-the-mud Lee?'

I noticed the other women in the office, perhaps for the first time since my marriage. Mrs Gwent, who had begun fixing me with a hard stare. She and her 'hubby', as she always called him, took their touring caravette to the same site in Margate every year. I felt that somehow she was annoyed at me going to Africa. It made me feel good. One of the partners walked through the office and said,

'Africa? Went there once. Sodding flies. How come black people can't swim? Ever seen a black Olympic medallist at swimming?' He looked pleased with himself and passed on.

My own work was to do with accounts. Chasing up overdue payers, that kind of thing. Not very exciting. I'd never expected life to be exciting. Before Cecilia.

Soon after this, the note appeared on my desk. It had been printed out on a word processor in large capitals, and it read

YOUR WIFE IS BEING UNFAITHFUL

Anyone could have typed it in. Anyone from the office could have dropped it on my desk. I picked it up, turned it over, and read it again. It still read

YOUR WIFE IS BEING UNFAITHFUL

I folded it carefully and placed it in my side pocket. I looked around at the other people in the office, all of whom seemed to be busy with their work. There was no clue who had written it. I got on with my own work.

That evening, sat in the living room, I took the note out and unfolded it in front of Cecilia.

'I found this on my desk at work.'

She read it, and a flicker ran across her face. Nothing more.

'I'm asking myself who it is,' I said, and quickly she replied, 'What?'

'Who it is,' I repeated, 'who could write such a malicious and poisonous note. Who could stoop to such lies?'

'Oh,' she said, and took the note up in her hand. 'I wouldn't know. I know nothing about the people in your office.'

'So what do you think?' I asked.

'I think someone is jealous of you,' she said. 'I think they know you have found real happiness and they can't stand it, because their own lives are shallow and boring and small. I think,' she said, and held the note up, 'that in a strange way this note is a compliment to the love we both have.'

I was silent for a moment as I absorbed her words. I put my arms round her and squeezed her tight.

'I have begun to find them all petty in that office of late,' I said. 'I've begun to tire of the place. Since you.'

'None of it matters, Lee,' she whispered. 'None of it can touch us. Our love is too strong, too far beyond them. You're changing. And they can't stand it. Because they will never change. They want the old Lee Norman. Well,' she ran her finger lightly down my cheek, 'they can't have him. He's gone for good.'

What happened next day took me by surprise. I did it instinctively. I didn't even think. I just stood up in the middle of the office and said:

'Someone left this note on my desk yesterday. It reads YOUR WIFE IS BEING UNFAITHFUL. I just want you to know both Cecilia and I find it pretty pathetic. We treat it with the ridicule it deserves. We love one another in a way you could not even understand. Whoever wrote it, we both feel sorry for you.'

No-one said a word. No-one made eye-contact with me. The silence in the office was broken when Frank, one of the partners, walked in.

125

'What's this, then, a minute's silence or something? Forgotten some major national ceremony, have I?' He walked out again, and everyone returned to work. I told Cecilia of the incident that night, and added, 'There's more to life than double-glazing anyway. I've a mind to leave.'

'And do what?' she asked.

'I don't know. Maybe nothing for a while. Maybe just be here with you.'

She took my hand. 'Lee,' she said, 'if you left right now, it would look as if they'd driven you out, that note and everything. They'd have won. Is that what you want?'

'I want to live life for the first time,' I replied. 'And you've shown me how.'

'All in good time, Lee,' she said, 'all in good time,' and she laid my head on her chest.

'Nothing is as important as loving you, Cecilia,' I said, 'nothing in the world.'

We travelled again. To Italy. I felt free, less cautious. Cecilia was right. Money imprisons you, and having more of it can just imprison you more. I spent freely, I enjoyed Italy hugely. And part of this enjoyment was witnessing the impression Cecilia made upon others, when she walked in a room, a bar, a restaurant, how stunningly beautiful she was, how the men would stare at her, how easily she could enchant them. And she was mine.

I bought new clothes in Italy. Bright colourful clothes, bold. I noticed how drab Englishmen were in their grey and black and beige.

'Have you noticed?' I said to Cecilia. 'The English are afraid of real colour, of its passion. Their clothes are dull, their houses are all white or tepid pastel.'

'You used to be afraid of passion, Lee,' she said.

'Not any more,' I said.

She stroked my hand. 'Poor Lee,' she said.

'Why poor?' I asked her and laughed, but already she was out of the room.

I felt my days of double-glazing were limited.

Some weeks after this I found the words on the telephone pad. It was the same period that I noticed Cecilia at times grew quiet, withdrawn, times when I could not get to her. This frightened me, but when she returned to me she assured me everything was well. The effect she could have on me, how her mood could affect mine, her happiness influence mine, was something new to me.

I mentioned the words on the pad. In fact they were the indentation of words which had been written on the sheet above, then torn off. The impression was still visible. The words were "Outside Odeon Wed. 2pm" and the handwriting was clearly that of Cecilia.

I had torn a message from the pad that morning before going to work, so knew this one must have been that day and therefore the Wednesday must be the one to come. As I read the words, I realised, with a mild amusement, how little I knew of Cecilia's movements while I was at work. I would ask her about her day, she would tell me things, but there was rarely anything specific. Until this.

I looked at the indentation again. A small playful plan came into my mind, a deceit but a harmless one which Cecilia would not later object to. Seeing the effect Cecilia had on people when we were away, I had the desire to witness it here, in Nottingham, but without her being aware of my presence at all.

I would slip out from work at 2pm and observe her meeting outside the Odeon. I would be invisible. The Odeon was on Angel Row, not far from the office. I found the idea exciting. Later I would tell her.

But how to get out of the office at 2pm? I began to think of all manner of excuses, but then laughed at myself. Why should a double-glazing firm any longer dictate my timetable? I would simply walk out.

On the Wednesday at 1.45pm I stood up from my desk.

'I'm off out,' I said.

'Out where?' asked Julia.

'Shan't be long,' I replied, and pulled on my coat.

'Do Frank or Jeff know?' asked Mrs Gwent. I didn't reply, and she continued, 'Is it company business?' By this time I was half-way out the door.

I walked down Pelham Street and through Slab Square, I felt good. I breathed in the air. The afternoon sun was slanting through the fountains, producing small rainbows. I ran my hand in through the jets of water, and this felt good too. A few mothers and toddlers were sat round the square. The odd tramp dozed on top of the low walls. How free it felt, being outside here during work hours. How ridiculous, I thought, that we were all chained up in offices, shops and factories for the majority of the day. Open the doors! Run out!

I strode across the square and up towards the Odeon. Cecilia was already standing outside, looking up the street and down. She had on a striking looking trouser suit in purple and pink. I was simply tempted to rush up to her, throw my arms round her, surprise her, but I resisted. I stood half-obscured in a shop doorway opposite, and saw how her long silky hair trembled slightly in the breeze. How I wanted to embrace her.

But somebody else did. The man walked down Angel Row. It all happened so quickly. A burly man, open-neck shirt, slightly rough looking.

He walked up to Cecilia and they embraced. Not the affectionate embrace of friends. The passionate embrace of lovers. They then walked swiftly into the cinema.

I was unable to move for a few seconds. The after-image of that embrace was burning into my retina, like those colour tests, when you look at the spot, turn away, but it's still there.

I hurried across the road. They were at the cash desk, then moving towards Cinema Three. I bought a ticket and kept my distance, following them into the dark muffled interior. The cinema was not very full. I waited at the back for my eyes to adjust, then spotted them on the back row.

I sat to one side, far enough down for them not to spot me easily, near enough for me to keep my eye on them, a light turning of the head. I saw how they came close together. I saw them kiss.

There was a romantic comedy on screen. Two lovers were on a train. Something about a third person getting on somewhere, complicating it. Several times I turned, and tried to see what Cecilia and the man were doing. They kissed several times.

And then they were gone. The film was only one hour in, but their seats were empty. I scanned the rows. Had they moved? No sign of them. Had they spotted me? An elderly woman in the row behind looked at me with suspicion. I stood and made my way out of the cinema, into the bleached brightness of the city centre afternoon. A melée of shoppers, traffic, buses, cars, taxis, shop windows. I looked up Chapel Bar, then back, down towards the square. Gone. No sign. Cecilia. The man. Their kissing.

I found myself standing once more in Slab Square. The fountains which previously had produced rainbows now seemed to pour only tears, and the tramps on the wall lay slumped in defeat. I sat down on a wooden bench. I sat all afternoon, pigeons occasionally scuttling at my feet. I remember little about it, except the thoughts racing through my head, a confused blur, and sometimes the cry of the newspaper seller on Long Row.

I returned home at the usual time. Cecilia and the house were exactly as normal. Had I dreamed everything? The lawn was neatly trimmed. The paintings were on the wall. What did I expect? That the furniture would be leaping around in shock? That the picture window might shatter into fragments at the awfulness of it?

Cecilia was on the settee, black leggings, a blue smock, feet tucked in beneath her, leafing through a magazine.

'Cecilia,' I said, but she leapt up and kissed me even before I could lean down to her.

'I've been worried about you, Lee,' she said. 'The office rang, said you'd walked out, disappeared, did I know anything about it,' and she hugged me close to her, then said softly, 'I didn't know where you were.'

129

'It's nothing, Cecilia,' I said. 'You shouldn't have been worried.'

'But I was,' she said, and then her face was close to mine and she was staring into my eyes. 'Of course I was.'

I was trying to make sense of all this. Trying to make sense of my wife and this stranger, kissing, intimate. Again the kiss on the pavement came to mind, the kisses in the cinema. And then them disappearing. Where?

'I've done you a nice tea, Lee. Lemon chicken, one of your favourites.'

After we'd eaten, Cecilia pulled me down onto the carpet and made love to me with such an intensity that she cried out several times.

The next morning, I told Cecilia that it was time for our annual accounts, and I would have to work the next weekend or two. A plan was forming in my mind, a cold, methodical plan. I needed time off work. I needed to find out what was really going on. I went in to see Frank immediately I got to the office.

'Captain Oates, eh?' he said. 'Except you've come back. You going to make a habit of it, are you, just nicking off like that?'

'I'm sorry,' I said. 'A crisis, something came up.'

'Crises are for non-work hours,' said Frank, 'understand?'

'I'd like to ask for some days off,' I said.

'What?'

'Just a few days leave. It's important.'

'What, just like that?'

'Yes.'

I didn't really care that much what he thought. He picked up a pen, and started twiddling with it. Then he stood up and looked out the window. When he spoke he had his back to me.

'Tell you what I'll do, then. One week, off your holidays. As from now. Any more than that, and don't bother returning. OK?'

'Yes,' I replied.

'Right,' he said. 'Now, I'm a busy man.' He didn't turn back to look at me and I walked out the office, and out of the premises.

I quickly arranged to pick up a hire car. I then called at a theatrical costumiers, hired a dark brown wig and some thick spectacles. I bought a tasteless loud checked jacket and a tie to match, or not to match, as the case may be. By the time I had driven the car and parked it at the far end of our own quiet cul-de-sac, it was still only mid-morning. The garage door was shut, suggesting our own car was still in the garage and, I hoped, Cecilia still in the house.

I was spying on my own wife. I felt a little absurd, and ashamed.

I noticed that Cecilia was coming out the front door. She opened the garage doors, reversed out the Granada, and drove off. She didn't give me a second look. I started the engine and followed her.

She headed east, through Wilford, and on to a council estate in Beeston, an unsavoury looking place where several properties were boarded up. The gardens were often untended, a few had abandoned rusty bikes and other things in them. On some corners, gangs of surly-looking youths could be seen. A few had cans of lager.

Cecilia stopped the car in one street and got out. She knocked at a front door which bore no number, though 48 was chalked roughly on the wall alongside. A man opened it. He was wearing a grubby white vest. Immediately he took hold of my wife and kissed her. She did not resist. He then took her into the house and closed the door. A few seconds later I saw both of them upstairs in the bedroom. As the man began to pull shut the drab yellow curtains I caught a quick glimpse of Cecilia. She was pulling her jumper over her head.

This was not the same man I had seen at the Odeon.

It was about one hour later that she emerged from the house, an hour during which several rather pasty-looking young men had peered in the car. They were dressed in

131

baggy denims, scruffy trainers and zip-up tops, and many
had inverted peaked hats on. Cecilia got into her car and
drove off. Again I followed. She returned to our house, put
the car in the garage and went in through the front door.

I sat in the driver's seat at the end of the cul-de-sac,
still gripping the steering wheel. For some reason I turned
on the radio. A man was being interviewed about a giant
mural he had painted in Leeds.

Who was that woman who had just walked in through
the door of our house? Who was this man, her husband,
who was sat in this car wearing a funny wig? What was
happening? To anything?

That evening Cecilia cooked a lamb casserole, and she
asked me, 'How was your day?'

I managed to reply, as calmly as I could, 'Oh, you know.
Nothing much. How was yours?'

What had I expected in reply? Cecilia said, 'About the
same.'

'Shall we go out tonight?' she added, and I asked
'Where?'

'Ice skating,' she said, and I said, 'But I've never done
that.'

'Reason enough, then,' she said. 'I'll help you.'

I slipped and slithered all over the rink. Cecilia supported me, held me up, led me gently like a child, round
the ice. How controlled she was, how poised.

How beautiful on that cold, white, ice.

'You see,' she said, as she slowly tugged me round. 'You
can do it after all, can't you?'

'Yes, Cecilia,' I replied. 'I can do it.'

The next morning I left the house as if going to work as
normal. I walked the distance to where I had parked the
car the night before, some minutes away, got in and drove
back to the end of the cul-de-sac. I put on the wig, the spectacles, the jacket and tie.

Suddenly I felt very very tired, drained. Defeated. I felt
tears welling up in me. I pulled myself together, sniffed,

blew my nose, and sat for my vigil.

Cecilia emerged around 11am, and once again got into the car to drive off. She drove north this time, through the city centre, out towards Sherwood on Mansfield Road, but only as far as Carrington (my old habitat!) then up the hill towards Mapperley, those large converted houses.

This time she let herself in with her own key. I looked up to the first floor bay window, and soon she appeared next to another man I had never seen before. After a long kiss they both sank out of sight. It was another hour before I saw my wife again.

The next day was slightly different. Cecilia drove north-east, towards Eastwood. She pulled the car into a lay-by, and a few moments later a large lorry pulled in behind her. She got out of the car, locked it, walked up to the lorry whereupon the passenger door swung open. As she climbed in she needed to hitch up her skirt and a pang of pain ran though me as her thigh was exposed.

I caught a brief glimpse of the driver. He was tousley haired, unshaven, slightly rattish looking. There were tattoos on his forearms. One was an anchor, I think. The door slammed shut, the lorry drove off, and I followed.

I turned into a quiet country lane a little further on and parked. It was impossible for me to park close without arousing suspicion. I left my car on the main road, pulled half way up the verge, and spied on the vehicle from a discreet distance. I did this by climbing over a gate, skirting a field, and emerging the far side of the lorry. Through a hedge I could look directly at the cab.

There was no sign of them in the cab. I knew they had not emerged, and thought of the long bench seats in such enclosures. At that moment I started thinking the cab would begin rocking, like in those sex-romp films. It didn't happen. I suppose it was too solid. There was just the blank staring eye of the cab window, and me, standing crouched behind a hedge in a muddy field, watching.

I suppose again it was maybe an hour, maybe less before they both sat up. They were adjusting their clothing. I moved swiftly back the way I had come, field and gate, and as I was scampering back to the car, heard the deep-throated sound of the lorry starting up. Firstly it moved further down the narrow lane, found a place to turn, and then emerged up it, its engine growing louder.

For some reason I felt very nervous as the large lorry came towards me. I sat bolt upright in the car, and for one second Cecilia stared down at me. She was applying lipstick at the time, that deep red lipstick called "Dusk" I knew so well. Our eyes met for an instant, though I had sworn I would not look. There was not a flicker of recognition in her eyes. Her eyes were dead, like those of a fish. Never before had I seen her eyes dead.

My intention had been to follow the lorry immediately. But I couldn't. I couldn't even turn the ignition key.

The pattern was similar over the next few days. Each time the location was different. Each time the man was different. She drove to a dog kennels in Colwick and I was forced to sit in the car and listen to the yelping of dozens of dogs while my wife and this man were shut up in a small corrugated hut at the bottom of the compound.

The next time it was Long Eaton. From the look of the man's oily dungarees he was a car mechanic, possibly on his break, as he and Cecilia arrived at different times at an upstairs flat, each letting themselves in with their own key. I assumed the man was married, and the flat belonged to a friend. They both emerged separately. I imagine he went back to his garage, carefully tuning a Cortina or something. Cecilia of course returned to our marital home.

The next day I followed her to Trowell, a glum-looking block of flats. The staircase stank of urine. I followed her up some stairs, but felt uneasy skulking, and was also given some strange looks by the inhabitants who seemed none too friendly. I returned quickly to the car and somewhat uncomfortably, waited for her to emerge. It took forty minutes.

It seemed absurd to go back to my — our — home, and

carry on as normal. Yet that is what I did, simply because at that stage I had no idea what else I could do. And how absurd, how pitiful, how degrading that, during this time, my wife seemed to delight in making love to me, and that I was unable not to respond, despite the pain she was bringing me. During these sessions I cried, and sometimes Cecilia seemed to cry too, but, I suspect, for very different reasons.

The next trip was to Calverton, a cramped terraced house with the taste of coal dust in the air. I assumed the man was a miner, he had that look of ingrained dirt and dust as he stood at the back gate down the untidy back lane, and waited to usher in his paramour. A small child on a tiny pedal bike stared up at her as she walked in.

There was no more. I still waited in the car, three more days. Cecilia did emerge, I did follow her, but the trips were innocent, to the shops, a walk in the park, once into the town centre. Somehow I knew her list of lovers was now complete. She had eight. My wife.

The pattern had become clear to me. She would see them all in a concentrated burst. Probably this made things easier for her to manage. And then? Presumably a gap before the next concentrated sessions. How on earth did she organise it? How long had it been going on?

I had been more content than any man in history, more hopelessly in love. I was more than happy with one partner. My wife needed nine. And so I had also been more fooled than any man in history, duped, swindled, ridiculed, misinformed, wronged, betrayed. I had been degraded.

'You've not been to work.'

'What?' My thoughts were interrupted by Cecilia.

'They say you haven't been in. That Frank rang. What's going on, Lee?'

'Going on?' I realised I had been off for longer than the agreed time. I had probably lost my job.

'Is there something you're not telling me, Lee?'

These words rang and rang round my brain. She was making an utter and complete fool of me. I had trusted in love and love had betrayed me, spat at me, turned a knife in me. I had believed love would complete my life. It had ruined it.

'Lee –' said Cecilia, but suddenly I was unable to be in the room with her. I turned and walked out, then out the front door. Where did I go? I don't know.

I returned the hire car. I burned the wig, the jacket, the tie. I trod on the ridiculous spectacles. I could not stop loving my wife, but each time she deceived me, another small part of me shrivelled and died. The love was a cancerous thing. Murderous.

Murderous.

'Your desk is cleared.' It was Harry. I'd returned to the office. The others looked at me as if I had a contagious disease.

'Mrs Gwent will sort out the details. Your successor starts tomorrow.' That was all he said. I caught a whiff of the after-shave as he turned and walked away, and that was the end of my job.

I walked again down to Slab Square. I stood in the centre, and stared at the straggle of people in the bus queues. What lucky people they were. How fortunate were their lives. What did any of them know of real tragedy?

In that moment it became clear to me that Cecilia must die. As this thought entered my brain, so a coldness ran through me, an icy finger. It was the only possible conclusion. How else could all this be reconciled? Sit down together, and agree to forget it? Pretend it never existed? Live our lives, either together, or apart, trying to ignore the black shadow it had cast?

I could no longer live with Cecilia as man and wife. Yet I could not bear to think of her living somewhere else, walking free from what she had done to me.

Fate had thrown us together. Fate had allowed us some brief time of utter bliss. And now fate was deciding it must end. So – let it be. I had lived 28 grey years, and one short time of brilliant emotion and passion. I was now to pay for this. Cecilia was to pay for this. Naïvely, I had believed life

136

could change. All it could do was offer an illusion, empty, like a card trick. And then we were back where we started. Even the lottery money now seemed of little consequence. Life had been made unbearable. Poisoned.

I decided the curry would be Madras – strong, hot, spicy. It was to be a special occasion. I told Cecilia. Just as I told her I had left my job.

'That's much bolder than you used to be,' she replied. 'Will you get another one?'

'I don't know,' I replied. 'Does it bother you?'

'It might have done – one time,' she replied, but didn't elaborate. 'So what is this special occasion? Celebrating getting the sack?'

'It's a landmark,' I replied.

How deadly she was. How beautiful. I could no more deny my love for her than I could the total futility of it. I had even thought of challenging her.

'Cecilia, why do you have eight lovers, one each in Beeston, Carrington, Eastwood, Colwick, Trowell, Basford, Calverton, and one whose home I have not identified?'

Perhaps all love was like this at base. Pretence. An illusion.

I spread the table with a deep red cloth. I folded crisp white napkins on top. I had bought her favourite flowers, fuchsias, for the table, and I placed them at the centre. One wedding present had been two ornate silver candlesticks, and I also placed them on the table.

I asked Cecilia if she would wear the simple black dress I had first seen her in, and she did. I looked at her small, perfectly formed figure, and for one second imagined it writhing naked with other men.

Carefully I laid the cutlery on the table.

She wore a very deep red lipstick.

It made that wide mouth seem even wider, more seductive.

'Just think, Lee,' she said, 'a tin of baked beans and a can opener was about as far as you got once,' and she laughed. I sensed a nervousness in that laugh, a tension. Did she suspect something?

'You've had a big effect on me,' I replied.

What had been her motives? Pure lust? Deception? Power over men? What did women think of? How long had she intended this monstrous deceit to continue? Were her lovers changing or constant?

We sat down to the starter, onion bhaji. I watched her delicate white fingers pick up the knife and fork, gently pull apart the yielding flesh. I had made the bhajis myself, just as within the last months I had come to do much cooking myself.

'It's lovely, Lee,' she said, and again that small nervous laugh. Had my actions given something away? Did she suspect I knew her secrets? How I longed to take her in my arms.

I knew little of poisons or how they worked, their effectiveness, only that getting them from the chemist was quite a complicated affair. Getting some strychnine wasn't easy and it was expensive, but money was hardly a problem.

I assumed it wasn't very tasty stuff, hence the strong curry. I'd also mixed the spices myself.

We finished the bhajis. She dabbed lightly at her mouth with the napkin, a small bird-like movement.

'Do you think this is all a new chapter then, Lee?' she asked, and I replied, 'Yes, that's what it is.'

'Most people spend their lives in fear, don't you think?' she asked, and I noticed she was talking rather rapidly. 'They are afraid to die, but they are afraid to live as well, which means they are afraid all the time.'

'Yes, that's true,' I said.

'I've not been afraid, Lee,' she said, 'whatever else, I've not been afraid. I mean, it's painful sometimes that kind of thing, but then you can't live life without pain, can you? You have to take risks. I think so, anyway.'

I was wondering how she would manage her lovers if I was at home, and realised that was why she had discouraged me from leaving my job. How did she intend to manage in the future? If there had been a future.

'It's worse for women,' she said, 'they're expected to behave certain ways, do certain things.'

I walked into the kitchen and began to dish out the portions of curry. Firstly I served the pillau rice, and on one plate I mixed in the strychnine. I then noted which plate was which and carried in the dish of madras chicken curry, and raised the lid for the highly spiced steam to escape.

I then returned to the kitchen and brought in the two plates of rice, which I positioned carefully.

'It looks lovely,' said Cecilia, and gave a little smile.

'I'll serve,' I said, and I ladled the curry on top of the rice. Hers first. After the second ladle, Cecilia held up a hand.

'That's enough, Lee – you don't want a fat wife.'

I served myself. I took some mango chutney, and I snapped off a piece of the poppadom I had prepared. Even at this stage I was hoping for some other explanation, other resolution. Yet I knew I was hoping in vain. My wife had cold-bloodedly betrayed me, not with one man, but eight.

'Why is this meal making me nervous, I wonder?' she asked, and again that small quick laugh. She looked across the table at me.

I remember small things at that moment. A distant dog barking, the chirriping of a starling in the garden, a revved motorbike on some nearby road. Part of me was a lifeless thing by now, a rag doll, a stringless puppet. The other part propelled me forward relentlessly to the conclusion.

Cecilia made small prodding movements with her fork, as if deciding which morsel of meat to eat first. As she raised the first piece to her mouth, a small dying voice inside me yelled "No! Stop!", but the voice was too weak, too close to expiring.

'You're staring at me, Lee.'

'I thought you liked me looking at you.'

'Yes. But staring – like that, it's –'

'It's what?'

'It's not like you normally look.'

'Well. I'm sorry, then.'

She half shrugged her shoulders, as if to suggest we drop it, and then the meat went into her mouth. I dug myself out a generous portion of curry and rice and also began to eat, and for a very short time we ate in silence. I knew the process, once begun, would be fairly swift. On the surface, I remained calm. I noticed I was fiddling with a cheese knife. There seemed something ironic about this, as the cheese would not be part of the meal.

At that moment her breathing became laboured. She slumped slightly in her chair, a hand went up to her throat.

'Lee, I –' A gasp came from her, and her large eyes darted this way and that, like a trapped deer. The breathing was more laboured now, and the expression on that beautiful face one of panic, alarm.

'Lee!' The voice, not her voice, but a half-strangled voice, was one of pleading, a cry for help. And then there spread across her face, as I sat passively watching her, a realisation, a falling into place.

Suddenly Cecilia knew, just as I wanted her to know before she died. I wanted her to see what she had done to my life, how she had destroyed me, just as I was destroying her. Retribution.

A rasping sound came from her throat as the breathing became more difficult. Both hands now went to her neck, and she slumped forward knocking over a glass of water which spread a dark red stain over the table-cloth. The stab of pain in my hand made me look down to where I had pressed the cheese knife deep enough into my palm to draw blood.

'My – my – bag – Lee...' My name was the last word she was to utter. Her hands fell away, her head jerked forward, and she writhed horribly until death.

The evening was now silent. The spilt glass apart, the table was laid as normal, the plate of poppadoms, the dish of curry with its curling steam, the pickles, the cruet. I sat still for several moments before I moved across, touched her gently on the arm, leaving there, inadvertently, a smear of my own blood from the cheese knife cut.

The flesh was still warm, a warmth that would quickly go. There was no pulse, no heartbeat. I gently raised her head. Those large dark eyes were open. But lifeless. They stared at me as they had stared from that cab window. I pulled down the eyelids, closed her off. I was released. I was freed. What happened to me now was of no importance.

A starling chirriped and I noticed it hop across the lawn. What was it she had wanted in her bag? Medicine? Help of some kind? Nothing could help her.

The bag was by the side of her chair. I took it, opened it, and slowly emptied its contents onto the table. The usual woman's stuff was there, lipstick, make-up, a small purse, loose change, a tampon holder. And a letter.

I picked up the letter. It was sealed. My name was on the envelope, and I could detect a slight hint of the perfume which identified her for me so closely, the perfume she had worn that first night we met, and many nights since. It was a wild passionate perfume. Its scent triggered me into a wild passionate response and smelling it on that envelope momentarily threw me.

I opened the envelope. The letter was hand-written on a textured vellum paper. This also threw me, seeing Cecilia's handwriting, seeing those words, "Dear Lee". I read the letter.

Dear Lee,

I should just be able to say all this, but I can't. So it's a letter. I'll give it to you after our special meal. I wonder how you'll react? It's pretty big stuff.

I'm not the woman you think, Lee. I'll explain. I know this guy works for a big building society branch in Nottingham.

He gets access to confidential account details, feeds me

141

info about people coming into loads of loot. Let's say I did him a few favours back. I've been able to make use of this info, and when he told me about you, and the lottery windfall, I came looking for you.

You were dead easy. Easiest of the lot. Candy off a baby. I didn't fancy you one bit. You were a drip. But a rich drip. This one, I thought, go for it.

See, I'm like lots of young women in Nottingham, but there again I'm not. Married to some dull oaf for forty years? No thanks. A life behind a Boots counter? No ta. I'd use my wits. I'd get on. I'd be someone different.

The plan was get access to your money, but live my own life too. I needed other men. Not soft gullible men like you, Lee, real men, men who could satisfy me. Same as you couldn't.

I started taking lovers. I was smart. I made the running. They didn't know where I lived. I always phoned them. I pulled the strings, arranged the meetings. What did they care? They got good sex, and usually keeping quiet suited them too.

I didn't mind a few years of you, Lee. Later, when I'd made good financial arrangements, I'd ditch you. And I'd still be a young woman. Meantime I wanted some fun.

You thought I was a loving wife. You thought I was broadening your horizons. It was all for me, Lee, everything. The trips abroad, everything. And I had eight secret lovers.

It all went great. You were as blind as a bat. You were stupid. Even when someone left a note on your desk (who was that?), you couldn't see it, could you?

But that note was important. Things started changing after that. I kept thinking about it, worrying about it. Why? It wasn't as if you suspected anything. You just loved me. Then I realised. Guilt. It was creeping in. I'd never let it mess me up, just like I'd never let love mess me up. Keep it all at arm's length.

But things were changing. Was it me, or you? Or a bit of both? You became bolder, more questioning, less of a mouse.

You didn't take things for granted so much. You didn't let life push you around so much. And you put it all down to me. It was all a big act, but you said it changed your life.

You really do love me, Lee, don't you? I mean, really, properly. It hit me, just like that, what it meant, first time. I'd changed your life. You were different. And I was falling in love with the difference.

This was crazy. I didn't want it. Love would just complicate it. I wanted you at that dull office all day, me here, doing what I wanted. Except now it wasn't that simple. I'd changed you. And it was working the other way.

I resisted. It wouldn't go away. What could I do? Falling in love with this person I'd duped.

Except he wasn't that person anymore.

I did something amazing. I decided to see all my eight lovers, on successive days. We would make love for the very last time. I would tell them I was now trying to love properly my husband.

They were pathetic, Lee. They couldn't see further than their own lust. They were shallow, like I'd been shallow. They mocked me, didn't understand. They insulted you. They just wanted to take, and I realised that's what I'd been doing. Just taking. Those eight meetings were terrible, Lee, but I stuck at it. I wrote each one out of my life. Now they're gone. They were not real men.

How could I even start to tell you this? I might lose you. I wouldn't blame you. But I want to love you properly. I want to try.

You might have noticed our lovemaking has been passionate lately. Just as you might have noticed I've been disturbed. Knowing how, and when to tell you. Then I took a decision. Something to symbolise this change, something positive.

You're probably feeling numb and sick inside to read this, Lee. Fair enough. I've betrayed you. You probably can't forgive me. But please try. Please make the effort to begin again. I want you to take two things into account. That for the first time in my life I think I know what it is

truly to love someone. And secondly that I am expecting
your baby. Our baby.

> *All my love,*
> *Cecilia*

I read Cecilia's letter once. Then I read it a second time.
The sky outside was darkening, like a recent bruise. The
starling had gone quiet. Opposite me, across the blood red
table-cloth, our wedding candlesticks, the spread of food,
sat my wife, propped up lifeless in her chair. Her eyes were
closed, as often they would be closed in sleep. I would stare
for long periods at her head on the pillow. Now not the
slightest movement came from her. All I could hear was
the fractured sound of my own breathing.

Organizer baggage
Robert Cordell

'Take me with you!' Jack said to his brother as the few oddments of luggage were thrown in the boot of the Peugeot.

'You bastard!' Marjorie thought, though she wasn't quite sure which of the two she meant, which of them was the more insufferable. There was her husband Jack, so full of *bonhomie* but so devoid of spunk. And there was his brother, Guy, obsessional in his tidiness and in his demand for order. He was obsessional in other things too — and, remembering his regular importunings, she found her hand gripping the strap of the shoulder bag as if it were a lifeline. Her fingers slid down the strap onto the curve of sturdy brown leather and the shining buckles. It was an organizer handbag. They were all the rage at the moment, with their myriad nested pockets and zippered compartments. Jack had laughed when he'd thrust this extra present at her on the morning of her birthday. 'There you are, sweetie,' he'd said, whacking her flank cheerfully, 'You can keep up with Guy now. Organization mania, the pair of you!' Then he'd laughed again and slapped her bottom once more as if she were some kind of flat-racing filly.

Abruptly, Marjorie tossed her head in the wind and put away such unsettling thoughts. She looked at her husband peering in through the driver's window at Guy Mallon, who was hunched and pale at the wheel. Even when he wasn't in one of his crises, Guy always looked ill. At 45, the 'seigneur' of Radlett Fovale was thin, short and lack-lustre. His face was like an aged eleven year old's and even his silly moustache looked like something a burnt cork had drawn on a kid. As the car moved off, she and Jack waved, but there was no response.

The wind was from the north, cold even for November,

145

and it pitched at her in a squall straight off the lake and pulled at her hair as if it were yellow bunting. The Peugeot, now so far down the hill that she couldn't hear its engine, was a tiny moving icon. Late sun caught its polished roof in a momentary flash then it was out of the gates and gone.

'You are a bastard. You know that, don't you?' she said to her husband. 'You no more wanted to go with him than he wanted you to.'

'Perhaps he'll actually do it this time,' Jack said. He hadn't responded to her jibe. Not that she'd really meant it as one, for both of them detested Guy. And as if to prove it, she was smiling and putting a hand on his forearm: 'Come inside, darling. By the fire... It'll be like old times.' And as he smiled back, she wondered how much they were both acting.

Guy could picture them close together over the fire. That's what they'd be doing, his predictable brother and his wife — giggling, sighing, acting like lovebirds after eight years of marriage. The windows of the car were black and cold, and the only spark of surrogate life to keep him company was the moving curve of cats-eyes that wound backwards beneath his wheels. He pressed the button of the CD player and let the repetitive beauty of Pachelbel's canon soothe him. After a long while, after all of Bach's violin partitas and then the quartets of Schumann, he found himself passing by the bright motorway lights south of Gloucester. The gauge, reset with his customary precision, showed the miles since he'd left Radlett Fovale. It was ten past seven. He should, he thought, reach Mendip by nine.

He was used to himself and his weirdnesses. The shape of his moods was as familiar to him as the shape of his hands that he gazed at so often. Or the shape of his body. He was always organized even when he was swept helplessly by his angers and by his feelings of revulsion for others. Setting the gauge was an example — of his organization, not his revulsion! He smiled to himself as he

146

clarified his unspoken words; even in his language he liked to be tidy. And phoning the hotel this morning and booking a room, that had been good organization.

'Certainly, Sir. It'll be a pleasure to welcome you again... Thank *you*, Sir Guy.'

He looked forward to it. It was a bijou hotel overlooking the lake. They served him properly. People did — for he took damn good care that he never over-stepped the mark with people outside the confines of his narrow family. What he said and did at home, the threats... well, outsiders simply would not believe it! Did he mean it? Would he ever kill himself as he so often threatened? He sighed in the darkness, and put the womb-like coils of Pachelbel on to play again.

He was very into womb-like images. That was why the dark rocky tubes of underground Mendip had enthralled him ever since his youth. *Youth!* Was he so very old at forty-five? Five years older than Jack and ten years older than Jack's wife. But not so old that he'd lost or forgotten the calls of his youth. His baronetcy, his acres in Rutland, his money... all were some compensation for his inadequacies. So was seeing Jack struggle as his Land Agent — and seeing 'La Belle Marjorie' balance herself between her husband and her role of honorary *châtelaine*. A pity she concealed her distaste for her brother-in-law so poorly. He, whose hand provided.

Tomorrow, he would go to Priddy and park his car. He'd check out of the hotel first, and say that he was going to London. The car park at the bottom of Blackdown was a public one, gravelly, unattended, only modestly used by winter walkers and winter cavers. He'd chosen the Peugeot rather than the Lancia because it was used and very ordinary. He swung into the paved yard of the hotel. Here we go...

'Welcome again, Sir. It's good to see you.' The woman at Reception looked around for his baggage, her eyebrows lifting in greeting. She'd been here last time; cachou-perfumed, delectable.

147

'Just the valise,' he said. 'But I'd like something to eat, please. Chicken sandwiches and a bottle of Meursault — a '78 if you have it. In my room. Can you bring it up yourself?'

Much later, in bed, he lay alone and cosy. The world of other people was safe outside the doors. He wormed down into a nest in the cocooning duvet, and the light of the lamp entered through the quilted hole and lit the well-thumbed pages. Poor Kafka, he too had had his trials. *The Trial*! Oh how droll! An accidental pun! But it was another of Kafka's stories that obsessed him. A retreat, a redoubt, a hole in the ground in which to hide. Like here in his bed, now that the woman was gone from it. In a cave, he'd often enough said, was the best way to end it. And end it, he definitely would; he'd told them that, time and again. They *must* surely understand? This time perhaps? Oh, please let it be this time.

The fire had burned through red castles and, replenished with black coals, had flared and re-flared again. The velvet curtains cloaked the stone windows and the November storm was shut out. Sod Guy, she reflected; just sod him. Marjorie looked sideways at her husband, lolling now in sleepiness. It was harder for her than him! Damn it, she had had to work for it!

She had first set eyes on Radlett Fovale when she was eighteen. At the time, there'd just been a serialization of *Rebecca* on the radio; and when this beautiful house, with its whispering poplars and green rich lawns crowded into her young existence, she found herself almost living an extension of that story. The 'Manderley' of the story and the Radlett Fovale of reality merged almost into one. But the duties of companion and secretary to Lady Mallon — Girl Friday was what the older Mallon brother, Guy, called her — brought reality and kept her busy. Emily Mallon was author, travel writer, one time explorer. Now, crippled with arthritis, she was tetchy and misshapen and in all but one respect mean-minded.

'My word!' Guy had mocked, 'It really is *Beauty and the Beast*, you with my Ma! Perhaps she got you down to service the Old Man!'

He was impervious to her anger at this and his other insults. For her, it felt like being harried by a grubby schoolboy. He was ten years out of his sixth form, yet had the face of a petulant youth and the mind and hands of a lecher. To escape Guy, she would have quit a dozen times in every month. But several things stopped her — three, in particular. One was books. The good side of Emily Mallon was her love of books and her encyclopaedic knowledge of all things literary. This she wished to share with Marjorie; and Marjorie, most heartfeltly, wished it shared with her. Another reason, which she tried unsuccessfully to hide from Emily, was Guy's younger brother Jack. And the last and greatest of all was Radlett Fovale itself.

And now, today, they were all dead, that former generation. All the proper servants were either in their graves or had left, and nowadays the estate was maintained by day-helpers and hired hands. Jack remained and Guy remained — and Radlett Fovale endured. Its very name, Emily had once told her, bespoke its ancient origins. Since Neolithic times, people hereabouts had grubbed in the ground to find the neat flat stones that made such perfect roofing. Often these were mined in small open pits and the derelict remains of these, ivy-covered and liverwort-carpeted, were still scattered round the estate; the caches of limestone tiling prised from them had been carried off long ago to make a roof for this or that fine building. Presumably the Romans and the Romanized Saxons had grubbed here too. *Fovea*, whence Fovale, was the Latin for pit. 'And God knows who Radlett was,' Emily had said; 'a local chief with cousins near St Albans?' And she'd cackled at her ludicrousness.

But now Emily was dead, the old Baronet was dead — and Guy Mallon was half mad and putting it all at risk. The coals slid in the fireplace and a red cave opened up, blue flames flicking inside it. It reminded them both.

'How many times has he threatened to crawl into that hole and die?' she said. 'I don't believe he ever will. He does it to taunt.'

Her husband said nothing.

'If he hadn't taken you there that once and showed you, I would not believe it existed.' She spoke again. But still he said nothing.

'Jack!' She cudgelled his chest with her fists: 'He says he wants a new Land Agent. He wants to be rid of us both.'

The hotel, the Meursault, and the woman's loins were objects now of the past; last night was so long ago. The day was crisp and wholesomely autumnal. Guy scrambled down onto the metalled road, glad to escape the wet dead bracken of the hillside. The Peugeot, over the hill and behind him, was three miles away as the crow flies and many more by road. He walked a hundred yards or so along the road, then veered right on to a track of rough stones alongside a brook. Head forward, small haversack on his back, he picked his way along the mud and rocks until the Combe and its road were out of sight. The small hills of this lesser combe — West Twin Brook valley was its name — rose on either side. Here in summer, the time that he'd shown Jack where he went, the narrow valley was flanked with slopes of rampant ferns and filled to the stream with rose-bay willow herb and the hum of bees. Now, in November, the low hills were bare and the brook was fuller and noisier.

At the concrete culvert that belonged to the water company, he turned left up the steep slope until he came to the smallish hole. This was, as the cavers called it, the 'tradesman's entrance'. Further up there was a bigger and easier entrance to the same system, but this smaller awkward hole was the one he wanted. Careless of the red mud, he lay on his belly and slithered in. The hand torch provided all the light he needed; he had been here so often. Inside, there was the standard and uniform cool of caves. No draughts, and as caves go it was gravelly and comparatively dry. The passage sloped gently down with even tinier tubes going off to left and right. If he went on, he'd either penetrate to the extensive lower series or loop round and up to the bigger entrance fifty yards and ten million tons of rock away.

But he did neither. Just where the passage widened slightly and where the floor was littered with boulders, he stopped at a small and inconspicuous tunnel. It was little more than a foot high and entered the passage at floor level. He'd first explored it twenty years ago and this was his chosen rocky womb, rocky tomb, crack of doom... He crawled in, moving flat out, arms ahead to stop them being trapped at his sides, until he was at the bulbous end of the rocky tube. Here he could move his arms, even eat from his pack of sandwiches. The floor was dry. One puddle fed by a solitary dripping stalactite was at the side. Drinks, if muddy, were on tap. Here he was and here he would lie alone — in an off-route tunnel where no-one ever came, and almost immured in limestone. He switched off the torch and wondered whether he would need to switch it on again.

He enjoyed the languid, timeless darkness of it and dozed and slept, no idea of time. Then Jack's voice, only slightly muffled by the turns of tunnel that led to his nest, called out: 'Guy! Are you in there?' Silence. Then again: 'Guy! It's me, Jack.'

'What do you want?'

Silence again. Then noises of rock and mud sucking, and rock on rock. But no more voice. With a great jerk in his gut, Guy knew beyond any doubt that his brother had dragged a boulder from the floor against the opening of his tunnel and wedged it completely shut.

'Did you smell anything?' Marjorie worked the oars while Jack checked the big canvas bag for the third time. It was more like April than February, except for the carpets of snowdrops along the path from House to lake. The sun was bright and the air temperature unseasonably high.

Yesterday, Jack had revisited the cave for the first time since Guy had driven off. Three months, they had left it. Three months!

'I wouldn't have expected a smell,' he replied, short of breath as he hefted the oars. 'He showed me the place in summer. The burrow, as he called it, is metres in; full of squeezes and twists and turns. In those conditions, he's probably mummified. You know, like in that magazine article, *prehistoric man fossilised in bog*!'

Jack Mallon scooped up the bag from the boat bottom and pushed the khaki straps through the metal buckles. The flap of the bag covered over the stones inside — the stones themselves packed in with the pieces of paper. He looked irritably at his wife. 'I can't think why you insist on sinking this lot. His diary, a few letters, a few books on caving. It's hardly incriminating, and no-one's interested anyway. Burning would have done just as well.'

'I'm just careful, Jack. Someone's got to be.' Her voice tailed off as she looked around.

'Oh come on,' he said, 'we *have* been careful. We waited till the end of November till we raised the alarm.'

'Careful?' she said. 'You were all for moving his car! That would have been madness. As it was, Cave Rescue made enough fuss. But there are hundreds of caves round there. And where he'd left the car was miles by road from where he is — and far enough by foot.'

'He's got to be found sometime, I suppose?'

The way he said it, it was more question than statement. At least, she took it so. 'The seven year wait will do me,' she said. 'Presumption of death? That's all right. I'll settle for that. But if he is found, the key thing is that you have now moved the boulder back to where it was. Since yesterday, that is. Well done, Jack darling! This'll do. It's about the middle. Drop the bag in, then. See how far down you can see it go.'

He shrugged, his response sulky. 'I still reckon that having me sneak back from a rented *gite* in Normandy to unlock his burrow — God, this bag is heavy — was unnecessary.' He knelt over the bow, the bulging bag balanced on the boat's edge.

She brought down the blade of the oar onto his head as hard as she was able and he fell back into the boat with the bag. It took her more time than she expected to lift the oar again and position it correctly in space for the second blow. But this time the blade had turned and its edge cut into him, and now there was blood. Unbelievably he still moved and, desperate lest this Frankenstein's monster should prove immortal, she scrabbled open the bag and found a stone to use on him. And at last, her frantic movements slowing, her bosom heaving and her skin bloodied, the job was done.

'It was *not* unnecessary.' She spoke her last words to his corpse. 'You are abroad right now — to the world, that is. Just as we are in the middle of the lake, for real.' She tied the heavy bag tightly to his ankle and to his waist, using nylon cord from her own shoulder bag. 'You were right, my adulterous darling, that there was no need that *you* could see to sink stuff in the lake. Not when the stuff to be sunk was you!'

She was quite an organizer, she thought as she tripped, almost skipped, up the grassy path towards the House. She could almost step outside herself and see how she looked: golden hair, Tyrolean blouse low on her breasts, full skirt joyfully swirling. Completely unsuitable for February, even when February masqueraded as May. She had guessed at the blood and had left a complete change, even of her underclothes, in the boat house. She'd stripped herself bare in the boat and crammed the stained garments into the bag of stones. Then, after she'd attended to Jack, sending bag, bloody clothes and brain spattered stone down with him, she had washed the boat as completely as she could, taking a long time over it. It looked perfectly clean, but she'd do more later. Then, quite naked, she'd rowed back, dried herself in the sun and dressed in the blouse and skirt. Good job it was Sunday and there were no staff... No, it was good *planning* that it was Sunday. That was what she had intended. She was an organizer — and how Guy used to boast about his bloody organizing!

'It had to be done...' she said aloud. The House had to be secured for ever. Dear Jack had, for far too long, been amusing himself with this woman here, that girl there and another woman somewhere else. How long before he might decide to replace a thirty-five year old wife with a twenty-five year old substitute? She would lose Radlett Fovale after all. And that was simply not permissible. The loss of Jack was no loss. Without a man in this place, everything here was hers. And, moreover, her body was hers as well — they were two for a pair those Mallon brothers, and a hearty good riddance to them both.

It would, on second thoughts, be better for Guy's body to be found. Sooner rather than later, she mused. Then Jack would inherit the title even though he, by then, would be posted missing. *Marjorie, Lady Mallon* sounded very good indeed.

'It had to be done...' she said aloud, again.

'You are so right; it had to be done.' The voice spoke into her ear. 'Don't turn round.'

She couldn't turn anyway, the arms were gripping her from behind.

'You see, little Marge, my nest had two doors and Jack only blocked one.'

She kicked at him and pulled at the encircling arm. The sallow hand and square cut nails she recognized all too well. He'd grabbed at her in the past, and she remembered his surprising strength.

'Don't struggle Marjorie. I used a whole thirty-six exposures on the lake scene just now. Remember my nice zoom lenses? Very touching. What porridge-like stuff brain is! And the exposure at the end was — just delightful. Titian would positively have adored you.'

She felt horror and sick anger boiling upwards together. But his words went on. Letters were already written and lodged at the bank. Even today's roll of film was already in the postbox in the perimeter wall. The thick stone wall was far too much of a redoubt for a feeble woman. Not to worry. No need to worry, my sweet. No worry at all, just so long as you...

Then his explanations. Four times in recent years he had waited in his nest, like a fly for the trout. Sooner or later the husband and wife would take the bait and bite.

'I did think,' he giggled from behind and she went cold at where he had wormed his hand, and what he was beginning to do with his fingers, 'that egging the bread with threats of a new Land Agent might finally do it. That you'd finally screw up Jack's nerve to sticking point.'

'But you couldn't possibly know what I intended to do about Jack.'

'Oh but I could know. I did know. You've both been very predictable — and I am an incredible organizer. And you,' he murmured, moving his hand again, analyzing but appreciating the territory, 'are a dishy bit of baggage. And quite well organized yourself! I will admit that, my sweetie.'

Maureen

Julie Myerson

Ian was near enough to seventeen when his big brother brought her home after an evening at The Trip. 'She's a teacher,' he went as they passed in the hallway, 'So mind your big mouth, arseface.'

Peter told him to fetch lagers, so Ian rummaged at the back of the fridge, found some cans. Blood from the chops on the shelf above had dribbled down on them. He wiped them off on a tea towel which whiffed of unwashed dampness. Then he combed his hair with his fingers and now his hair had the same smell.

In Sherwood, the night was hot, airless. Down the road you could hear the pub emptying, people shouting, disagreeing, throwing up. They sat out in the yard — him and Pete and Maureen — and shared the takeaway they'd brought. The yard stank of other people's detergent crashing through the pipes and the shit of next door's terrier. Ian felt conscious that he hadn't showered and he still had on his paint-spattered boots and the rough bitten skin on his hands was still caked with emulsion. Crown Expression, No. 5567, Lucid beige.

He'd been watching the box and hadn't expected company. Being dirty meant he'd nothing to say.
He watched Maureen prise open the little foil containers with her short, dark blue fingernails. Her long black hair snaked down her back like an Indian squaw. 'Where'll I put these?' — the cardboard lid had grease rolling off. Peter got the carrier bag, held it out. Ian watched the procedure and you'd think he'd never seen a lid chucked in a bag. She was so attractive, his brain went soft.

For the rest of his life he remembered what she had on that first night: short, black skirt made of glittery stuff, and a little purple disco top. No straps. Skinny shoulders, the sexy arch of her breastbone, not a lot in the way of tits,

157

but pointing the right way. Round her neck a gold cross, maybe gold plate. And then, when she lifted the fork to her mouth, he saw a crawly insect tattoed on her wrist.

He watched her and his insides went erotic.

'She's never a teacher,' he told his brother when she excused herself to go to the toilet 'That tattoo? Those nails?'

'Fuck off,' said Pete, 'What do you know? I reckon I'm in there, so you can go fuck yourself.' He stabbed at his food, he was pretty pissed.

Maureen told Pete she was a teacher, but it turned out Ian was right, she wasn't — she worked at Argos.

How he knew was easy. He went in there one afternoon and she served him — he was standing in the line marked C with his receipt for a power drill (special Argos price of £69.75) and there she was, blue suit and striped shirt and all. Her hair was up and he might not've recognised her from the back, but from the front? That way of standing like she knew who she was, those apologies for tits.

It wasn't that he fancied her. But looking gave him goosepimples in his groin.

'Bloody hell, Ian,' she hissed — cos she was stuck into going out with Pete by now, 'Don't tell Pete you saw me, OK?'

She got him his drill, stuck it in a plastic carrier, looking sulky and worried all the while. Ian watched her and felt his bones loosen with anticipation. So she'd lied. He thought he'd get her for it.

'So what school is it exactly,' he asked her, 'Where a teacher has a tattoo on her wrist?'

She jumped as if he'd hit her. 'School of life,' she said — and they both laughed.

Ian was the last son — a mistake, as well as a disappointment for not being a girl.

They hadn't set eyes on Greg for two year — he was out in Oman, shagging everything in sight, which wasn't much,

158

from his letters; Pete had a desk job with the paint firm in Arnold and he'd pulled strings to get Ian the decorating. It paid the rent on the flat in Winchester Street him and Pete shared, but he knew the reality was Pete wanted out, was champing at the bit to have a woman permanently in his bed and head. Pete was after a lifestyle like in the adverts: new things, nice cars, a bunch of slobbering kids.

And what did Ian want? Not a life up the top of a ladder with a pot of emulsion, they could all go stuff themselves. He was thinking of doing a night course, studying electrics. If he could get his diploma, he could swing a job in theatre or TV. Fancy lighting, canteens full of people — he had his eye on the big time, the Media.

He said nothing to Peter. You shifted your expectations all the time, didn't you?

Up until then, he'd have said his ideal female was blonde, leggy, big up top. Maureen was none of these. Did Pete know she worked at Argos? Did they never talk at all, Maureen and Pete, just fuck? And when they talked, did he believe her?

These were the questions Pete wanted to ask, but didn't. Where would it get him, anyway? They go on about how love is blind, but no-one ever said about it being stupid.

Actually it made him feel good that she'd lied to Pete, made him feel Pete was excluded from something and he was in there, snug and knowing. Pete was a stupid fucker if he believed her thin stories. Just showed you could bonk with someone and not know anything.

'How's the teaching going, Maureen?' Ian asked her when Pete was there.

'Oh, I gave it up,' she said without a shake or a shiver, 'Got another job now.' She looked away, then flicked her eyes back at Ian, then away again.

And Pete bragged that they got a ten per cent discount on goods at Argos, which was handy because of all the electrical appliances.

At a party in Beeston, at a house which he'd decorated as

159

fluke would have it, Maureen got him in a corner. 'Come here, Pete's little brother,' she said.

Ian looked around, to see if Pete was in the room. He wasn't. The stairs curled round into the room, the sort you could see through, like a ladder. The door was open, some people were out on the fire escape. Maybe Pete was out there. The air was black and throbby with the Commodores. Maureen's shaven armpits were shadowy, blackish blue. 'Come here,' she said.

When she kissed him, the room lurched only he wasn't drunk, not yet. His erection almost hit his belly button. He panted between kisses, to catch his breath. She parted her legs, pressed him back against the wall. The wall he'd painted back in June. Crown Expressions No. 0042. Babybird.

Maureen and Pete married in the October. Maureen had no roots, no strings, all family dead and left, which was convenient or else another lie. The wedding was quick and small at the registry office, drinks in the pub afterwards. Pete's face was glossy with happiness, like the paint which fills your chest with purplish fumes.

Maureen's body was thin and tight and miraculous in her strapless red frock, her hair was cut short, trimmed and lacquered into wings.

Ian kissed her on the cheek, like rubbing up against a piece of cold fruit. 'Preferred the hair how it was before,' he went. 'Liked it long.'

She frowned. Since the snog at the party, it'd all gone wrong between them. Every time he tried to speak to her, all he did was slag her off.

She just looked at him without looking. The booze'd already tilted her features, blurred her eyes. She wasn't that attractive if you thought about it. That was a relief. She looked at him and shrugged, as if she'd snuck inside his mind and had a look and decided no thanks.

*

160

They'd been married about six months when Pete let slip one night in the pub that they were having no luck in the baby department. 'Not for want of trying,' he went, and told Ian how she was randy as anything and they were at it all the time.

Ian didn't want to know. The mere thought of Pete and Maureen at it ached his gut.

He had his own new girlfriend by then — Libby. Lib was a beautician, worked on Parliament Street — big-boned and solid and blonde and willing. She did Aromatherapy massage. They were thinking about a week in Ibiza, at Easter. You could get a great deal if you flew last minute. Lib had started a course of sunbeds.

The following week, he shoved the brochure under his brother's nose, but Pete barely bothered to look. 'We've had some tests done at Queen's,' he whispered. 'To rule certain things out.'

Through the kitchen hatch, they watched Maureen shake frozen chips onto a tray. She seemed fine, unworried. She was the best. She did not look up.

They were just off to the airport when the phone went and it was Pete, voice all racked with pain. 'She can't have kids,' he told Ian. 'Something in her tubes. Sorry, mate, I didn't want to spoil your holiday — just that there's no-one else to tell.'

In the Duty Free, Ian dodged among the mirrors and glass while Libby sprayed things on her wrists. Glancing up, he saw Maureen. His scalp went hot and cold and then he rushed at her and shouted her name, but as he said it — 'Maureen!' — she was already gone, sucked into the money-spending crowds.

He told Libby. Libby laughed and said he should lay off the booze. On the plane, he settled his hand on her thigh and thought of Maureen. 'They could always adopt,' said Libby, sipping her Vodka and Britvic Tomato.

Lib flicked her hair over her shoulder. Her tubes were

intact as far as she knew and she never had much time for Maureen anyway.

That night, in the thin double bed in their sultry white rectangle of a room, he dreamed his first Maureen dream.

In the dream, he was straddled on top of her and he thought they were fucking at last, only every time he moved inside her, he lost breath till it was all sucked out of him and he woke sweating, gasping.

Then he really woke — sweating like a pig and gasping.

'What's the matter with you?' moaned Libby as he held the heavy heat of her tit inside her bikini, rolled her startled brownish nipple between his fingers, 'You've gone sex mad all of a sudden.'

In the heat and the harsh light he couldn't tear Maureen from his head. He and Libby lay around, swam, clubbed, fucked, but he went every night to Maureen — woke in the greenish, pre-dawn light with a hard-on and an inside-out sourness in his belly.

Libby slept with her mouth wide open, fillings on view, a line of perspiration around her newly sun-reddened breasts.

One night Maureen was there before him on the nylon carpet and between her parted legs there was this insect — brownish, violet-veined, smudged with dust and trembling. A thickish, dark body, tired-looking.

'Your tattoo's come off,' he said.

'Our kiddy,' she said, 'I was cut up to get it out,' — and taking his hand she pressed it against the long, horizontal slit in her belly, just above the lines of her pubes.

Her wrist where the tattoo had been was naked.

On the plane home he couldn't look at Libby, he just couldn't do it, 'I've a lot on when we get back,' he said, hoping she'd get the picture.

She shrugged, blinked, plucked her eyebrows frowning into a little hinged mirror. She drank a Vodka tonic. Sneezed. Cried-into tissue was balled up in her sun-tanned

162

fingers. He lost her in the terminal and took a cab straight to Pete and Maureen's.

The street lights were a fuzz of orange, the air smelled of wax, of blossom. She opened the door. He went shy — he'd never have thought a bunch of dreams could alter so much. 'Hey,' was all she said and the first thing he saw as he went in the living room was Pete's stretched-out legs and the static shudder of the telly.

In the kitchen, she flung Maxwell House into mugs, ran the tap to fill the kettle. He wondered why he was there. Demerara sugar lay in crumbs on the white melamine counter. She wiped it down, flung the J-cloth in the sink. 'Well?' she said.

'Well what?' he said.

And every night the dreams got more, not less: X-rated, pornier and hornier. Easier than sex, better than wanking and telly, more reliable than sport or women. Sometimes he'd just snog and lick and cram, move onto each surface of her shape and find a hole and fill it.

Sometimes it was more than he could bear. Sometimes he wanted to go round there and tell her. Sometimes he was buried so deep in her, his mouth so deep in the cave of hers, that he thought he'd never get out. 'Man lost in Woman's cunt.' Like the dead potholers you hear about and don't feel sorry for, because why do such a fucking stupid thing in the first place?

Ian didn't feel sorry for himself.

'We've thought about adopting,' said Pete as they trailed round IKEA together in search of a sofa-bed, 'But I'm not sure I could — you know, bring up another bloke's kid as my own.'

Maureen was ahead of them, pulling dhurries from a pile, comparing the patterns. She didn't hear. At the queue for the till, she smiled at Ian, eyes blackly, viciously crazy. Did she know what he knew?

It wasn't possible. He was safe — in his own head he believed he was safe.

163

That night, Maureen blew his cock till it was three times its normal length and then demanded that he put it into her.

'Jesus Christ, are you sure?'

A warm wind was blowing off the sea and Maureen pulled down her little black and red nylon pants and said, 'Look at my scar,' — a cross-hatch of livid stitches — 'Look, you did that to me,' and this time she grabbed his hand and he felt his fingers slip on the hot soup of her insides. He pulled away but the flesh had knitted over. He vomited.

Pete's voice, when he phoned a couple of weeks later, was cracking with joy: 'I can't believe — you won't believe it — she's up the fucking duff. We've done it!'

Ian sat himself down and took a breath. He felt so out of it, so tired.

That Sunday, a lunch — Maureen beside him in a white strappy sun-dress passing the dishes, serving the roast. She smelled of talc'd skin, showers, sex without the stickiness.

'It's a miracle,' Pete said, 'A fucking miracle. Shows how much those doctors know.'

'When's it due?'

'March,' said Maureen, 'We're going private. I'm narrow about the hips.'

When she cleared, he followed her into the kitchen. He just stood there and watched her body fold as she bent to get dessert bowls out. The cane chair had left its criss-cross patterns on the back of her thighs.

'What about you, Ian?' she said, 'Still no woman in your life?'

He knew it was the wrong thing before he did it as well as during. It wasn't so much that he placed his hand on her breast — the breast was offered to him in its cup, the nipple tucked away. Have one. No, it was the look on his face, the look in his eyes, the look that didn't let them off.

She wouldn't forgive him the look. He knew too much,

she knew he knew too much. In the kitchen with the dessert plates in one hand and the carton of double cream in the other. She stayed there a moment, that drop-dead darkness in her eyes. She didn't have to say anything. He knew. They both did. Moving away now.

The dreams, of course, had stopped.

Maureen and Pete's baby came six weeks early, delivered by Caesarean section, Valentine's Day. The doctors did everything they could, but it died four days later, in its parents' arms, big, elderly head, small greyish limbs, too ungrown and brain-damaged to breathe.

No-one's fault, one of these things. Try to talk about it. The nurses made a little, cheery diary of the four day life, with polaroids. Everyone took off their masks and gowns. You saw the whole face again. You breathed.

'I'm so sorry,' said Ian and meant it.

Maureen, yellow in her hospital bed, looked at him and almost laughed.

Pete — stopped in his tracks by grief — thanked everyone so much it got embarrassing.

Three months later Maureen just upped and went, packed her bags and moved to Milton Keynes, the divorce already in process. 'She's taken everything,' Pete told Ian, 'Presents she gave me, all our snaps — even the bloody wedding photos. You'd think she'd never been here at all.'

He finally admitted to Pete that they'd had their problems and that, once Maureen knew about her tubes, 'She wouldn't let me near her. We had sex only the once that month, so it was a miracle we conceived at all.'

But it would have taken a bigger bloody miracle to save their marriage, he said.

Pete was OK. He chatted up one of the Special Baby Care nurses who'd been there for him through the whole thing and they went out a bit and eighteen months later, he proposed. Got her pregnant on the honeymoon.

Now and then, Ian thought of getting in touch with Maureen and one night he tried her name with directory enquiries, but nothing was listed.

People don't change. They get restless, they tell different lies, but they don't change.

And why should he care? Why should it matter when he has her anytime, often as he likes, every night, in every conceivable position?

Moving above him, spoonfeeding him his climaxes, wetting him with her various wetnesses, soothing and sating as if it's her sole task in life.

Which now it is. He's heard Pete say it, especially since the twins were born, but it's true. Forget the egg and sperm race — sex is so much better once the pressure's off, once you're back to doing it just for the sheer hell of it.

Or heaven.

Oh, he'd forgotten how good it could be, sliding between the sheets each night and demanding Maureen's inevitable, chilly kiss.

No Smoke
Michael Eaton

The first class carriage pulled up closest to the station exit,
so Becca was soon wrapped in protective greeting by her
P.A. and whisked into the waiting car. By the time Professor Pascal had hawked her bags down the entire length of
the platform from standard class — looking for, yet never
finding, a trolley — the end of the taxi queue stretched outside into the drizzle. She caught sight of a Tourist Development billboard displaying the silhouette of a medieval
outlaw with capacious thigh muscles who flexed a taut long-
bow and who wished her:

'Welcome to the City of Legend'.

It is extremely doubtful whether the co-incidence of
the arrival of these two eminent women on the same
train and for the same purpose would have meant anything to either of them. Extremely doubtful that Becca
would have ever read Joan Pascal's (highly-regarded, if
only in the discipline) ethnographic monograph on the
comparison of witchcraft accusations in three East
African societies, nor even her most recent (and more
popular — she'd even been on Woman's Hour to promote
it) study of the anthropology of psychotherapy: 'Talk Is
Never Cheap'.

Harder, perhaps, to credit but it was also extremely
doubtful that Joan was aware that Becca (whose name was
invariably accompanied by an Exclamation Mark) was
British television's Confession Queen. Since Joan had been
inveigled to accept the Chair she rarely managed to turn on
the goggle box, as she alone still called it, before Newsnight
and watched little besides.

But here they both were in this overcast provincial town:
searching for Satan.

*

167

The tweed suit Joan had bought when she had given a guest lecture in Edinburgh was already dampish by the time she gave the taxi driver the name of her B & B. She was greeted with not even ill-concealed contempt as he slurred out that it was only ten minutes walk away and he had sat on that rank for thirty five minutes. She had never known what to wear and she had always felt more at home squatting in a Nyakyusa compound than she did whenever she set foot outside the Senior Common Room.

She still couldn't quite understand why Jack Crossley had asked her onto his patch. His evident and hesitant anxiety had been palpable even over the phone — uncharacteristic, both professionally and personally, of the Superintendent. What exactly had he meant by: 'nothing official at this stage'?

The bilious cabbie seemed signally inappropriate as an informant but old habits die hard. She leaned forward 'I suppose you must of heard about these devil worshippers?' 'Nobody wants to talk about ought else.'

'What do you think?'

'Well, there's no smoke without fire, is there?'

'Yes, you may well be right.'

'Here's your hotel, missus. See, could have walked it no trouble.'

As she leant through the window to pay him he looked up at her:

'You know what I think: it's them Freemasons. Got this bleddy town sown up.'

Becca, meanwhile, sat in the back of her car on the way to her country house hotel critically scanning the call sheet for the shoot which Rupert had handed her. In her long career in television Becca had undergone more physical metamorphoses than any heroine in Ovid. It was only since she'd publicly come out as a victim of an eating disorder that she'd gracefully, if not exactly lightly, effected the tricky transformation from Game Show hostess to People Show presenter. Now she was twelve-stepped back to fame as the

168

personification of the Victim as Survivor, the Compassion Bulemic who gorged on the sufferings of others only to splurge them up before her targeted audience.

She glanced through the drizzle at these ordinary streets and murmured, as if only to herself:

'Those poor children!'

Then she turned to Rupert. He always felt a mounting sense of inadequacy whenever Becca smiled:

'Can't we do anything about this weather?'

There seemed to be not one right-angle in Joan's guest house room. The furniture shook every time traffic changed gear outside. She looked out of the window to the row of shops across the street, among them a hairdressing salon called Snipping Image and a chip shop, Fryer Tuck. Not for the first time in her life did she feel that she was the only person in the world without a sense of humour. She put down her luggage and opened the large manilla envelope that had been waiting for her at reception. Inside was a thick bundle of photocopied police files and interview transcripts. Stuck onto the top sheet was a Post-It note with the hand-written scrawl: 'For Your Eyes Only, Jack'.

Later that afternoon Joan sat in front of the empty desk of Richard Wall, the Director of Social Services. He shuffled in bearing two plastic cups of brown liquid which were evidently searing his finger tips.

'It might be tea, coffee or vegetarian oxtail soup. I'm afraid it's the best I can offer.'

He placed one before her. His smile seemed to Joan to be designed to signal to her the ease he felt in his own territory rather than as any token of welcome.

He was in his middle 40s, casually but in no way carelessly dressed as befitted the image of a senior member of the caring professions.

'Certain members of my team have been asking me exactly why your presence is required at such a time, Professor. To tell the truth, I haven't been able to furnish them with an entirely satisfactory answer.'

He took a biro from his inside jacket pocket and stirred his cup. He offered it to Joan, she declined.

'I'm sure it would have been sufficient to explain that my presence as an outside observer was requested by the local police.'

He sighed, trying to draw her into a comprehension of his delicate position.

'I'm afraid that only rubs salt in the wounds. I do realise the Superintendent thinks very highly of your expertise, but, after all, this is England not Africa. Nothing personal, Professor...'

Joan was well aware he meant exactly the opposite:

'But my team feel we are at a very sensitive stage in the investigation. Any outside interference at this time could prove highly detrimental.'

It sounded rehearsed, but none the less heartfelt.

'Exactly what evidence do you have so far, Mr. Wall?'

'The evidence of the disclosure sessions.'

'From the girl... Sheena Phillips?'

'That young person has provided us with cast-iron proof of a Satanic ring...'

'But no criminal charges have been levelled as yet, I understand?'

'To tell you the truth my team have the distinct impression that Superintendent Crossley has been less than sympathetic to the content of the disclosures...'

He added ominously:

'Which may, some might say, be hardly surprising.'

'What exactly do you mean by that?'

Wall noted the force of her reaction. It was clear to him now that he had been correct not to regard her as ally. He smiled again:

'Merely to suggest that it is hard for some people to think the unthinkable. I have a very small window this afternoon, Professor. How exactly can I be of help?'

'I shall have to talk to the Case Officer and I'll need to visit the foster parents.'

It seemed to pain him to say:

'That can be arranged.'

'And I shall, of course, want to see Sheena.'

'Nothing I can do about that, I'm afraid. She's in a place of safety. Well protected. I've been assured there can be no question of contamination at this time.'

'Very well... Then I shall need to see transcripts of all her interviews.'

For the first time his response seemed definite:

'Absolutely not! Until the C.P.S. decide to move on prosecution those tapes remain the sole property of this department.'

The rain had stopped when Becca's car pulled up to be met by Mike, the cameraman.

'You'll love this, Becca!'

The Victorian cemetery was on the crest of a hill looking down upon the town. Mike led Becca past the draped urns, the broken columns, the angels with sooty faces of the necropolis commemorating long-forgotten members of the city's bourgeoisie. The very dilapidation only made the place more wistfully Gothic.

As Mike turned a corner:

'O.K. Shut your eyes.'

When he asked her to open them again he had his thumbs and index fingers framed in front of her face 'So we start high like so... tilt down to find you up picking your way through the grave stones... then we pan across: Dah-dah!'

He stopped — through his fingers Becca could see a line of eerie sandstone caves carved into the rock wall and framed by cypress trees.

'What do you think?'

It was a beautiful end frame: Hammer-esque. Even the most unimaginative viewer could manage to picture Christopher Lee, a black opera cloak shrouding his features. Becca couldn't help but look impressed:

'Why the devil not? It's perfect, Mike... really cinematic. So this is where they hold their ceremonies?'

Rupert was equivocal:

171

'We-ell...'

Becca stared him down.

'Yes, it could well have been.'

But she was already off, pacing it out. She stopped at the entrance of the cave and turned towards Mike:

'And it was to this very cemetery... not a mile away from the bustling city centre... that the children were brought... no: dragged... against their will...'

She stepped inside the cave and looked around, suddenly disappointed at its shallowness and the fact that it could be seen so easily from the top deck of any passing bus. Mike was encouraging:

'We can cheat the nearness to the road.'

As Becca walked into the cave her feet sunk into the years of detritus that covered the floor:

'I must say it looks better from the outside.'

She looked across at Rupert:

'I trust someone will clean this out before I go on camera?'

Suddenly a thought hit the young man, he mustered his courage:

'Becca, what if you were to find something inside. You know, ritual stuff... that they use. Something visual. I could easily find something in town, it's almost Hallowe'en. It could be really cinematic.'

Becca's expression showed outright disdain:

'Really, Rupert, didn't they cover ethics on your Media Studies course?'

Rupert wished that one of these graves would open and swallow him down. He knew that this was not the right time to remind her that, actually, his degree was in philosophy.

Back in the guest house Joan looked at the contents of the package Crossley had been so anxious for her to examine and Wall had been just as eager that she shouldn't. She studied the photograph of a pinched, sallow-faced teenage girl and tried to reconstruct the order of events from the

172

case notes of her half-life in the city which existed in parallel to the one outside the window: 'Welcome to The City of Pain.'

Ever since she had been taken into care three years before, Sheena Phillips had a history of casual self mutilation. She had repeatedly absconded from her Social Services home and had been periodically picked up by the police for soliciting. Even before she'd gone on the street she'd acquired a benzodiopate habit — prescription Temazepams she'd filched from her mother's handbag. Now sixteen, Sheena had been finally sectioned after an unsuccessful suicide attempt. In therapy she had started to talk.

She claimed to have escaped from an organised cabal whose members seemed not only to come from the neighbours on the estate where she had grown up but was made up of an ever more exalted constituency of doctors, lawyers, even a high-ranking policeman. Whenever a name was mentioned it had been inked out with indelible black marker. As the sessions progressed, Sheena's memories became ever more ghastly: from secret ceremonies involving blasphemy and the invocation of evil spirits she began to remember the ritual torture of domestic animals and brutal sex orgies involving herself and other, younger, children, not all of whom had been allowed to survive. She went on to describe how she had been forcefully drugged, how her body had been abused to provide a foetus for sacrifice.

The detail was relentless but not, it increasingly seemed to Joan, entirely unfamiliar. When she read the section where the girl described how one member of the cult worked in a crematorium and so could dispose of the bodies without leaving any traces, Joan remembered similar allegations in an American case... was it Oregon? Washington State?

So, in spite of the complete lack of any corroborating forensic evidence, on the basis of Sheena's allegations Social Services had already taken five young children from the estate into care. Joan had seen their shocked parents on the news: incoherently denying the outrageous rumours circu-

173

lating about them. Joan began to scan the transcripts of their disclosures but before long called reception and asked for the number of the University:

'Department of Social Psychology... Professor Evans, please...'

She was connected with a voice she hadn't heard for some years but one which seemed very pleased to hear from her. He asked what she was up to:

'You won't believe it, Trevor, but I'm up here hunting the Devil and all his works...'

Mike set up his lights in the suburban sitting room. The houseproud woman on the sofa tried not to think about the muddy trails left by the tangle of cables on her carpet as he swooped up close to her face brandishing a light meter. As Amanda, the sound recordist, moved in to fiddle with her microphone he took up the offer of a cup of tea from the husband of the interviewee. By the time Amanda came into the kitchen to tell him she was set, Mike had his photos out:

'There's the paddock at the back of the property. You can't quite see the river bank where I moor the boat. Hang on...'

Mike fanned out three of the snaps together making a domestic panorama. The husband looked more envious than impressed:

'You must make a bit, then, at this game.'

'Not anymore, mate. Those days are over. It's all deals now. They've done away with the old Spanish customs.'

He nodded at Amanda and picked up his walkie-talkie:

'O.K., Rupe... Ready for Her Beccaship.'

The neighbours peered through lace curtains as the celebrity was ushered up the driveway.

After the interview the woman felt drained:

'Was that what you wanted?'

Becca was already in a huddle with Rupert. She made a perfunctory turn to the householder:

'That was perfect, Pam.'

Rupert ran his finger down the clip-board:

'Don't you think that where you said: "And how did you feel about your foster-child's involvement" it might be stronger if you say: "...about the little boy being a worshipper of Satan?"'. Then we can maybe use this answer of hers about how she'd heard of these things but never thought they were going on in this town?'

Becca nodded. Mike had swivelled the tripod around and was repositioning the lights. The lady of the house dangled around, excluded from these esoteric rites. She seemed embarrassed as she plucked up courage to ask:

'There was one other thing, Becca...'

Mike intervened:

'Would you please just mind waiting in the kitchen, love, while we do Becca's cutaways?'

'I wondered if I could have your autograph?'

Becca flashed her trademark smile and Rupert handed her a ready-signed photo.

'Why the devil not?'

As Pam was cleaning the carpet the following day her husband grumbled:

'It's getting like Slab Square in here.'

But she was proud, she knew what she was doing was important. Not, of course, that a Professor could live up to a visit from Becca!

Joan had been picked up by a Social Worker who looked as if she was not long out of education and who acted as if she'd left without a particularly high class of degree.

'You're very young to be in charge of this case, Miss...?'

'I'm Karen Pearson... no, I've been liaising with the foster parents. I'm to take you over there.'

Joan made it clear that she'd been expecting to meet the Senior Case Officer who was handling disclosures and who was yet to return her calls. Karen told her she was away for the weekend so Joan said she'd see her on Monday.

'Oh, will you still be here on Monday?'

'I shall be here as long as it takes. Have you been present at the disclosures?'

Now Karen was really unsettled:

'Please, I'd rather not say. We have to be very careful. We have no idea how far this network might stretch. We've never had anything like this before.'

Joan's look exposed all Karen's uncertainties. Why did she suddenly feel like she was back at school again?

On the drive over Joan had done little to hide her displeasure when Karen had also explained that only one of the foster families was available. Pamela Berridge was an experienced carer whom the department had entrusted with Davy M., aged six.

'Will I be meeting him?'

'Not possible today, I'm afraid. He's away on an outing.'

By now Joan seemed entirely unsurprised with this answer. She was careful not to give away the source of her knowledge when she asked:

'From what I've been told you had him for several weeks before he said anything that could be remotely indicative of any abuse.'

'Yes. He was in denial. Terribly. He's a very disturbed young person. Not surprisingly. He's giving us some amazing stuff now, though. Amazing.'

Joan sat on Mrs. Berridge's sofa, awash with tea. She was often aware how uneasy people felt in her presence. Maybe it was the ground bass of Caledonian sternness which she still projected, even though she'd left Scotland in her teens. Maybe it was her title, or the unfashionable way she dressed. Maybe it was the resolutely precise way she framed her questions which marked her out as indelibly middle-class. Whatever it was, it had never been an issue in what was then Nyasaland, but it had remained one ever since she came back home.

Though Pam had felt free and easy chatting with Becca, in spite of the lights and the camera, her words now came falteringly:

'He's such a... damaged... young lad. In all my years... I've never seen anything like it.'

'Does he talk to you about what is supposed to have happened to him?'

'Oh no, he doesn't have to. I know.'

Pam suddenly stopped.

'What do you mean?'

'I mean... it's there... you know...'

'I'm not sure I do, Mrs. Berridge.'

'In his play... he's always drawing ghosts... monsters and such, poor thing.'

Joan suddenly remembered a particular gruesome image from Davy's disclosure:

'Does he ever draw cats?'

She knew right away she had a struck a chord.

'Don't talk to me about cats!'

Joan turned to Pam disingenuously:

'Does young Davy ever talk about them in his interviews?'

Karen interrupted:

'Please, Professor, Pam can't be privy to the contents of the disclosure.'

But Joan continued:

'I'm told he seems particularly upset about seeing a cat eviscerated...'

Pam looked blank.

'Killed in front of him and disembowelled.'

Karen looked shocked:

'Where did you get that from, the police?'

Joan persisted:

'Has he ever mentioned that to you?'

And suddenly Mrs. Berridge was off:

'If you ask me it was the best thing that could have happened in the long run. That damned animal. I never wanted him to bring it here. It's not that I'm against pets, Professor, we've had them before. But that... creature. I knew right away. I was glad when it was run over...'

'When was that?'

'About a fortnight after he came here.'

'Whereabouts?'

'Outside there... in the road.'

177

'And did Davy see that?'

Karen seemed suddenly upset by this line of questioning:

'I really don't see what...'

But now Pam's erstwhile hesistancy was entirely overcome:

'It was evil that animal. You could see it in its eyes. It was devilish. I'm glad it's dead. I'm sure it was God's will...'

Joan looked across at the young social worker — even Karen seemed amazed by this outburst.

When they left Joan asked:

'What do you honestly think about all this, Ms. Pearson?'

It still came out like a mantra, but without the poker-faced, party-line certainty she had hitherto displayed:

'I think we should believe the children.'

'Yes, I'm sure. But doesn't it rather depend on what they're trying to tell us?'

Becca mentally ran through the material as Mike set up in the cemetery. She must admit that the interview with the police Superintendent hadn't gone too brilliantly. He gave nothing away, just came out with the same non-commital blah-de-blah over and over. He must have been on some bloody media charm school course, like the one her ex-husband ran for New Labour politicians. She'd have to make it work to her advantage. Maybe if his denials were cut in with the foster mother stuff — she was perfect People Show. Who could argue against that kind of first-hand experience? She — what was her name: Pam — even managed unprompted tears when she spoke of these evil men who destroyed the most precious thing in the world: a young child's innocence.

'Somebody should do something. Somebody should listen. But nobody wants to listen. Perfect! But the policeman... maybe they should just use the bit where he he came out with:

'I must stress that all of these claims come ultimately

178

from one unreliable source: a drug addicted prostitute. She is a very disturbed young girl.'

And quick as a flash Becca had told the heartless creep:

'It seems hardly surprising that she is, does it?'

Brilliant. That had really rattled him.

'I must repeat, my enquiry has found no corroborating evidence for any of these alleged offences.'

'Perhaps that's because you haven't been looking very hard, Superintendent! O.K. Cut it! Thank you, Plod and good night.'

And now for her *pièce de résistance*.

'Ready, Becca?'

'Sure.'

Becca crept towards the mouth of the cave. The suspense was palpable:

'And it was here...'

Then that bloody whining lesbian sound recordist started moaning on about the traffic noise. Becca threw her hands in the air as Mike bellowed:

'Fuck it, Amanda. We can fix it in the dub.'

A second take. This time as she neared the entrance, atmospherically lit by flickering candlelight, Becca suddenly felt a twinge of regret: maybe the lad had been right, maybe the discovery of ritual paraphrenalia, even the sight of a pentagram smeared upon the sandstone wall might have given the shot a bit of a lift. But she instantly dismissed the thought — her reputation was paramount. She turned round to face the camera on Mike's shoulder as it came in closer and her lowered voice echoed:

'And it was here... in this very cave...'

'Who exactly conducted these "interviews"?'

In his widowhood Trevor Evans' domestic environment had gradually taken on the contours of the rooms Joan remembered him occupying at St. Cat's. There were antique cabinets filled with his late wife's china collection in the alcoves, but they were barely visible behind the rising piles of books and academic papers that made an obstacle course of the floor. Joan wouldn't have been at all surprised if he'd have stuck a crumpet on a fork and toasted it on the gas fire. She found herself entirely relaxed as he freshened her glass from his bottle of Highland Park.

'Primarily, I gather, a Senior Social Worker whose current role in life seems to be the avoidance of myself at all costs. Was anyone in your department involved at all, perchance?'

'Never bloody asked, dear heart. First I knew of any of this palaver was when I read about it in the papers. Though I did offer.'

'Then, for my sake, don't tell anyone I showed these transcripts to you.'

'You don't happen to know what the qualifications of this "caring professional" are, by any chance?'

Like every academic she knew, herself included, he habitually put inverted commas around words — it was an article of faith to them both that verbal concepts meant little outside the context of those who were using them.

'The director told me: "she was fully trained in the therapeutic technique of counselling abuse survivors". Which, as you know, could cover a multitude of sins.'

'An evening class at a portakabin "university", at best. A weekend school at an "alternative health" centre, most likely. Christ, my students have to study for seven bloody years before they're allowed to practice. This one has no training in Child Psychology, that's apparent.'

'Is it, indeed?'

'Eminently. In fact, I would go so far as to say that this is a paradigmatic instance of how not to conduct interviews with children — "normal" or "disturbed".'

As the level of the bottle lowered Trevor became more and more infused with anger. He enumerated the ways that the interviewer had asked leading questions, had put words in the childrens' mouths, had given confirmation to answers she wanted to hear and veered away from those that didn't fit her thesis. When the children refused to confirm the scenario Sheena Phillips had outlined they were

180

"in denial". When they later contradicted apparently con-
firmatory detail they were "in retraction". And Trevor's
lucidity was "in decline" by the time he said:

'Interesting how these "therapists" — by the by, it's not
even an anagram of "the rapist"...'

Joan smiled:

'You read that in my book.'

Caught out.

'I might just as easily have said it myself, Joan.'

Anyway... they know sod all about dear old Sigmund and
all his works yet one concept which seems to have sunk in
mightily is "repression". If you are not doing or saying what
I want you to do or say then ergo you must be "repressing".'

Trevor was sprawling closer to Joan on his torn leather
sofa now. She could smell the nicotine on his cardigan and
in his hair. She found herself surprised that she didn't seem
to mind over much.

'Don't get me wrong, Joan, I do have some residual
respect for the Viennese mountebank but you do have to
know how to read him.'

'Isn't that what true believers say about the Bible?'

He laughed. It was rare for him to have any company on
a Saturday night. Joan thought for a moment:

'Trevor, what if... just suppose... what if all this were
true?'

'You can't be suggesting...'

'Indulge me for a moment.'

'You mean: that Satan is alive and well and living and
working on planet earth? Then, dear heart, everything you
and I stand for must not only be worthless but positively
harmful. And that is a thought far too horrible for the likes
of us to contemplate.'

She seemed more serious than he was expecting and less
clear than he was used to from her:

'But that's what they'll say about me... isn't it? If I con-
clude all this is patent rubbish then they'll say that I have
a vested interest in saying so, won't they? They'll say I've
only been wheeled in to say that. That my mind was made

181

up in advance. That my world-view means I'm not prepared to think the unthinkable. Do you see what I'm saying? You do, don't you?'

She heard her speech slurring, she heard her repetitions, the way now she seemed only to be thinking of herself. Trevor was closer to her as he leaned over to charge her glass.

'No, no. I'd probably better go, Trevor. I'm starting to get a bit squiffy.'

'You could always stay here, you know.'

She knew she could. She saw him now not as the prestigious head of a university department but as an ageing man, lonely and passed-over.

'I mean... I've lots of room these days...'

They both knew what he meant.

Opening the window in the taxi back, trying to clear her head, Joan couldn't help thinking back to Africa. For her, witchcraft had always been an object of study. When accusations were levelled it was her task to examine who was making them and against whom they were made. There were different patterns of accusations in different societies which reflected the power relations in those societies. Witchcraft had a sociological existence, not a supernatural reality. It was what anthropologists called "a social-strain gauge", indicative, not of dark forces at work in the world, but of how the world wasn't properly functioning. Like the taxi-driver had said: there was no smoke without fire — but why had that fire been lit, who fanned the flames, and who ended up burnt?

Her people (damn, she should stop thinking of the Africans who had allowed her to live among them and from the study of whom she had gained her doctorate as "her people"). They, of course, explicitly believed in malign paranormal entities and she was well aware that, from their perspective, believing often made them real. To the imperial authorities an outbreak of witchcraft accusations had been another bloody nuisance, proof of the primitive superstitions of their child-like colonial charges. But the missionaries... the missionaries often seemed to share the people's belief in the absolute reality of supernatural forces, and for them, of course, they were manifestations of the Biblical principalities and powers. She remembered a Protestant evangelist once saying to her:

'I don't think I'll ever understand what you are doing here, Miss Pascal. The other civil servants want to control the natives' behaviour, you just seem content to take notes.'

She asked him what he thought it was he was doing, suspecting the answer in advance:

'I'm here to save their immortal souls from everlasting damnation.'

Was it all she could ever do — take notes, study, analyse and look down on those other professions which seemed to have no uncertainties about interfering in social situations they had never really bothered to understand?

She thought of little Davy M., denied his parents, even his proper name. She had no doubt that the authority which had removed him from his home genuinely believed that he was under a terrible threat from agents of Lucifer, even though his stumbling testimony did little to confirm that. She equally had no doubt that his troubling answers, interpreted by that authority as evidence of his presence at animal sacrifices, were produced out of the more mundane trauma of witnessing his poor pet cat run over before his eyes.

She thought of Sheena Phillips' hideous case history and couldn't help but equate her with the powerless young girls in her village, equally convinced that the important male elders had brought misfortune down upon them through sorcery. For the first time in Sheena's life, perhaps, she was being listened to by representatives of an authority which had never hitherto wanted to know. But only when she said the things they wanted to hear.

She knew that the social world could not be just an object of study — that it had to be acted upon. But had she ever managed that? Sheena's meaningless life was enough

183

to convince anyone that the world could be wicked. But she couldn't help putting the academic air-quotes around the word 'evil' in her mind and never once felt tempted to precede it with the letter 'd'.

The taxi-driver cocked his ear as she heard herself thinking out loud:

'Those poor children!'

'What's that?'

'Nothing.'

The interview with the Social Services director had been brilliant — lots of really hot stuff, Becca could barely turn him off: 'What we do suspect is that there exists in this town an evil conspiracy to abduct and abuse children.'

We do not know how wide it stretches or how high up it goes but we do believe that it is done in the name of Satan. And we have become increasingly convinced that the police have been dragging their heels in bringing this network to justice.'

'And why do you think that might be, Mr. Wall?'

Ever reliable Mike had caught the moment and zoomed tight in on him before he said:

'I hesitate to think, Becca.'

Now a few grab shots of the town to stress its drab, provincial, Sunday-morning ordinariness and the crew could forever shake the dust off their feet. Should make a hard-hitting five minute intro to the studio discussion: Satanic Ritual Abuse — This Demonic Plague Sweeping Our Nation!

She had to admit it: she had the magic touch. Who else on this side of the pond but Becca could consistently craft programmes which managed to be both hard-hitting and ratings-heavy? Her critics — mean-spirited, over-educated wannabees to a man (yes, come to think of it, they were invariably male, weren't they?) — they envied Becca her audience and her high-profile. They wouldn't recognise the popular touch if it poked their short-sighted eyes out. They accused her of making 'tabloid television'. Sure, why not?

184

Nothing wrong with that, is there? She should be proud of it. She shouldn't let their spite get to her. That had always been her main fault: her rhinoplasty surgeon had told her she was much too hard on herself. She should be more self-confident. Her work spoke for itself.

As they drove out of town they passed a sign "Come Back Again to the City of Legend".

It wasn't only because it was Sunday morning but probably, if she were honest, because of all Trevor's malt, that Joan felt like a loose thread waiting to be tugged. The last thing she felt she could face right now was writing up her notes.

She already knew very well what she wanted to do, what she knew she would do. She had an overwhelming desire to see little Davy. To see if she could see him. Perhaps if she went over to the Berridges, perhaps if she hung around the road discreetly she might find him playing, she might even approach him and talk to him. She might even simply ring Pam's doorbell and demand to speak to him. She knew she shouldn't be doing this, that she was out-reaching her brief, that she risked jeopardising her status even amongst those who supported her intrusive presence.

And now she found herself dangling around at the end of the Berridges' street. How could she possibly imagine that the sight of a five year old fostered boy would put her marginal and unwelcome involvement into some kind of human perspective? Why did her confidence in her own dispassionate analysis seem to dissipate whenever she thought of the time that others had spent with that wee lad? It couldn't be that she was envious of the work of these others whose predispositions she instinctively felt were unsound?

And then she saw Mrs. Berridge come out of her neat semi- and then Davy after her, spit and polished, impotently complicit, held tight in her secure, benevolent, fostering grasp. So she followed them.

Up the clinging-on-to-respectability-by-the-fingernails-because-the-alternative-is-too-ghastly-to-imagine of this suburban street; through a urine-stinking shopping

185

precinct with its axiomatically boarded-up stores — one of which, a lace curtain emporium, showed a sale sign which read, without irony: Last Few Days; onto a playing field where youths of all races ducked and weaved around twirls of canine faeces as they kicked balls at each other, exhibiting a surly, self-conscious codified masculinity she had no time to observe, let alone decode right this minute; across a busy main road — jammed with leisure-pursuited cars aspiring to inflict upon the weekend countryside an arterial sclerosis in which their presence wouldn't seem out-of-place; past a Do-It-Yourself warehouse from which couples emerged clutching furniture in brown cardboard packages, deliberately dis-assembled in order to give those consumers something to do-for-themselves when they got back to their soul-less nests — another contemporary ritual of couple-dom she must suggest to one of her graduate students as worthy of analysis.

"Welcome to the City of Signs".

Joan suddenly started to despise her thoughts. Maybe this was why people were so uneasy around her — she was so bloody patronising. But then she watched as Pam Berridge dragged Davy towards an old wooden building with a perfunctory brick extension which was decorated with the optimistic legend: Gospel Hall Of End-Time Prophecy. Its Wayside Pulpit read: "CH—CH. What's Missing? U-R!".

Joan took out her notebook but suddenly found she couldn't write for laughing. Joan thought it was choice: that exclamation mark! Evidently she must have a sense of humour. But not one this congregation could share.

It was only at the door of this cut-rate chapel that Davy seemed really to put up any kind of a struggle. Joan immediately stopped thinking of herself. She recognised at once that powerless resistance of his infant body language, more articulate than any patent confrontation.

Where had she seen it before? Of course: it reminded her of the expressions on the faces of those aboriginal children she had seen in a mission school in the Northern Territory when she was teaching in Australia. She still had no way of assessing exactly what might have happened to Davy before he was taken 'into care' — those air quotes again, dammit, probably justified — but right now Joan could see only a frightened little boy in the clutches of culture shock.

And, as Mrs. Berridge and the reluctant child in her doubtless capable charge were ushered into the bosom of the throng, Joan's hypotheses were abruptly halted. A car pulled up in front of the church and a middle-aged man slid out of it.

She didn't recognise him at first: in his pressed black suit and crisp light blue polyester shirt he bore all the lineaments of an executive from an American corporation. He carried a large, soft leather-bound zip-up Bible. But as he gave a firm handshake to the white-haired black pastor at the threshold she suddenly had a clearer view of a man she had seen only two days before. Before she had started to analyse, before she'd commenced comparing and contrasting, before she'd allowed herself to get drunk and emotional and involved. It was Richard Wall.

Joan wondered for a moment whether she should join the congregation as a "participant observer", but then she decided that her role in life would be best served, in this instance, as a snoop. So Joan hung around the side of the building, eavesdropping on the worship, the exhortation of Wall's millennial address and the accompanying "Hallelujahs" which bled out through the planks of the jerry-built tabernacle. And then she heard the sounds of a language that was momentarily unfamiliar to her. She couldn't help herself, she had to peek through the arch of the window to see elderly matrons falling down upon the floor, twitching and convulsively laughing, filled with the fruits of the Holy Spirit. Then she realised what language it was they were speaking: glossalalia — the Pentecostal vernacular. They were talking in tongues.

Joan carried on staring into the church, an outsider as always, as Pamela Berridge gabbled in divine possession. And through the glass all she could see now was the fear in

187

little Davy M.'s eyes as the born-again — as if once was not enough — Director of Social Services approached him and shoved his healing palm onto his forehead:

'Cast out, cast out, O Lord, these demons. In the name of Jee-sus!'

Becca's Satanic Abuse show aired just as Joan felt she was about to get something definite out of Superintendent Crossley. But his vanity made him stop to watch himself on the box in his office and he became visibly annoyed when he watched his interview, slashed in the cutting room to misrepresent him as a total uncaring, authoritarian — pardon his French — arsehole.

'I never said that... well, I must have done. She's made me look a right prat, Prof. I'll turn the bugger off!'

But Joan shut him up and insisted they suffer through the rest of the show — for research purposes.

In the studio, backlit to avoid identification, was Davy's dad, shuffling uncomfortably, struggling in vain to maintain some semblance of dignity:

'All I want is the lad back.'

And Becca, before the nation, was accusing this dad of unspeakable crimes against the body and soul of his own son.

'What is it I'm supposed to have done, then? Nobody's ever told us. We've had bricks chucked through us windows. We've even had shit shovelled through the letterbox...'

'Please, Mister M., this is a family show. But you don't care too much for the sanctity of the family, do you?'

His very denials labelled this uneducated tattooed monster as someone who must really have something to deny:

'If I've done summat to that lad then have me up for it, why don't they? But I ent done nothing to our Davy. Honest. I just want me lad back.'

Joan turned away from the crumpled face of the man on the box towards the now respectable bruiser she had first met fifteen years ago when he had barracked her ad nauseam from the back of the class as a dyed-in-the-wool, bigotted DC on her (some of her colleagues said "pioneering", others "misconceived") Ethnic Awareness course at the police college. They say you know that you're old when policemen look younger than you. But you really know that you're past it when your pimply-necked former students turn into stocky Superintendents. With tears in their eyes.

'Allright, Prof, you know I didn't really ask you to come here just as a potential expert witness. I wanted you to tell me that you thought all this was a load of cobblers. I can't explain why I feel that. I may be wrong, I don't know. But that's why I wanted you around. I'm using you to get me off the hook.'

Joan thought hard before she asked:

'Tell me something, Jack...?'

Why did he always feel, when she spoke to him, that he was back at school, in the headmaster's study?

'You're not, are you perchance, one of those trouser-rollers?'

He tried to look disappointed in her:

'Prof... give me some credit.'

'No. I can't quite see you wearing an apron.'

And then they stopped to stare at the set as Becca swept away from her instantly-abandoned studio audience and addressed us in our living rooms:

'Satanic Ritual Abuse — This Demonic Plague Sweeping Our Nation. When will we believe the children? Join us next week on 'Becca!' as we probe an even more terrifying threat: we have startling claims from victims of the extra-terrestrials as we ask: Alien Abduction — Is There A Government Cover-Up? Goodbye and look after yourselves.'

The Anthropologist looked at the Policeman. They couldn't help it, they had to laugh.

Joan had wished more than once that she had never boarded that train to the City of Legend. Now, five years later, she was back on it again. She scanned the cutting that Professor Evans had included with his letter. The account of Sheena's successful trip to eternity figured in the local

189

free sheet under the headline: Abuse Girl — Death Wish? It barely clung onto page seven, opposite 'Poet's Corner' and an inventory of car boot sales. Joan was halted once again by that same picture of that young girl with the soul-stolen eyes.

Joan had long since tabled her report. She had concluded that the existence of a conspiracy of internationally net-worked Satanic abuse was a total illusion and that the disclosure sessions had been conducted by unqualified agents determined to assert their own misguided agendas.

It was subsequently circulated throughout the Caring Professions but never made public. Those amongst them who chose not to ignore it completely were disposed to accuse the anthropologist as being, at best, an establishment tool, at worst, an apologist for the Satanists.

Joan's book: *Idle Hands — The Devil Finds Work — An Anthropological Study of a Modern Witch-hunt* — had yet to find even an academic publisher. Nevertheless, she took some small comfort in the fact that the Chief Constable, on Crossley's recommendation, had decided not to proceed with any prosecutions and all of the children who had been taken away by Social Services were now back home. The Local Authority had eventually agreed to an out-of-court settlement with an undisclosed payment, provided the families signed a gagging clause. But it had not been a straightforward rehabilitation for Davy M., not by any means. More often suspended from his secondary school than a pupil in it, he was now, in that ominous phrase, 'well known to the police'.

Trevor's letter had informed her that he had been petitioning for the children's files to be surrended to him with the stated aim of burning them unread on Bonfire Night in the Market Square as an act of public contrition. His Vice-Chancellor, he told her, was endeavouring to shut down his department on the grounds of unprofitable conduct and had offered Trevor early retirement. The younger members of his staff were being redeployed in the burgeoning School of Cultural Studies. Joan could hear the Cambrian inflection

190

in his voice as he compared his fate with that of the Director of Social Services. Richard Wall had resigned from his post with a generous golden handshake and now spearheaded The Healing Ministry Of Divine Psycho-Succour, working from a mansion on the outskirts of his native Swindon.

With a couple of hours to kill before Trevor would shake the dust off his feet at his retirement do, Joan walked about the town aimlessly, looking at the people. She knew they were not her people. She didn't, any more, know what to make of that. All she did know is that all her thinking, all her concepts, seemed not to have touched the lives of any of them.

She knew very well where she wanted to go, where she knew she would go. She found herself staring through the chicken wire, looking into the playground, watching out for little Davy. She had no trouble spotting him, though he was not so little any more. These days he was really quite big. He was the one all by himself. He was the one without any friends — the one banging his head against the school wall.

Brothers

Alan Sillitoe

In the ten minutes or so while Ken dealt with his large white mug of tea he didn't take his hand from the handle once, not even when the mug was resting before him on the table as if, Tony thought, he was frightened of somebody coming in and snatching it away.

'I don't know what I'll do. I can't even think.' Ken's voice sounded vacant and forlorn. Though not aware of pitying himself it was beginning to get through that you only lived once. He'd always known — and who didn't? — but regarded the fact as not worth bothering about. The green progress of summer made it more insistent however, as also did the discouraging fact that he had lost his job at the factory.

Thin rain fell noiselessly into the backyard beyond the window. In work you could choose your friends, but out of it you couldn't, so he had come to see his brother, and he didn't know why, because they had never felt much sympathy for each other. He didn't expect any help. His problem was too big for that, and problems were always your own, but he had just wanted to say hello. The only time he looked away from his tea was to glance at his own polished boots, which unaccountably made him put his hand to his throat and realise he wore no tie.

'I don't know what you can do.' Tony stood. It was his dinner time, and soon he would have to get back to work rewiring the canteen of a local small factory. Ken wanted something, and Tony didn't like to think so because he wasn't sure what. He'd never seemed much in contact with the world, our Ken hadn't, and Tony recalled their father saying about him that he was just bright enough to realise he wasn't all there.

Ken had never understood how they could be brothers, being so physically different. He was tall and lean, with a moustache, and almost bald (or so it had seemed in the mirror that morning) but Tony was short and stout and round faced. Eyes almost closed and a wide smile showed he was thinking of something funny, but he was too tight-arsed to share the joke with anybody else, certainly not with his brother. Only when they looked each other square in the eye did they know they came from the same family.

Ken took a final swig at his tea. 'Well, I didn't come here to ask for anything. I suppose we ought to meet now and again, though. We're brothers, after all.'

Tony had to agree. 'That's true enough,' but as if he'd also been wondering what they had in common. Behind him was a big colour television, and half a dozen shelves of video films arranged in the recess like books in a library.

Ken lit a cigarette, and leaned back in his chair. If Tony wanted him to go, let him say so. 'The gaffer gave me five hundred quid when he laid me off, so I don't suppose I can grumble.'

'That's the trouble, working for a boss,' Tony said, puffing his thin little cigar. 'Sooner or later you get the push.' He told the familiar tale of how, on coming out of the army, he put a card in his front window saying: ANY-THING REPAIRED. 'I couldn't lose. If it was a wireless, you knew nine times out of ten it was summat to do with a plug or a loose connection, or a dud valve. Wireless was easy, in them days. If it was a watch or clock it was either a bit of dust in the works, or it wanted winding up. Or one hand was so close to another it stopped both from moving. You'd be surprised how many people don't know a watch wants winding up. Or they didn't then anyway. The same with most things.

'I'd sometimes get called out only to mend a fuse. And if it was owt more complicated I'd tek it to a place in town, and charge the customer a commission. You can always mek a bob or two in this world. After a while there wasn't much I couldn't fix in the electrical line: vacuum cleaners, fridges, televisions. Then I moved out of the front room, and rented my own workshop. Took on another bloke to

194

help. Got my own firm going in no time.'

The most successful cowboy in the business, Ken thought, but now he knew so much he wasn't a cowboy any longer. Last year he went to Benidorm, and this year he was taking Molly to Greece. 'I like to go abroad now and again,' Tony went on. 'Got a taste for it in the army, after my year in Germany. Anyway,' he winked, 'I like to see all them topless girls dodging about with a volley ball!'

Ken didn't begrudge him any of that. Nor did he really mind being out of work. He was nearly fifty, anyway, and would get the dole. He didn't suppose he could be thrown out of his flat, though sometimes he wouldn't mind, seeing as how far above the ground it was. Then there was the noise from neighbours, and it got damp when rain blew horizontal from Derbyshire.

All his life he had gone from one job to another because there were plenty to be had and none had seemed good enough. He'd got on well with most gaffers, though, working hard because he liked doing the best he could, and because time went quicker that way. When he realised that even doing the best bored him he opted for another job. Nor did the gaffers want him to leave, but what changes they offered to make him stay had never seemed interesting enough.

When they sat in the armchairs Molly came in with the after dinner cup of tea, and Ken was surprised to see one for him. He remembered her being as ripe as a plum and very good looking, but now she was a dowdy little woman with a few teeth missing. She apologised and said she'd broken her plate that morning, and Ken was surprised that Tony hadn't been able to fix it. He didn't say so, but there was a slight glint in Molly's eyes as if she'd known what he was thinking, and she smiled on handing him a cup of tea he didn't expect because he'd already had a mug. On the other hand he supposed it was a signal that after he'd drunk it Tony would say he had to drive back to work. His little red van was parked outside the terraced house for which he paid only fifteen pounds a week to the

195

council. Then Ken knew he would be sent on his way.

At election times Tony put a Conservative poster in his window, not a big one, only a label really, and Ken wondered what his brother had to conserve. He was the opposite, but didn't put anything in his window. If he did only the birds would see it as they swooped by, because it was ten floors up, one of the high-rise hencoops nobody liked living in.

'I expect you'll have to sell your car,' Tony said, putting three spoons of sugar in his tea. 'Won't you?'

He sounded as if he would enjoy seeing him do it, so Ken laughed. 'I'll be lucky if I get enough to buy a push-bike, and even then it'd be secondhand. I only gen fifty quid for my old banger, and it's bin more trouble than it's worth. You're right, though. I shan't be able to afford the tax and insurance.'

'Cut your coat according to your cloth,' Tony said. 'That's my motto — allus has been.'

Ken had done that all his life anyway, because he'd had to. That was the sort of family they came from, with six kids altogether, and their father earning just enough as a shop assistant at the Coop to keep them alive. But the more cloth Tony got, as it were, the more he put into the bank, though he was no miser when it came to holidays and a bit of enjoyment. Apart from the van he had a new Cavalier, which he kept locked in a garage off Alfreton Road for fear somebody would set fire to it in a riot, or drive it away and push it in the Trent for a bit of fun when they'd finished, which could always happen these days. Black or white, the boggers stopped at nothing. Ken stood at his window once and saw some lads down below looking at his car. One of them shook his head, and they went away laughing, to look for a better one.

Too much time was going by, and the ash from Ken's fag fell onto the carpet. Tony noticed: 'I don't think it'd suit me, being without a job.'

'I'm out everyday looking for one,' Ken said, 'don't worry about that.' Not that he would worry. But he'd been

196

turned down at half a dozen places already because of his age, he supposed, so he might not bother anymore, though if he did he wouldn't go to the job centre and apply through them.

Tony with a wider grin suggested that if his brother didn't stick his nose into their office every day and get that bit of paper, and go out to try for a designated job, he wouldn't go on being eligible for the dole. Maybe that's how far he would fall, then he wouldn't care anymore, knowing — as their mother always used to say — that you couldn't fall off the dogshelf. Then he might plonk himself onto me, Tony thought, either to borrow something, or to cadge a bed for a few nights when he was slung onto the street.

The street had altered during the stay at his brother's house. Tarmac and pavements turned into silk and every car was washed clean, even his own as he stooped inside and twisted the key. More often than not it started first time now that his job had gone west.

He had to go home and change the budgerigar's water, and smiled at the thought that that was all he had to do. In one way he fancied being out of work, or would if he had enough money to keep him halfway happy.

He raised his foot from the accelerator and flashed a bus out of its stopping place. A gentleman of leisure, that's what I'll be. Shooting along the boulevard by the supermarket and hosiery factory, he turned left at the traffic lights. I've done my stint since I was fifteen, so somebody else can have a go on the treadmill. He was a bit slow at getting away, and a souped-up white van to his right set a horn screaming that almost blew him out of his seat, followed by a bawled curse as it leapt forward.

What was the hurry? They'll get to the coffin soon enough. It parked only a couple of hundred yards ahead, and the driver, a shaven-headed bully with an earring, ran into a shop with a parcel under his arm.

Maybe he had a girl friend there, though it seemed as if everybody in the world had an irritable form of St. Vitus flu, people either half doped, or in a rage to set on each other and do murder at the slightest provocation.

He used to amuse himself imagining how an unstoppable civil war might begin: late on Saturday night a man, well satisfied with his evening's boozing, and all set for home, stood on a pub step for a moment to clear his throat. Someone in the dark nearby thought his sound was the beginning of some sneering remark aimed at him, so clocked him one. At the noise of the fight people came out of the pub, and joined in for the fun of it. It turned into such a set-to that the police were called, and the riot spread over the whole area. When TV cameras were set going the people started throwing petrol bombs, just to give the crews better footage, and those seeing it on their screens in other towns sent their streets up in flames as well. Finally they had to bring in the army to mow the boggers down.

In a way he liked the picture, but while parking hoped that one day everybody would be cured of their madness and be able to live and let live with each other. That'd be the day, he thought, sorting out the four keys to get into his flat as if it was Fort Knox. He didn't see why not, and hope never did anybody any harm.

A ladder leaned across the pavement and Ken wondered about the old fashioned saying which told you never to walk under one because it brought bad luck. Surely such notions are now forgotten or no longer believed in. But no, during his time standing there to take out a fag, strike the match and light it, three people avoided the ladder by walking out onto the road, all of them a lot younger than him. He did the same, and went on his way up to the Castle.

He'd struck lucky, and got two hundred quid for the car, from somebody who was into vintage makes. It wasn't that old, but would be in a year or two. He'd be vintage as well soon enough, though doubted whether anybody would pay as much for him. Even he would think twice about giving more than a bob or two.

On the other hand he knew himself to be priceless, getting up to the Castle top without too much heavy breathing, and walking along the parapet which used to be known, and probably still was, as Suicide's Leap. At least the air's good up here. Used to be all smoke, and now it's clear as far as the hills and the power station. One time you heard the noise of mayhem from the scruffy houses of the Meadows, and the grunt of trucks, but today it was muted except for motor traffic on the road at the bottom of the sandstone escarpment.

The way to the bottom was long, and the body would bounce forever before hitting the railings. A few bushes growing out from the stones might stop your fall, as if to brush the dust off your coat so that you would be tidy before strolling into Heaven, though it might be Hell for doing something like that.

The body would spin a bit, it was bound to, and you wouldn't end up tidy at all. If you chucked yourself off on the q.t. — and funnily enough there wasn't anybody about at the moment on the long wide terrace — the only witnesses would be the birds, who wouldn't be surprised because they'd seen a lot of people doing it over the years. 'Another bloody fool,' they'd say. 'Christ! Just look at him,' — then go on whistling.

After the final wicked thump which he could hardly bear to think about he knew there would be no bloody Heaven or Hell for him, just blackness. Having imagined the smash so vividly, almost with real pain, he felt as if he had done it, and thought that would have to satisfy him till death came for real from he didn't know where.

A loop of approving wind spun from behind a corner of the stark Castle, and he buttoned his coat against it. Loving his life, whether joyless or not, he lit a fag and walked smiling down into the town for his morning cup of coffee. Then he would buy a paper and go home to read, and feed the bird which had always seemed happy enough in its cage.

And maybe somewhere at the back end of the newspaper there would be a few lines about a silly old sod who had stood on the wall of Nottingham Castle and got a medal for not slinging himself off.

But they don't print things like that do they, then, my pretty little budgie? Tut-tut-tut — come on, and get this lovely birdseed in my hand. There, I knew you would. Tastes like the best steak to you, don't it? What nice smooth feathers you've got. I wish I had a coat like yourn. That's right, eat your fill.

After I've fried myself an egg I'll close all the windows and let you out of your cage for half an hour. You'll like that, won't you? Brothers, did I hear you say? Don't talk to me about brothers.

From the Cradle
Keith Wright

The nurse was really quite pretty. Her thick black hair was tied back behind her head, her smile instinctive. Claire had that tired, worldy-wise look in her eyes that gave away the trauma she had witnessed in her eight years in the Casualty Department at the Queen's Medical Centre. The University Hospital was world renowned for its pioneering medical research and for accommodating Prince Charles after a polo accident. It was, however, a vast working hospital, where normal people visited and were taken by ambulance to be treated. Its NHS status, by definition, ensured a continual flow of people through the Accident & Emergency Department. Claire spoke concisely but sympathetically, occasionally glancing down at the wad of paper in her hand.

'The Ambulance arrived at 0733. Both parents were with the baby. Distraught, as you might imagine, bless them. The paramedic had attempted resus. but to no avail. Mr Ortega, the on duty Registrar pronounced life extinct at 0745. It appears to be a case of IDS.'

The two detectives had listened carefully. The Detective Sergeant; Andy Chase, a man in his mid thirties with swept back hair had been to A & E many times, and knew Claire to speak to. She always had a smile for everyone. The reason for their visit was not a smiling matter. Andy had a young detective with him, slightly shorter than he; Chris Ferrigno, an Anglo/Italian who was almost dribbling at the lips. Not only was the girl attractive, she was clever and charming also. The DS toyed with his watch and took the lead in the conversation.

'Any sign of injuries, Claire?'

'I'll let you have a look for yourself, Andy, she's over there.'

The three moved slowly towards the perspex see-through cot. The area was cordoned off by screens, but the general hub-bub of people going about their business could be heard.

Chris Ferrigno was trying to conceal the fact that this was his first cot death. His black hair glistened slightly with sweat as it met his tanned forehead. He had bitten his lip when Claire had alluded to IDS, and was glad, as he eventually managed to work out that the acronym stood for Infant Death Syndrome. He'd seen a programme about it on morning telly once. So much for police training. At twenty two, he was the youngest Detective Constable on the force. He had a lot to learn, but was as keen as mustard. His main mistake was trying to mask his obvious inexperience by bravado or over-confidence. Ferrigno looked less than comfortable being confronted with this situation, and all his swaying and chewing gum could not disguise it. He peered tentatively over Claire's shoulder at the baby. The baby looked like a doll, the skin was very white and almost porcelain-like. She was clothed in a pink cotton suit with a rabbit motif, the same clothing she was wearing when admitted.

Chris blurted out. 'What's its name?'

Claire frowned. 'ITS name is Sally. She's in pink, you know pink for a girl, blue for a boy.' She cast a glance at Chase, who raised his eyes skywards.

'Go on then, Chris, take the baby's clothes off and let's have a look at her.'

Ferrigno reached forward and began fumbling around the clothing, turning the baby on its back, searching aimlessly for buttons to undo. By chance his finger caught one of the press studs along the inside of the baby's leg and he began pulling them open. The baby had just begun to stiffen up with rigor mortis, which made the removal of the clothes slightly more difficult. Once the suit was removed he saw the nappy. His heart sank and sweat began to bead on his forehead. Ferrigno swiped through his hair, primarily to remove the sweat. He grunted.

'Come out of the way, will you, we'll be here all day.'

Claire removed the nappy, which was dirty, and cleaned up the mess.

Ferrigno felt sick as the foul stench of green slime floated towards him.

'Jesus! There's got to be something wrong with its insides to produce that. Christ!'

Chase grinned. 'Newly born baby poo sometimes looks and smells like that. Beautiful isn't it?' He smirked at Claire. 'Can't you tell he's a bachelor?'

Ferrigno was eager to see Claire's reaction. She merely muttered an 'I can tell alright.'

Chase put out his open palms and shrugged, he had tried to get a response from her for him, but you can't win them all. He spoke.

'Right then Chris. Get hold of the baby and let's see if there are any marks of violence.'

Ferrigno took hold of the small body and examined it. Lifting the arms up with the tips of his fingers, the stiff limbs preventing any great amount of movement.

'Nope. Can't see owt.'

'Pass her to me.' Chase instructed.

He held the face of the baby very closely to his own, scrutinising it.

'Mm.'

Ferrigno responded. 'What? What is it?'

'Probably nothing.' He put the baby down in its cot and covered it with the small white blanket. He grimaced and shook his head slightly. 'Thanks Claire. See you again no doubt.' He grasped her forearm and squeezed it. Giving her a smile. Chase turned and walked away, pursued by Ferrigno. He was still puzzled, and had to almost jog to keep up with his detective sergeant.

'What did you see, Sarge?'

'As I said, probably nowt. I thought I could see a slight mark on its cheek. The post mortem's later, we'll sort it then I guess.'

*

Mortuaries stink. Their smell is almost indescribable but is a sort of mixture of rotting cabbages and bleach. You can never seem to relax whilst in one. They have large clanking shutters at one end of the room to allow undertakers' vehicles to drive in, and a wall of large drawers covers one side, the contents of which need no further explanation. Opposite this is the PM room, next to the office-cum-tea mashing room.

Andy Chase and Chris Ferrigno stood in their white coveralls, the hoods down and plastic covers over their shoes. Normally, there are large tools on display at adult post mortems, hack saws, trepans, hammers and chisels; to access the brain and other internal organs. These are not required for babies. A saw is required to cut through a tree trunk but only scissors to cut through cardboard.

The pathologist was a grey-haired gentleman. Away from the mortuary he could easily be mistaken for a retired businessman strolling through the grounds of Nottingham Castle, or perhaps blending in with other tourists picknicking in Sherwood Forest. He wore a surgeon's garb of Lincoln Green with green calf-length wellington boots.

Chris Ferrigno never made it all the way through the obscene, but necessary butchery that unfolded. Chase didn't blame him too much. Thankfully such sights are restricted to a handful of people in society and only a sense of duty rooted him to the spot. As they discarded their disposable clothes the pathologist joined them.

'I share your concern, Sergeant Chase.'

The DS was hopping around trying to get the waxed paper coverall over the heel of his foot. 'Okay.'

The grey-haired gentleman leaned against one of the trolleys which bore a naked obese victim. 'The two main factors of concern are the petechial haemorrhaging in the whites of the baby's eyes and then more so the bruising at the side of the mouth. Three spots...'

Chase cut him short. 'Finger marks?'

'Looks that way I'm afraid. The cause of death is; 1A: Lack of oxygen and 1B: Heart failure. The Coroner is going to need a full investigation, Andy.'

With that the pathologist returned through the clear plastic doors back into theatre for the heart attack victim to be given his autopsy and subsequent cause of death.

Chase glanced at Ferrigno who asked for a translation.

'Petechial Haemmorhaging are small red dots found on skin and more commonly in the whites of the eyes if the victim has been deprived of oxygen. The small blood vessels in the eyes burst and pop leaving the tiny red dots.'

Ferrigno looks slightly puzzled. 'Yes, but surely we all die of lack of oxygen once we stop breathing. There's no dead body that I've come across yet who is still pulling breath!'

Chase grunted a laugh, as he rubbed his stubby fingers through his hair, returning the displaced strands. 'True, my old mucker, but the give away is the bruising once the surface of the cheek was cut away showing the darker red clotting underneath, seemingly caused by the placing of a hand over the mouth. We may well have a case of murder, my duck, and I don't think we need to look much further for our suspects do we?'

'You mean the parents.'

'Ten out of ten, we'll make a detective out of you yet. Come on.'

Eastwood is a former mining village which marks the border between Nottingham and Derby. It is a quaint little country town surrounded by beautiful countryside. Like most places it has a small area that is dedicated to lawlessness and disregard for others. Phoenix Street was as infamous to the local police as the nearby birthplace of DH Lawrence was famous to the local community. Phoenix Street was formed by a seemingly endless row of terraced housing that ran parallel to the town's main street. As the two Detectives parked their car and walked down the slight gradient towards the street they could not fail to take in their surroundings, shrouded in a hue of what smelled like rotten vegetables. A trail of smoke filtered across the row of gardens emanating from a distant garden fire. The terraced housing, skewered by streams of sunlight spewed out all manner of contraptions and miscellany onto their back gardens; prams, bicycles, car engines, motor bikes, dolls, dirty washing, clean washing, old washing machines, cats, dogs, rabbits, dead birds, live birds, bird muck, confectionery wrappers, crisp papers, bins, rubbish bags, loose rubbish, coal, fag ends, beer bottles, beer cans, used contraceptives, nappies, babies' dummies, babies' bottles, babies, children, people, pots and pans.

It was a strange quirk of fate that almost all the local criminal population lived on the street that ran parallel to the main shopping area. 'If the devil should cast his net' was a popular saying about the street. A place that even an inquisitive and needy Lady Chatterley would not be seen dead in. There was certainly little evidence of gardeners employed in the locale, judging by the long grass and lack of flora or fauna. Interspersed amongst the degradation was the occasional decent person. Some poor sod that happened to exchange one Council House for another and find themselves knee-deep in domestic disputes, late-night swearing, fighting and fornication.

Paul and Mary Saunders were two of these unfortunates. Not highly educated, but certainly not criminals. Chase and Ferringo stood at the door and after casting a glance at each other, Chris knocked on the door.

Paul Saunders was in a right state. His hair was matted and it was clear he had been crying. He needed a shave and his twenty eight year old face appeared forty eight.

Ferrigno raised his open wallet. 'Pol...'

'I know. Come in.'

They followed him into the house. The living room was veiled in semi-darkness, the curtains drawn, but a small gap afforded a shaft of light to pierce the cigarette smoke that lingered like a fog. Several mugs were on the floor and a large glass ashtray was brimming with cigarette ends. The room had not been decorated for some years and was

206

stained with a yellowy tint of nicotine. Mary sat, huddled in the corner of the room and did not look up to greet the two men. DS Andy Chase took the lead as he adjusted himself into the seemingly springless chair.

'Can I just say that, we are very sorry for the two of you. It's unfortunate that we have to speak to you at such a time but, I'm afraid we simply have to.'

Chase was aware that there was a strong argument for him to just walk in and arrest both parents. He was not going to do that. The law does not always fit into the lives of real people. Sure, the PM revealed suspicious circumstances but he needed to get a feel of the people he would be dealing with, to get an account first of all. There may be some innocent explanation, mightn't there?

'Can you tell me how you came to discover your child... erm, you know...'

'Dead you mean.'

Chase sighed. 'Yeah.'

Mary was sobbing quietly into her handkerchief, her fingers twisting the cloth, her eyes closed tightly and tears spilling from them. She was a very thin woman with bony knuckles and chipped nail varnish.

The father mirrored the sigh. 'It was four in the morning or just after. I got up to go to the toilet and, as you do, I stuck my head around the door. I thought she was asleep, she may have been, but when we got up, she was... she was...' His voice distorted into a cry as his emotions took over. 'Fucking dead. Dead. Fucking dead.'

Chase looked briefly at Ferrigno who widened his eyes.

Mary spoke for the first time. 'You know we're glad, don't you?'

'Mary!'

'They're going to find out, for Christ's sake, they're not stupid, you know.'

Chase spoke quietly, his voice attempting to disguise the anticipation.

'Find out what, Mrs Saunders?'

She began rocking backwards and forwards. 'Sally was

ill. Well not ill, you see we had just found out that she had a bad case of cerebral palsy, she would have had a life of hell, she would...'

Paul interrupted. 'She was going to be a spastic. A spas. A fucking dudoo.' He was visibly shaking and he took in a deep breath before continuing. 'I'm sorry. What she means is, not that we are glad, well we... it's a blessing she's gone, it's for the best, that's all.'

There was a pause, before Chase commented. 'I see.'

Ferrigno spoke for the first time. It was all too clear to him what had happened. 'Look Mr Saunders I'm afraid we are going to have...'

Chase cut him short.

'When did you find out about this? You know, when did the hospital tell you?'

Paul answered. 'They rang two days ago. They said the test had come through. That they were very sorry. All that crap. I couldn't believe it, have they got the first idea what this was going to mean? Did they give a shit? Did they fuck. Well I know we sound hard, but as I've said, it's for the best, and that's it. That's all there is to it.'

Chase cupped both his hands and placed them over his mouth and nose, breathing through the space between his fingers, in a loud exaggerated fashion. He sighed.

'Can you show me where the baby was sleeping?'

'Yeah sure.'

Paul stood up. The detectives did likewise. Chase motioned to Ferrigno to sit back down. 'You stop here a minute, mate, will you?'

Ferrigno looked puzzled, but complied, still feeling ill-at-ease with the distraught mother who was now his sole companion.

The bedroom was small, but tidy. There was nothing much in it other than the cot in the centre of the room and a Moses basket propped against the wall and some baby clothes piled neatly on top of a pine dressing table. It was undoubtedly the cleanest room in the house. A mobile was descending from the ceiling above the cot. Sheep and cows and clouds. Only the baby was missing. He peered into the cot. There was no sign of blood or other obvious signs of violence. No vomit. No indentation in the sheets. In fact the cot was bare, bereft of anything whatsoever. The scent of the baby was still in the air. Scenes of crime would do their examination in the fullness of time.

Chase dwelt over the empty cot for some time, lost in his thoughts as Saunders stood behind him. Saunders spoke first.

'Difficult to know how to say it, isn't it?'

'Sorry, say what? What do you mean?'

'Look. I know you have to take me to the station. Can you keep Mary out of it? It's nowt to do with her. She knows bugger all, my duck.'

Chase held his gaze at the cot. 'Sorry, Paul, she'll have to come as well.'

'There's no need, it's...'

Chase spun around and raised the palm of his hand as if stopping traffic.

'Shut up, Paul. Just keep your own council. We're talking serious shit here. So let's just get down to the nick and then take it from there, understand?'

He shrugged. 'Fair enough.'

Chase organised the patrol car to collect them. He arranged for Ferrigno to take Mr and Mrs Saunders along with the constable to the station. He would drive the CID car back. He had to call in somewhere on the way.

Andy Chase had arranged for an experienced female DC to take the lead and interview Mrs Saunders. He had told her not to labour any points too much, but to try and get as detailed an account as possible to be able to use as a working contrast with whatever, if anything, Paul Saunders would have to say about the fateful night.

There had been a protracted technical discussion about whether they should actually arrest the two parents, the father in particular. It was a difficult one to call. The three small marks visible underneath the cheek of the baby were the only tenable evidence of foul play. Indeed they were the crux of the whole investigation. They were not categoric evidence, nor did they show who might have caused them. However, there was the scenes of crime examination to wait for, the check with the hospital, the house-to-house enquiries that were ongoing and the time restraint of an arrest ie; twenty four hours, to consider. It would also mean putting the distraught parents into a cell. This was a lesser consideration. They were police officers not social workers, but having said that Chase felt it better to start soft and see what happened from there. The snag was that if the investigation did not reveal anything further, the law was quite clear that one cannot just choose to arrest someone when it is convenient tactically. If there was sufficient evidence to arrest at this stage, he should arrest immediately. If he did not make this decision he would have to wait for some other piece of evidence to enhance the current level of suspicion, to then place them in custody at a later time. It was problematical that if Saunders decided he wanted to leave the station he could, in theory, merely get up and go. They had no right to arrest him just to prevent him from doing so. The law did however state that an officer should arrest only if it was 'necessary'. Chase decided to nick him if he did leave and work out why afterwards. This was a dangerous game to play. He could well be punished for his compassion should it happen. But what the hell.

Paul Saunders leaned with both elbows on the table in front of him. His greasy hair and baggy blue tee shirt had clearly adorned him since the tragedy occurred and there was a smell of body odour permeating the windowless interview room.

Ferrigno went through the obligatory instructions as soon as the tape machine had finished its introductory loud and sustained bleep. Saunder's solicitor sat next to his client scribbling notes, his balding head glistening with a film of sweat, the heat and the charged atmosphere undoubtedly contributing to his perspiration.

210

'You are not under arrest, you have the right to free legal advice, which you have undertaken and you may leave at any time. Do you understand?'

Saunders nodded.

'Can you please answer, Paul, I have seen you nod, but if you can try to answer verbally in order that the tape can pick it up.'

'Sorry, yes, I understand, my solicitor told me that as well.'

'I must tell you that you do not have to say anything, but it may harm your defence if you do not mention when questioned, something which you later rely on in Court. Anything you do say may be given in evidence.'

Saunders raised his head. 'Does this mean that I will definitely go to Court?'

His solicitor was quick to answer. 'No, Mr Saunders, it is something the police must tell you. In other words whatever you say can be given as evidence and it's no good not mentioning anything today and then suddenly saying in a Court, if it ever got to Court, that something else happened. Because if you do then the Court can draw an inference from that.'

Ferrigno stared at Saunders. 'Does that make sense to you Paul?'

'Yeah, I'm with you, it's all a bit strange, that's all.'

Ferrigno glanced at his Sergeant. They had agreed that the handsome young DC should lead the questioning with Chase jumping in with any salient points.

Ferrigno smiled, and leaned back in his chair. 'Can you tell us, Paul, and I know this will be distressing, so take your time, in your own words exactly what happened last night.'

Saunders looked over at his solicitor.

Ferrigno tried to be understanding. 'Take your time, there's no rush. Just cast your mind back to last night and what you were doing, Paul.' Saunders shuffled forward in his chair and said. 'No comment.'

Ferrigno did his best not to appear too concerned by

this stance. It was often the case. The right to silence applied in practical terms. It was just as obstructive to get a no comment interview. The solicitors knew it may cause the defence problems at Court, but the police had to get enough evidence to get the damn thing to Court in the first place, so it was usually worth sticking it out unless there was quite a bit of evidence in the first place.

'Who put the baby to bed?'

'No comment.'

'Was it you, Paul, or your wife?'

'No comment.'

'Was anybody else at the house when the baby was put to bed, did you have any visitors?'

Saunders gazed at the desk in front of him. 'No comment, look I don't want to appear...' His solicitor jumped in.

'It's alright, Paul, you do not have to say anything, the police have told you that themselves.'

Saunders nodded.

Ferrigno smiled benignly at the solicitor who mirrored his gaze. He continued. He would treat each no comment response as if Paul had given an answer, giving him time to actually form the image of the answer in his mind, even if he did not actually say it.

'It was you who found the baby dead, wasn't it, Paul?'

A pause. 'No comment.'

Ferrigno tried a different tack. 'I'm sorry, Paul I keep saying "the baby", what was her name, again?'

'Sal...' Saunders began his reply at the same time as his solicitor commented; 'Look Mr Ferrigno, I am sure you have the child's name in your file, so can I suggest that you refer to it.'

The solicitor was well versed in many of the tactics used by the police to get a client talking. He had been around long enough. Ferrigno continued, ignoring the solicitor.

'Thank you, Paul, Sally. Yes, that's it. A nice name.' He shook his head. 'This is all so tragic, it really is. I want you

212

to know Paul that some of the questions we have to ask are necessary, but not pleasant. It's just the way it is, I'm afraid.'

Saunders nodded.

Chase spoke for the first time. 'You told me at the house, Paul, that you 'looked in' on Sally. Can you explain to me exactly what that entailed?'

Saunders looked up at the Detective Sergeant. There was something about Chase that bothered him. Something he couldn't quite put his finger on. In his haze of pressure and grief, it was Chase who was impacting on him.

'I just put my head around the door, that's all.'

'Was she lying still?'

'Yes, she...'

The solicitor wouldn't let a second answer go by. 'Sergeant I'm not sure where this is leading.'

Chase took a cigarette packet out of his shirt pocket, and he pulled out a cigarette. He tapped it on the side of the pack and leaned back, averting his gaze from the cigarette to the balding solicitor.

'I will tell you where it is leading. Your representation of the client Mr Saunders is verging on being obstructive and I must warn you that if it continues I shall have no other option but to have you removed and replaced with somebody else.'

The solicitor threw his pad on the desk.

'Sergeant Chase, I have a duty to...'

Chase cut him short. 'Look, let's not pussyfoot around here. You have a duty to advise your client, sure, but I have a duty to put questions to him. You are preventing that process. We have told him he doesn't have to say anything, he knows his rights, so let us get on with it shall we?'

Chase had nothing to lose, the guy wasn't answering questions so he might as well let the solicitor have both barrels; plays him at his own game. The brief knew that if he was replaced, a letter would be sent to the Law Society and that could mean grief to him, particularly in such a sensitive case.

The solicitor tutted and began animatedly scribbling on his pad which he had retrieved from the desk in front of him.

Chase continued talking to Saunders.

'Paul, my colleague has pointed out that there are a few awkward questions we have to ask you. The sooner we do that, the sooner the interview will be concluded. So let's get down to the nitty gritty, shall we?'

Saunders nodded. 'Can I have a cigarette?'

'Sure.' Chase reached for his packet but the solicitor beat him to the draw and passed him a fresh packet.

Chase continued. 'Paul, did you want this baby?'

Solicitor; 'You do not have to answer that question.'

'Yes, I did want it, we both wanted it, that's the truth.'

'Okay. Had you been trying long?'

'You do not have to answer that question.'

'A while, six or seven months I guess. We were pleased, you know when we found out, Mary especially.'

Chase, had by now totally blocked out the solicitor. 'Was the marriage going well? You know sometimes, people think that having a baby can, you know, make things better?'

'You do not have to answer that question.'

'No the marrige was okay, we had the normal arguments like everybody else, but we were alright, she's a good wife.'

'Have you ever hit her, you know, Mary, ever given her a slap? A lot of men do.'

'I advise you not to answer that question.'

Saunders almost grinned. He shook his head. 'No, never, I'm not like that. I don't like falling out, arguments, all that sort of thing, it's just not me.'

Chase blew a cloud of smoke into the air which mingled with the billow emanating from Saunders. 'What about Mary, has she got a temper?'

'I advise you not to answer that question.'

'Yes, a bit, but not with Sally, she loved her, she did,

214

loved her to bits.'

Chase nodded his head. Time to go for the jugular. 'Right, okay. Who killed the baby, Paul? You or Mary?'

'I strongly advise you against answering that question, Mr Saunders.'

Saunders met Chase's gaze. 'It wasn't Mary. I think you know that don't you?'

Chase offered a warm smile. 'It doesn't matter what I think or what I know, Paul. So you killed her, then?'

'Do not answer that question.'

Saunders flicked some ash into the metal bin at his side. There was no answer. Any silence over seven seconds becomes superfluous psychologically. Chase let it run its full course.

'Nobody is judging you, Paul, to have the news that you had, to learn that Sally was a spastic, that must be horrendous.'

'That's true, you've no idea, what the...'

Chase interrupted. '...implications are. Maybe we don't know, and now you'll never know will you Paul? Because you did it, didn't you?'

'These are leading questions Sergeant.'

Chase ignored the comment and continued.

'Ever heard the expression, a crime of passion, Paul? Maybe it was the right thing to do, who can be the judge of that, unless they have lived through what you've had to.'

'I advise you not to answer that question.'

Saunders was staring into space. 'Nobody can tell, nobody understands what that news meant to us.'

He was almost there. Chase followed up.

The solicitor sensed it. 'I want another consultation with my client.'

Chase leaned back. He had no choice. The law was clear. 'Do you want another consultation, Paul?'

Saunders looked at his solicitor who nodded.

'I think I better had. I'm sorry.'

Chase smiled, and held eye contact with the suspect.

215

'I've heard enough. DC Ferrigno. Stop the tape.'

It was 15 minutes before they resumed. Saunders had been schooled during the break. He was to answer no more questions.

And so the interview continued in a similar vein. Every time that the officer managed to elicit a response, it was smashed down by the well-trained solicitor, with either the answer to the question or an 'I advise you to remain silent'. Every now and then the solicitor would exaggerate a sigh or tut, or query the relevance of the question.

The bright red digit on the tape machine clock displayed 32 minutes as DS Chase excused himself.

'DS Chase leaving the interview room, the time is now 5:37 with the interview room clock.'

Ferrigno, not for the first time that day, appeared puzzled at the actions of his DS.

No sooner had he left the room, than he returned, clutching a small brown paper bag, bearing an exhibit label.

Had it been a saloon in the old west, the pianist would have stopped playing.

Chase took over the interview, breaking the silence. 'I have in this bag something that may be crucial to our investigation, and more importantly to you, Mr Saunders. I must say that I am puzzled by your responses, and I am surprised you haven't mentioned it before. Chris has explained to you about the bruising to Sally's cheek, and questioned how the bruising got there. Could this be the reason?'

He produced a baby's rattle. It was turquoise in colour and had hard plastic serrated edges.

'What...'

The solicitor touched Saunders' arm to silence him.

Chase continued. His DC's mouth wide open, agog.

'I retrieved this from the cot when you took me upstairs this morning. Is it fair to say that this could have caused the bruising if the baby had inadvertently rolled on to it?'

Saunders stared at the DS. It began to dawn on him what the DS was doing. A tear rolled down his cheek. 'Yeah, thank you. Thanks... thanks a lot.' He broke down crying into the crook of his elbow which he rested on the wooden table.

Ferrigno stood with his Sergeant in the front living room of Chase's house. He was still thoroughly fed up with the day's events and all the way over to Andy's house he had said what a lucky bastard Saunders was and how he still wasn't happy with it. Chase had suggested that in the light of other evidence the Coroner would be forced to make a judgement of accidental death. Ferrigno had never been to the Chase residence before. He felt a little awkward, despite the friendliness of Chase's, blonde, attractive wife, Laura, who fussed around them. She supplied them with drinks and a warm smile.

Chase spoke. 'Where's the little 'un?'

'He's playing out in the garden.'

'We'll come out in a minute.'

She smiled. 'Oh, boys talk is it?'

'Go on bugger off and play with your son, before I give you a good hiding.'

'Promises, promises.'

Ferrigno shook his head as he clutched his cold beer. 'I can't believe that you never mentioned that rattle to me. I mean what was the point of going through all that crap, when he had got a way out and what's more you knew all about it?'

Chase smiled. 'You've got a bit to learn about life yet, me duck.'

Ferrigno interrupted. 'Oh, hold on a minute and I'll start swinging the lantern.'

Chase grinned. 'Cheeky git. Anyway it was good experience for you, wasn't it? I wanted to see how he coped, to be as sure as I could, get a feel of him. Make sure I was certain about him.'

'Well he didn't say a fat bloody lot did he?'

217

'No. But that was his brief wasn't it, not him? There were never going to be any winners with this one, Chris. He's got to live with this tragedy for the rest of his life. Poor bleeder. It's another case for us tomorrow, someone else's life to deal with.'

Ferrigno wiped some beer from his lip, the result of an overzealous swig of beer to vanquish the thirst that the hot summer's day had created. 'I suppose so, Andy. He was a bit of a toe-rag though wasn't he? Saunders I mean. It wouldn't have been much of a loss to society if he'd been sent down, now would it?'

It was Chase's turn to shake his head. 'Oh Christ. He was alright man, bloody hell. The bloke was skint, in the mire, living in the middle of a shit hole.' He took a drink from his can. 'There is an old Indian saying, mate, "never criticise your neighbour until you have walked a mile in his moccasins".'

'Bloody hell, Andy, you steady on. You'll be quoting the bloody Bible to me next.'

Chase slapped his colleague's shoulder. 'I'm sorry. Come on, let's join Laura on the patio.'

It wasn't like an ordinary wheel chair. More like a metal frame. The boy inside it looked around seven years old. His face was covered in phlegm and saliva and he thrashed around grunting and jerking. Only the straps over his shoulders and around his waist prevented him from tipping out onto the floor. The boy seemed to recognise his father as he bent to kiss his hair because the child urinated into his trousers. A smile flickered briefly across the lad's face before a painful grimace returned, defeating his moment of joy.

Chase turned to Ferrigno who was rooted to the spot.

'You've not met my son, have you?'

Chase spun the wheelchair around to face Chris. He stroked the boy's head as he spoke to him. 'Tony, this is Chris Ferrigno, ace detective, fine fellow, and all round good egg. However, he does still have a bit of living to do.'

Ferrigno stood there, his mouth agape, ashamed,

218

embarrassed, confused. He slowly began to realise what the last eight hours had all been about. He blurted out, 'Hold on a minute... Jesus Christ... So the cot...' He stopped himself and took hold of Chase's arm leading him to one side, now speaking in a whisper. 'So the cot was empty all the time then? That's why you wanted to go upstairs alone, why you came back to the nick on your own. You bought the rattle yourself didn't you? Andy that is wrong, this is serious shit, you just can't do that sort of thing.'

Chase looked tired. He reached for a cigarette and took his time in lighting it.

'Do you believe that all life is precious, Andy?'

He had a quick response. 'Yes of course, it is.'

Chase blew out some smoke. The crows' feet around his eyes enlivened an embittered smile. 'Come on then.'

'Come where?'

'Come on, let me tie YOU to the chair. Precious, my arse! Come on! Let me watch you piss youself, shit yourself. Oh it's so precious, isn't it? Let me watch YOUR eyes pleading with me to ease the pain. Let me riddle you with pain, let me humiliate you. Come and let strangers stare at you, let them show compassion to you for a minute, for five minutes, for an hour, then watch them bugger off into the sunset shaking their heads. Come on, what are you waiting for?'

Ferrigno had fallen quiet. Chase's wife came over and held her husband's hand tightly. Tears were visible.

'Do you know what shame is, Chris?'

'Andy, I...'

'Let me explain something to you, Chris. Shame is holding a pillow over your own son's mouth, wanting him to die, but not having the guts to see it through. Watching your own small child try so damned hard not to struggle; desperate to try to make it easier for me, but still I can't do it. Still I fail him.'

Chris felt himself shaking his head. 'Andy. I didn't know. I'm sorry, mate...'

219

Andy took a deep breath. He knew he had said too much. 'No, I'm sorry, pal, I shouldn't say these things to you, you're embarrassed, it's wrong of me. Look forget it, let's have a beer.'

They had reached the door before Andy spoke again. 'And just to put your mind at rest, there was a rattle in the cot.'

'I don't give a shit, Andy, but if you say so, that's fine by me.'

'There was a rattle all right. The fucking hinges were loose!'

An Exile's Tale

Brendan Murphy

My daughter speaks like an English girl. And after such a
short time. I sit here, in this thin sunlight, where the free
newspaper is easier to read, and smoke near the open window. More and more I need this time to myself. More and
more she gives it to me. I am conscious of my hands which
hold the newspaper, wonder at their slight swelling, at
how seldom they now seem to be without bandage or
elastoplast. My left thumb is still darkened and yellowing
where a piece of tubing fell on it. It saddens me to see it so.
Once my wife, Grainne, took my two hands and kissed
them as she admired some wood carving I had done. She
said, 'The hands of a craftsman, Frank.' A craftsman?
Now they use a pick and carry heavy concrete piping
around.

My daughter shuffles back in in her flip-flops. She is
wearing that Indian-type dress she always puts on after
she has had her bath. I know this means she will study for
two hours now and then go out with her friends. The first
job I had here was laying the tarmac and we had to live in
a caravan for nigh on three months. Pat hated it so much
but it was just behind that nice school. That's how she
started going there. She got to like the teachers. She made
her friends quickly.

'Dinner will be ready in half an hour. I want to ring
Elspeth.'

'I'm just after making a cup of tea.'

'I wish you wouldn't say "after making". It's an
Irishism. The English say, "I've just made a cup of tea."'

'Is Elspeth the horsey one?'

'Daddy, don't be a bore.'

It's on the phone that Pat sounds most English. She
tells her friend Elspeth that she can't 'muck out' on Saturday. She says it like 'mack aut'. I'm not sure what 'muck

221

out' means exactly. Elspeth has horses. It's got something to do with horses. She can't 'muck out' on Saturday because her Aunt Brigid is coming. Pat has developed a way of saying 'Aunt Brigid' with mock desperation. She raises her eyes when she says it. Elspeth can't be allowed to meet Aunt Brigid. My sister. The woman who risked her life for me. Aunt Brigid who sings quite loudly sometimes after a few whiskeys.

When Brigid came at Christmas she began to sing in the club. Pat reddened and looked daggers at me. Like it was all my fault.

My wild Irish rose
The sweetest flower that grows.

Some people were frowning and whispering but a man who wore a black sweater and a brightly coloured waistcoat looked pleased. He had a mop of white curly hair and winked at me. When Pat saw this she threw down a box of matches beside her glass and drew deeply on her cigarette. 'God, how we fulfil the English's expectations of us! More Irish malarkey! Can't you stop her, daddy?' And then she goes, 'It's so vulgar... and trite.'

I did not know what 'trite' meant.

My daughter has a boyfriend. Trevor. From Attenborough. His father is a solicitor. Trevor dresses like a paddy with holes in his jeans and has lank, greasy hair. Grainne would have hated that. He sometimes smells of cannabis but I like him. He calls me Frankie. I never got Frankie before, always Frank. Trevor's accent is that of a British officer. I saw a major killed in Belfast. In Belfast everybody has a claim to fame. That was mine. It happened not far from where Fintan McCoy and I were standing chatting. The major was standing giving instructions to a group of Brits. They were running round supervising a clear-up Op after an explosion when the sniper got him. One shot. He fell like a stone. It was quiet and clinical, no death sounds. No one noticed for a while. Everyone was trying to locate the source of the shot. We moved away in case we got picked up. He looked quite a decent sort. He wore a cravat which peeped up over his uniform.

Grainne and I had an argument over it when I said that it wasn't right he had to die, that he'd looked a decent sort. She said he was just another name to add to the list. She said British soldiers had been dying in Ireland since the fourteenth century. Said not one of them would have died if they'd stayed in their own country.

That night our lovemaking was strained. I could tell she didn't want me. Our argument over the major had soured us. There seemed no way back. We went through with it. I sensed she was edgy and impatient for it to be over. No words were spoken. Afterwards she got out of bed and chain-smoked while she watched the late movie on TV. I lay there naked, feeling alone. Cheapened. In later days I felt the nagging of the pain and aggravation of that night, when our coldness towards each other pressed on me more than the death of the major. What was his name? I would wonder. Where had he been from? How would you ever go about telling his wife, his father, his children that the failure of our lovemaking that night had rankled with us more than his death?

When did Grainne and I stop being lovers? She hadn't always been cold and unfeeling. I had held her as she wept when the first soldier was killed in Belfast in the early days of the Troubles. February 1970. So long ago now but his name I know I'll never forget. Gunner Curtis. Grainne said, God help his mother — just a boy. That night and all winter with the house full of bitter cold we made love in front of the fire and she would keep me inside her as long as she could, pressing me tight to her while the stutter of automatic gunfire echoed across the city.

My daughter is a reader. She has her own room. I sleep in here. The sofa becomes my bed. Her room is like a library, brimful of books. Twice I have built her shelves and now she says she needs more and points to the pile of books in the corner. Once I made a mistake and bought her a book.

Last Christmas. The man in the shop said everyone was reading it. On the back it said it was 'undoubtedly the love story of the year'. I could see she was disappointed though she tried to hide it. I know she has never opened it. She is reading a thick book with very small type. Nine hundred and twenty six pages. I can't remember its name. She plays her flute in her room and sometimes when her door is open it drifts out here. It is music which makes me feel at peace. I recognise the pieces and know the names now, but can't put name to music: Bach, Haydn, Mozart. When she is not here I play my own double cassette, 'Songs of Ireland — Past and Present'.

My daughter is going to Oxford. Her form tutor stared at me during the parents' evening over those fancy half-glasses perched on her nose. She had a mole at the side of her mouth and wore too much make-up. The room was unheated, the classroom chair was uncomfortable. I had a cold and was wheezing and coughing every few minutes. She looked at me in a very peculiar way even though I'd put on my Sunday suit and shaved for the second time that day.

'She's definite Oxbridge material. She could do either History or English Literature.'

'She takes it after her mother. Her mother's a very intelligent woman. Very well read she was.'

'Oh, I didn't know, is she — ?'

'Oh no, we've... she still lives in Belfast... separated but.'

'Trish — Pat — well, she gets Trish here you see, well, Trish seems very happy with us. Well adjusted. She settled in very quickly. Intelligent girl. Good worker.'

The teacher seemed to be making a great effort to stop staring at me. I knew that she would be wondering to herself if I was Pat's real father. Pat is so blonde and is tall and elegant, every day more and more like her mother. I am dark and short, thick set — squat, Grainne used to say. I know I am not handsome and my hands are scarred and calloused now. The teacher's face was all screwed up as she leaned towards me to interpret my Belfast accent. I remember thinking that I'd like the interview to have had sub-titles like the foreign pictures on TV. 'Sorry?' she said. I repeated myself as slowly and as clearly as I could. Maybe it was the cold in my head. After a while she gave up and just spoke about how well Pat had done in the Spring examinations. Pat learned the fancy accent not from the nuns at school but from her mother's poetry recitations. For all her Republican philosophy Grainne was still a great one for what she called 'the rounded English vowel sound, clearly enunciated'. Pat rarely asks about her. It's as if she died way back in the dim past and we had a pact to leave her behind the scrim of fading memories and forget her.

'Jesus, how I hate that woman!' Pat shouted at me one night when she caught me brooding, close to tears.

'Don't call your mother "that woman"!'

And yet, when I see the flash of anger in her eyes, I see Grainne.

My daughter is ashamed of being Irish. She says she hates the way my world has become the world of paddies, of All-Ireland Hurling Finals and pints of Guinness in Carlton, an Irish whore in St Ann's, Father Michael hearing confessions at Easter. She calls it 'reverting to type'. Says I should date. Said it real Yankee. 'You should date, daddy. Proper dates'. She doesn't understand. I did tell her I couldn't have another woman — properly like — while her mother was alive. Pat was doing so well at her school in Belfast. That's where she was that afternoon I surprised Grainne, the afternoon I came home early from work after I'd taken ill. It was easy working for Mister Stevens. He knew I was a good worker. Twenty years I'd worked for him. If I was complaining, I must be ill. He didn't hesitate to ring a taxi right away, said I looked dreadful, that the flu bug had finally got even me. As I sat in the back of the cab I thought to myself: maybe Grainne will be at home, maybe she'll make hot whiskeys and come to bed with me. It made me aroused and I began to feel better.

But I find them in the kitchen. Grainne, Sean O'Dowd, young Mattie McGrath, the singer, who'd been in the 'Mikado' with our Pat. They mustn't have heard me close the front door. I am among them, standing in the kitchen before they notice me. They are drinking tea and Grainne has a piece of paper in her hand and is reading to the other two. They are shifty-looking, embarrassed. My first thought is: this is the feeling of betrayal, what it's like when you catch your wife in bed with another man. They look so uncomfortable, pathetic. Even Grainne — as if it isn't her house either. Then she glances over towards the table.

'What's wrong, Frank? You're home early.'

'I felt poorly. Mister Stevens sent me home in a taxi. Thought it might be the flu. What's this then?'

I walk over to the table. I know immediately it is a Kalashnikov when Sean O'Dowd moves his big arse away from the table from where he is trying to screen it from me. The light gives it an ominous sheen and I think how sleek and elegant it looks. It lies proud on brown sacking, like a piece of modern sculpture against the background of the white formica table top. There are three pieces of string on the table, a milk bottle and dried-up tea bags on the brown-stained saucer.

'We're off then,' goes O'Dowd. He wraps the sacking round the rifle and ties the cord carefully round the outside, like he's preparing the presents on Christmas Eve. Mattie McGrath has a bulging Man U shoulder bag. I wonder if his school books are inside as well as the ammunition. *Modern Europe, 1815–1939. Senior Mathematics. The Ambleside Book of Verse*. Grainne puts on her old anorak, fluffs her hair and says, 'I'm going too. Make yourself a cup of coffee.'

'That thing's not coming back in here.'

'Go and have your tea with Brigid if you don't want to be here when we come back,' she goes. 'Pat's going to stay

226

with her friend for the night after school.'

'No, listen to me, Grainne. No. No. Talk and poems and songs in pubs are one thing, but I'm not going to let our house be used for guns or —'

'We're off, love. That's a terrible cold. Put a wee nip in your coffee. There are aspirins in the cupboard.'

The other two sidle out first. She stands for a moment, looking back at me and smiling. That makes it harder for me. The only other thing she says is, 'Frank, love, you can't stand back from the people's struggle for ever, you know.' Then she sashays out. The door clicks shut behind her.

I bolted the back door and put the snib up on the front. Then I sat on the sofa in the front room, twisted round so that I could have a permanent look-out. My nausea had gone but I was shivering and felt miserable. I knew I should have made that coffee but I couldn't move. I kept remembering things about Grainne, or not so much remembering things, events, but just seeing pictures of her. In the club Grainne never sang. Brigid was the singer in our family. Every Irish song you could ever have heard of, our Brigid could get up and sing it, every word. Grainne recited. She was the only one in the club who did. There was never any shortage of singers on a Saturday night but Grainne always had a great memory and she could learn poems off by heart. I loved the burr of her voice, the way she smiled and then would change suddenly, becoming very serious before she began to recite.

I heard her sing only once. On our honeymoon. It was a peculiar, low, rasping voice where she never got the top notes quite right. She lay back in the rowing boat and pushed her white sun hat down over her eyes.

As I came down through Dublin city at the hour of twelve at night,

Who should I see but a Spanish lady washing her feet by the candle light.

She used to stand still on the stage till the noise had ceased. There was always silence for Grainne. She'd hold

227

the microphone just below her chin in her right hand, with her head bowed and the other arm limp by her side. Then she would look straight down at the audience.

'There are many well-known poems about the revolutionary struggle in Ireland. In this one the famous poet, W.B. Yeats, reminds us that victory and freedom can only be won at the cost of suffering and our own sacrifice, our own blood... "The Rose Tree" by W.B. Yeats...

O words are lightly spoken,
Said Pearse to Connolly...'

I must have fallen asleep, even though I was cold, for when I woke the street lights were on and the sodium glow from the lamp outside the house made our front room look like a stage set. My immediate thought was that I had heard shooting but I didn't know if I had been dreaming or not. There was that waking taste in my mouth and my head ached. What if someone had died as I slept: What if it had been Grainne herself? Or O'Dowd? Or Mattie McGrath, still a schoolboy? Or some young British soldier who never asked to be here in the first place?

I didn't move when I heard the car draw up. In the street light I could see Grainne and McGrath get out of the car which was driven off immediately, the gears whining as the clutch was let out too quickly, the tyres screeching. McGrath held the rifle awkwardly under his arm and the bag hung from his shoulder. I could hear the jingle of Grainne's keys. The impatient turn as she tried to force the key.

'The bastard's locked us out.'

The bell rang and rang. I couldn't believe that she didn't have some sense that I was only six feet away from her. That I could have opened the window, leaned out and touched her hand. Her anorak hung loose and I remember she was wearing her black woollen sweater. It was tight fitting and made her breasts stand proud and her blonde hair hanging over it made her body look so inviting that I had to close my eyes because I could feel myself wanting her again, trembling and near to tears with my longing.

'Christ, Grainne, we're goin' to be nicked with this stuff. The balloon'll go up round here any minute. There'll be Brits everywhere.'

'Go down to White's wasteground and dump it there.'

'Dump it? They'd fuckin' do their nut.'

'Dump it. Do it quick. Don't hang about. Meet me in Gerry's Bar in half an hour.'

I had finally got round to making the mug of coffee in a mechanical sort of way, my hands shaking, still shivering, when the phone rang. It was Brigid. She was frantic. She called me 'brother' as she always did when she thought I'd done something stupid.

She goes, 'Brother, get a bag, a few things, all your money and stand at the bottom of the entry. Don't be seen. Run into the car when I park. Don't ask questions. Just move fast.'

She hung up before I could say anything and the dialling tone was a final and frightening sound. I stood like a fool holding the phone in my hand, listening, not understanding at first. I found it hard to think clearly, like the way you do when you've got the flu. I remembered that my tool bag and my carving chisels were at work. I went and got my good suit, my electric razor and tooth brush, my Post Office book, the wallet with some cash in it. I ran down the entry thinking 'I've left the lights on'. Brigid was already parked there with her engine running. I opened the door and lay on the back seat.

'For God's sake stay down, we'll probably pass them on their way to the house. O'Meara and Hagan. Top men, brother. You're no more than five minutes ahead of them.'

As I lay there I shivered with fear and desperately needed to pee. I kept my hand between my legs.

'How did you know?'

'Don't ask questions, Frank. I'm taking you to the ferry. Get the train to Nottingham, to your Aunt Pauline's. I'll take Pat to Glasgow. She'll want to join you later. She won't mind England. She's always been a bit on

229

the posh side has our Pat.'

'Did Grainne set me up, Brigid? Was it her? My own wife. I have to know.'

'You don't have to know anything brother,' she goes. 'Just thank God you've got away. Kalashnikovs don't grow on trees, you know. The Brits got it and young McGrath too.'

My daughter will soon leave me. Sometimes the way she sits and stares into space with a book lying on her lap, with her blonde hair and her black silk blouse, I'm disturbed how alike her mother she is. The way she'll take a hair and stare at it and then brush the blouse with the back of her fingers.

She makes a face at the talk of ceasefires, of peace processes, of new dawns. For her and for me it is all over, she says.

I am her last link with Ireland. She will never return to Belfast. She never wants to see Grainne again. She says she will die of shame if anyone here finds out that her mother is a terrorist.

After tea she will once more go to her room and her books and her music. I will snooze in the dying sun that is still coming in through the window. When she goes out with Trevor and her friends I will have an early night. And before I sleep I will say a prayer for her mother who recited poems about Ireland, taught my daughter to talk posh, joined the people's struggle and once loved me.

Character Witness
Frank Palmer

'You are Phillip Todd and you are a chief superintendent.'

No inflection lifts the last syllable so it comes out as more of a statement than a question.

Advocates always open their examinations-in-chief as though you're a patient recovering a lost memory. One of these days some witness is going to cause total confusion in court by replying, 'Never heard of him, mate.'

Today is not that day. My side's mouthpiece is so young and seems so nervous that to add to his discomfiture would only alienate the jury. For reputation's sake I need the right result in this case. Besides, I've just sworn to tell the truth. 'Yes' is the only truthful answer. I don't add a patronizing 'Sir'.

The judge, a middle-aged woman wearing the pale blue of civil courts, looks to my left, addressing the jury in the fashion of a schoolmistress.

'This is the witness,' she says, waving a slender hand in my direction, 'over whom there was some difficulty this morning when he was otherwise engaged giving evidence in another court.'

Actually, I was testifying at a private disciplinary hearing back at HQ against a boozy inspector who groped a clerk. Since the clerk was male and the good name of the force is involved here, I'll not correct her.

She had, she recalls, agreed to an application that my evidence for the plaintiff, the Regional Police Authority, could be heard after the defendants, the Crime Writers' Association, had closed their case.

'Those of you who have been taking notes...' With the long-windedness of so many jumped-up judges, she goes to complicated lengths to make the simple suggestion that what they are about to hear from me this afternoon should be read as being given in evidence this morning.

231

It gives me time to look down on and size up the jury sitting in three rows in their box next to me. They are equally divided by sex. Somewhat out of fashion these days, they are uniform in smartness of appearance.

I peg them as mainly middle-class and am not sure whether that's good or bad. Jurors from working-class backgrounds have always voted for the underdog, given half the chance. A mate of mine in a county further north reckons he hasn't had a conviction since the miners' strike.

Ever since radical lawyers and a meddling media began the process of demystifying the British legal system with that welter of miscarriage of justice cases, middle-class jurors have taken some convincing, too.

There are two black faces among them. One is thumbing through a red exercise book, presumably looking for a gap she sensibly left in her notes this morning. The other is gazing yearningly beyond the packed public gallery to a big black clock high on a cream wall. Its hands are at two-twenty.

Having finished her lecture, the judge looks back at me, promptly demoting me. 'Superintendent, you are aware that this is a case of alleged defamation, a civil matter...'

'Yes,' I interject, immediately deciding she merits an added 'Ma'am'.

'...and, as such we are dealing here with the balance of probabilities, not with proof beyond reasonable doubt as in the criminal cases in which you so often appear.'

Having tried and failed to cut her short, I'm not going to prolong the boredom of the clock-watching member of the jury by explaining it's some years since I stood in the witness box of the much bigger criminal court across the foyer giving evidence against striking miners accused of riot. Nor am I going to reveal that all were acquitted. If it's right that juries shouldn't know of the previous convictions of the accused, then, in my view, they have no claim to know about the past failures of the accuser, either.

Billed as a show trial by civil liberties groups, even that

232

case didn't attract this sort of turn out. Every seat behind black wrought iron railings of balconies on three sides has been taken. Both rows of the Press bench at right angles to the jury box are filled. Botham v. Khan failed to pull this size of crowd down the Strand.

'Yes, ma'am,' I repeat.

She looks at me doubtfully, not sure that I've fully understood, making me feel like the dunce of the class.

Now she nods briskly at the Regional Police Authority's boyish-faced brief to tell him to proceed.

He does so, reading in a voice that owes nothing to elocution lessons from a pack of white postcards on which he's clearly drafted his questions. 'You've been a police officer for ...'

I'm half expecting another one of those 'welcome back from amnesia' questions, also beloved by TV news presenters ('You are at so and so,' just in case the on-the-spot reporter has forgotten.)

Abruptly he looks up, pleadingly '...how long?'

'Twenty years,' I say, suspecting he can't decipher his own handwriting.

He resumes reading. 'During which time you have not only investigated several major crimes but been badly wounded in the leg in the course of your duty?'

Pointlessly, he nods at the front of the solid oak witness box behind which my gammy right leg is, like most of the rest of me, clad in midnight blue mohair, my Sunday best for this special occasion.

Should have created a bit of sympathy by putting on a more pronounced limp when I climbed the two steps up here, I realise, replying with a modest nod.

'Please answer yes or no,' says the judge sternly.

'Yes, ma'am.'

I appear to have upset the old crow, because she's not finished with me yet, motioning with a sweep of a hand to three girls with their heads down over notebooks with wire spines. They are sitting in the well of the court at a huge polished table shared by my questioner and an age-

233

ing man who is thumbing through a book from two stacks in front of him.

'Sorry,' I say to their bowed heads.

My brief again, his head down over his cards: 'And you have strong views on the way the defendants in this action have depicted your force and, indeed, this city as a whole over recent years?'

'Yes, indeed...'

'In what way?' The advocate is not only abandoning his cards, tossing them on to the table, but me, too. Police witnesses like to be guided, only having to answer 'yes' and 'no', giving nothing away for the opposition to latch on to. In the trials where I've previously testified, judges and juries want facts, proof, not opinions.

This old crow of a judge is right. This is not my sort of case.

Well, I begin slowly, crime writers seem to have bred and multiplied in these parts in the Nineties. Sadly, they are no longer content to make up picture postcard villages and let little old ladies run from rose-covered cottage to haunted vicarage solving crimes.

They use real locations, describe in great detail land-marks, hotels and pubs I know well. Far more ethically questionable and legally dangerous, some draw on real life characters, particularly police officers, with very little or no disguise.

They are invariably depicted as dunderheads, the sole purpose being to make their own invented main character look good by comparison. 'You know, the on-the-road mav-erick and his resentment against chairbound authority, the old cliché.'

Into my stride now, I nail the lie that major crimes are solved by one inspired middle-ranker and his sidekick when the truth is that success comes through team work and painstaking routine.

Well warmed up, I add, 'Even the so-called heroes of their pieces frequently go down blind alleys in pursuit of red herrings, consuming time and paper merely to create a build-up of tension for the climax.'

At the word 'climax' two females in the subdued light of public balcony snigger, heads close together.

Even more off-putting one of the jurors is absently scratching something a nasty yellow (drippings from lunchtime junk food, I presume) off his blue striped tie.

I decide to play on the old school tie. 'It's very bad for morale in a fine force in which I am proud to serve.'

The juror, sitting on the front row nearest the judge's bench, the spot usually taken by the foreman, goes on picking at his tie, not really listening.

Unnerved, I have dried up. My side's man helps me out. 'What about the effects on the city?'

At this the ageing man next to him rises wearily from behind his piles of books. 'Is this germane?' he asks pompously.

Two members of the jury look at each other quizzically, as if they have never heard the word before.

The judge throws herself against the thick leather backing of her high, heavy chair. Seated there, plush red curtains and marble columns behind, lamps on golden twists either side, she looks like a petulant queen.

The opposition is raising a technical objection that the issue of the effects on trade in the city is a problem for the City Council who are not joined in the action. 'A mere police officer,' he adds sneeringly, 'is not competent to answer.'

The judge leans forward, resting her elbows on each side of her notepad on the ledge of her bench. So many judges have adopted this pose over the years that the leather on top of the ledge is holed like the arms of an old jacket.

'Evidence,' she says with a sigh, 'was heard this morning on this issue and the time to object was then, not now. Your point on relevance is not well taken at this late stage.'

He sits, crestfallen.

I nip off a gloating grin as she turns to me. 'Proceed.'

Well, I say, the way the city is forever being publicised as full of homicidal maniacs who took weeks to capture could not be good for the tourist business.

There's coughing and rustling of street coats and papers. The public galleries are becoming restive, having heard it all before, I reason.

'Thank you,' says my young interrogator. Sensing torpor overcoming his audience, he perhaps wisely leaves the questions on the rest of his crib cards unasked.

Sounding as if he's watched too many Hollywood court dramas, he mumbles, 'Your witness.'

No coughing, no rustling now, as the man beside him rises as my brief sits, seesawing past each other.

He is mid-fifties, beyond pensionable age in my job. His mousey brown hair is thinning. Black framed bifocals are too big for a small, creased face, altogether an unimpressive figure.

'You'll appreciate, Mr Todd...' His accent is flat and local, unlike most barristers '...that I represent the Crime Writers' Association in this matter?'

I nod, then follow up immediately with, 'Yes.' No 'Sir' for him either, I decide.

'Tell me...' A sugary smile. '...do you read crime novels?'

'When I've the time.'

'And when you find time in your ultra busy life, who do you like?'

A difficult question that, and I mull for a moment, noting that the piles of books in front of him have marks in them. Their jackets are too gaudy for legal tomes.

Still smiling, he breaks the short silence. 'I don't want to embarrass you or anyone in this court so discount home produced writers. Americans, say?'

'Well, Chandler for Marlowe...' I pause again, wondering if I'm talking myself into a trap.

He seeks to encourage more with an insincere smile. 'And, this side of the Atlantic, here in Europe?'

'Simenon for Maigret, naturally.'

Surprisingly, he latches on to neither name, changing the subject and, with it, his expression to solemn. 'The fact is, isn't it, that this city was indeed — and this is a statistical fact — the most violent place in Britain?'

I relax. This is going to be easier to answer than his soft openers, all the more so since I'd researched the topic for a little speech I had to make, as a last minute substitute, at a tourism convention six months ago.

True, I concede. Home Office figures had once put the city at the top of the league table for offences against the person, attracting unwelcomed national publicity.

What Fleet Street failed to grasp, I point out, was that the records had been badly distorted by the high rate of crime that had occurred in one, just one, inner city block of flats with dark, covered walkways, havens for muggers and handbag snatchers.

I tell a tale of a top tabloid writer who'd visited the city, intent on stealing the title of locally-born Alan Sillitoe's book about life in the back streets 'Saturday Night and Sunday Morning' for a feature article on a weekend of violence. Not a noteworthy crime was reported during his stay. 'No news is bad news for a journalist, so the story never appeared and the mistaken impression of the city was never corrected,' I complain.

'But the figures were official,' insists my interrogator, swaying back on his heels, a boxer being outpointed. 'The writers I represent did not make them up, manufacture them out of thin air.'

He is seeking to compel me to agree, but I'm not falling for it. 'Since the flats were pulled down,' I reply, 'the figures for muggings and other violent street crime are no more than the national average.'

One up to me, I congratulate myself.

'Yes ...' His face is wreathed in a self-satisfied smile, '...but wasn't Robin Hood the greatest local mugger of them all hereabouts and he's done no harm at all to the tourist trade, now has he?'

Not a bad counter attack, so I grudgingly grant him a

tight smile as a ripple of light laughter flows right round the three sides of the gallery.

'Ah.' He points a finger at the high pink and white ceiling. 'A titter in court.'

Head up, ignoring me completely, playing to the gallery, he begins to tell a story of an English diplomat visiting darkest Africa in our colonial days to inspect their system of justice.

'Impeccable,' he declared. 'What did you use as your model?'

'We followed all the law reports in airmail copies of *The Times*', replied the chief proudly.

'One thing puzzles me,' the diplomat goes on. 'Why every so often does a man with a feather dash round the public gallery tickling the bare bosoms of all the women spectators?'

'Because,' explains the chief, '*The Times* is always reporting that "A titter ran round the court."'

It's an old courtroom tale, but I must be the only other person here to have heard it, because the titters become a gale of happy laughter that must be flowing outside across the foyer and into the crime court beyond.

The judge smilingly chides, 'Now. Now. Let's get on with it. I must have the jury out by three-thirty if we are to complete this case today.'

The cunning old sod has been grandstanding all day, I brood.

Still playing to his captive audience he gets on with it. 'Let's not waste time on the repercussions of these books on commerce...'

This is too good to miss. 'In that regard I doubt that John Harvey's own adaption for TV of his Resnick series was helpful to the tourist trade.'

'Why so?' he asks querulously.

'It did nothing but rain cats and dogs on screen for three nights running, made us look as gloomy as Manchester.'

He fixes me with a hostile expression. 'I thought we'd

agreed to leave home-based writers out of your testimony.'

'You may have suggested that...' I gesture to the short-hand writers '...but you'll find nothing in the record to indicate that I concurred.'

'Yet we hear no criticism from you of Keith Wright's work.' With heavy sarcasm, he adds, 'Could that be because he is both a police officer and a crime writer?'

Below the belt that, but I'll respond with good humour.

'If, as I suspect, one of his bumbling senior officers is based on me, he can certainly expect no early promotion.'

I smile to myself at what's a rather nice aside, both sardonic and self deprecating. I switch off when I see that no one appears to have spotted it; too much of an in-joke.

My adversary's face has become serious again. That's your trouble, isn't it? You don't like the truth?'

'Not at all,' I answer, unrattled. 'I have no objections to true crime books — the arrest on this patch, for instance, of the Black Panther. My own favourite in that field is Joseph Wambaugh's "The Blooding", an account of the first killer to be caught in DNA screening; a classic in true detection.' An effective pause. 'Completely factual.'

'You don't understand, do you, that sometimes you can only get at the truth via fiction?' he continues with a pitying expression.

'If that were so,' I reply, a touch testily, 'then every jury trial such as this would be a waste of time.'

'Why so?'

'Because the duty of the court is to seek the truth as opposed to the fiction of any case.'

'Not so, surely?' He picks up a glass jug of water from beside his pile of books, pours it noisily into a glass, sips and smacks his lips, hamming it up all the time.

'Surely, trials don't seek the truth? They seek proof. Truth is sometimes the first casualty of legal proceedings.' Belatedly, to turn another statement into a question, he adds, 'Is that not so?'

Without waiting for an answer, he turns his bespectacled eyes from me to the jury. He launches into what, in

239

effect, is a longish speech, disguised as questions by throwing in the odd 'surely?'

A detective might know the truth about a case — a murder, for instance, he postulates. There is no admission of guilt because the killer is too cunning to have confessed. Or, indeed, the detective may have obtained a partial admission which the judge has ruled the jury cannot hear because the manner in which it was obtained infringed procedure.

The detective will, however, have certain corroboration of his case in the form of the accused's movements, motive and so on.

When that case comes to trial, truth is not the issue, he argues. Proof, and only proof, is the issue. If you can't prove your case beyond reasonable doubt, he must go free, whatever the truth. 'Is that not so?' he adds.

I enter into the spirit of what's become a philosophical debate, nothing like the quickfire question and answer of criminal hearings I got used to across the foyer. 'You are doing what all good defence lawyers do.'

A hurt expression, 'And what, pray, is that?'

'Muddying the waters.'

'Explain, please.'

I accept the invitation, opening a policeman's heart about the frustations felt about lawyers who nitpick over every small detail in the prosecution case, suggest wildly improbable scenarios to explain away cast-iron evidence against their client, then don't put him in the witness box to give his side of the story because his lies will not withstand cross examination.

Head tilted, he gives me a perplexed look over the top of his spectacles. 'But it is the duty of the Crown or state to prove their case without the assistance of the accused, is it not?'

I'm not going to give a direct answer. 'All people in your position ever do is seek to throw doubt on the evidence of honest witnesses like me.'

'Exactly, and if that doubt is reasonable enough, then

it is the duty of the jury...' he waves theatrically towards their box '...to find in favour of the defence.'

No time to respond as he continues, 'The fact is that you fail to appreciate that fiction can sometimes lead to the very truth you so relentlessly pursue.'

I open my mouth, shut it again, as he monotones on, 'Certain police officers are corrupt, have fabricated evidence, bent your precious truth, have they not?'

I stand firm, proud, nothing in my body language to suggest I'm on the defensive. 'There are no more bent police officers per head of professional population than there are crooked lawyers.'

'Point taken.' He nods briefly. 'And there are also racists, bigots, incompetents in your and every profession and you, within your own force, investigate them and other law breakers?'

'Correct.'

'And having completed that investigation you submit your report to the Crown prosecutors who decide whether or not to proceed in public courts. On what basis is that decision made?'

'They have to satisfy themselves that there is a more than fifty per cent chance of the evidence securing a conviction.'

'And,' he asks with an oily smile, 'if the case comes to court, everything said in that court, every accusation made, can be reported to the public without fear of libel proceedings being taken against the publisher?'

He is feeding me easy lines. 'Yes, it's known as privileged information and no one can be sued for repeating it, provided their account is fair and accurate.'

'But, if there is only a, say, forty-nine per cent chance of securing a conviction, then there is no court case, no public hearing and no privilege applies to repeating the details of the case?'

'That follows.'

'And so the public will never know the facts of the case?'

'True.'

'Unless, of course, a writer, either by using his or her imagination or research finds out...'

I break in. 'He or she could be sued...'

He holds up his hand like a cop on point duty. '...wait one moment. And changes the names and the locations, fictionalises if you like, and describes the crime. Then he couldn't be sued, could he?'

'Not if he's covered his tracks cleverly enough, but I don't see the point.'

He puts on an impatient face. 'The point is that information that would otherwise remain secret is shared with the paying public. Not all of it, the names, for instance, but certainly the method, the motive. Thereby, the public is given an insight into the criminal mind which would otherwise remain a closed book to them.'

I'm not having this. 'You don't write as a public service to psychology or crime prevention. You write to make money.'

'Ah...' He sighs deeply and sadly. '...would that were so.'

'Isn't it?' I dart back.

'May I remind you, Mr Todd, as well you should know, that I ask the questions here.' He shrugs. 'But since you inquire, hardback authors do no more than eke out their meagre pensions.' A deeper sigh. 'And the pay is even poorer for short stories.'

It's a blatant pitch for a sympathy vote from the jury. Even the judge who, to my admittedly prejudiced mind, has handled him with kid gloves, demurs. 'No one compels the defendants in this case to write.'

Hear, hear, I think privately.

He sits down. The judge leans over her ledge, looking down at my brief who for sometime has been idly shuffling the cards bearing his unasked questions. 'Any re-examination?' she asks.

He gives his head an uninterested shake.

The judge prompts him. 'Your final speech then.'

242

Reluctantly he heaves himself up, reading yet again from his cards, relying heavily on evidence given this morning by a tourism official who'd whinged about the city's castle being rich enough in real history without Johnny Come Latelies making it up.

Spotting me stranded in the box, the judge gives me her first warm smile. 'Thank you. You may leave.'

I back down the steps and walk round behind the high wooden wall of the jury box, dragging my right foot a touch in the hope of reminding its occupants of my sacrifice to their safety. By the time I've sat down on a ground floor bench at the back of the court so has my brief.

His opponent rises again, demolishing the tourism officer's evidence by pointing out that most of the kings who had stayed at the castle were bigger cut-throats than anyone any crime writer had invented.

He's briefer and even more scathing about my evidence. 'Far from being a seeker after truth he stands exposed as a censor of it.' Hurtfully, he adds, 'He's a typical establishment man, cover it up, keep it secret, in case it reflects badly on the powers-that-be.'

The judge sums up for a little longer, carefully spelling out that the Regional Police Authority had to establish that the written words of members of the Crime Writers' Association had, on the balance of probabilities, unjustly provoked hatred, ridicule or contempt towards the said authority.

As promised, she gets the jury out of their box by 3.30.

Five minutes later they are back. 'We find for the defendants,' announces their foreman, his tie picked clean.

With the judge so anti and our case so poorly presented, that's no real surprise.

'With costs,' he adds.

Costs, I think, gloomily. I'm never going to live this down.

*

243

Crossing the slabbed foyer, I catch up with my mouth-piece dawdling disconsolately beneath a colourful collection of heraldic shields on the cream and green walls.

'Never wanted the bloody job in the first place,' he grumbles. 'Should have gone to rugger this afto.'

We step out of double doors into September sunshine. At the foot of a set of worn stone steps a red Barton's bus is waiting on a yellow line in a narrow bricked street. Out of the rear window of the bus the foreman is grinning maliciously and giving us the thumbs down.

The judge, a white raincoat over her blue dress, is chatting to the victor, who has a stack of books under each arm. 'A great idea of your's hiring this place, Mr Jackson. The PTA want to make it an annual outing, more instructive than classroom teaching, much more atmospheric.'

Jacko Jackson nods.

She turns to me. 'Will you be free again?'

'I'll see,' I reply, thankful that she's given me twelve months to come up with an excuse, any excuse, not to be repeat the ordeal of mock trial with a nobbled jury of urchins as my judges.

Jacko Jackson declines her offer to join her and his young son on the school bus home. 'I'm going to claim my costs,' he tells her with a sly smile.

As the bus pulls away, he waves at his son, a rather good looking lad, who, mercifully for him, takes after his mother. Everyone cheerily waves back.

Jacko throws an arm across my shoulder, propelling down the steps and across the street to the County Tavern. It's a favourite old haunt of ours, beams in the eaves and leaded windows in weathered stone, one of many lovely buildings in the Lace Market.

At our backs are the sand-coloured colonnades of the Shire Hall, the assize courts until ten years ago, the Galleries of Justice now, a museum.

'Could have been worse from your point-of-view,' he says.

Ever since Jacko, a museum piece himself, retired from

244

CID to write his fifteen quid dreadfuls he's sprinkled his conversations with arty phrases like 'point of view', 'sense of place' and 'narrative drive', the boring old fart.

I can't possibly think how my humiliation could have been much worse and, with no one within earshot, say so, rather obscenely.

'Well,' he says, 'I could have revealed in court that you're the prime source of my new series.'

On second thoughts, yes, it could have been worse, I accept privately, stepping up to the copper-topped bar, the drinks on me in lieu of costs.

Notes on Contributors

Catharine Arnold read English at Girton College, Cambridge. She is the author of *Lost Time* and *Changeling*, published by Hodder.

David Belbin's short stories have appeared in many magazines and anthologies. He is the author of a Nottingham based police series *The Beat* and many other *Point Crime* novels for young adults.

Robert Cordell teaches Biochemistry for the Open University and has written an A-level text book on the subject. This is his first published story.

Michael Eaton's screenplays include *Signs and Wonders, Shoot To Kill*, and *Fellow Traveller. No Smoke*, his first short story, is a companion piece to his Screen Two play, *Flowers Of The Forest*.

Raymond Flynn is a retired Police Inspector. Hodder publish his *Body* novels, which include *Seascape with Body* and *A Fine Body of Men*.

John Harvey is the author of nine Resnick novels. The tenth, *Last Rites*, will be the last for the time being. Smith Doorstop will publish his second collection of poems, *Bluer Than This,* in 1998. In his spare time, he runs Slow Dancer press.

H R F Keating is the author of the *Inspector Ghote* series and many other crime novels. He is a past chair of the Crime Writers Association.

Robert McMinn is doing a PhD in the American Studies Department at Nottingham University. Several of his short stories appeared in the late, lamented, *Slow Dancer* magazine.

Stanley Middleton is the author of thirty-six novels, including *Brief Hours, Married Past Redemption, Two Brothers,* and *Holiday,* which won the 1974 Booker Prize.

Peter Mortimer was taught English at High Pavement Grammar School by Stanley Middleton. His thirteenth play, *A Change in the Weather*, goes on tour shortly with Theatre Sans Frontières. He also finds time to run Iron press.

Brendan Murphy was the East Midlands regional winner of the 1992 Heinemann Fiction award. His stories have appeared in magazines and on Radio Four. He teaches Creative Writing at the University of Derby.

Julie Myerson is the author of two novels, *Sleep Walking* and *The Touch*, both published by Picador. She writes regularly for the *Independent on Sunday* and *The Observer*.

Frank Palmer is the author of the recently completed *Jacko* series and the new *Todd* series, both police procedurals set in the East Midlands. He quit journalism to write full-time in 1990.

Alan Sillitoe recently published both his autobiography, *Life Without Armour,* and his *Collected Short Stories*.

Keith Wright is a CID sergeant. Constable have published four of his police novels, including *One Oblique One* and *Addressed to Kill*.

Another short story collection from Five Leaves

THE SLOW MIRROR
and other stories
New fiction by Jewish writers

Edited by Sonja Lyndon and Sylvia Paskin

There I discovered the mirror. It was sitting on top of a dusty seventeenth century Portugese dresser in the twisted-and-turned style made popular following Vasco da Gama's first trip to India, and it caught my attention because it was shaped like a lyre.

The Slow Mirror and Other Stories is a collection of contemporary fiction by British, American and South African Jewish writers. The stories are as diverse as the writers. The haunting title story, by Richard Zimler, concerns a mysterious mirror which reflects the past. Others describe the new South Africa, the erotic possibilities of shoes, the lost Jews of outer space and the search for Kafka in Brontë country...

Carol Bergman, Tony Dinner, Moris Farhi, Rachel Castell Farhi, Elaine Feinstein, Ellen Galford, Jack Gratus, Dan Jacobson, Zvi Jagendorf, Gabriel Josipovici, Robert Lasson, Shaun Levin, Deena Linett, Marci López-Levi, Carole Malkin, Rozanne Rabinowitz, Nessa Rapoport, Frederic Raphael, Stephen Walker, Michelene Wandor, Shelley Weiner, Jonathan Wilson, Tamar Yellin & Richard Zimler

232 pages : 0 907123 81 3 : £9.99

Postfree from Five Leaves, PO Box 81, Nottingham NG5 4ER.